A SCALED HAND TOUCHED HER SHOULDER...

"You are the new concubine? Come."

*** ***

The room beyond was small and nearly bare. It held a chair with straps and wires and a switchboard; she recognized the electronic torture machine which leaves no marks on the flesh. In a chair more peculiarly shaped crouched another being that was not human.

"Sit down," the creature ordered. A thin hand waved her to the electronic seat. "...Sufficient pain will disorganize your mind until questioning will bring out inconsistencies. Should there be any we can go on to the probe. Let us get you secured." He gestured to the other, different alien.

Rough hands closed on her arm. Whirling, she jabbed fingers at his eyes. He ululated and backed away.

"Ah-h-h," breathed Sarlish. He drew a stunner and took judicious aim.

"Not recommended, comrade," said a voice from the doorway.

Sarlish dropped his weapon. "Captain Flandry, is it not?"

"In person, and right in the traditional nick of time."

POUL ANDERSON

AGENT OF THE TERRAN EMPIRE

Afterword by Sandra Miesel

SF

ace books

A Division of Charter Communications Inc.
A GROSSET & DUNLAP COMPANY
360 Park Avenue South
New York, New York 10010

AGENT OF THE TERRAN EMPIRE

Acknowledgements

"Tiger by the Tail," *Planet Stories*, January 1951. Copyright ©
1951 by Love Romances Publishing Co., Inc.

"Warriors From Nowhere," *Planet Stories*, Summer 1954, under the title "The Ambassadors of Flesh." Copyright © 1954 by
Love Romances Publishing Co., Inc.

"Honorable Enemies," *Future* combined with *Science Fiction*,
May 1951. Copyright © 1951 by Columbia Publications, Inc. Reprinted by Belmont Books, Inc., 1964.

"Hunters of the Sky Cave," *Amazing Stories*, June 1959, in a
short version under the title "A Handful of Stars." Copyright ©
1959 by Ziff-Davis Publications, Inc. Reprinted 1959 by Ace
Books, Inc., under the title "We Claim These Stars!"

"Lurex and Gold: Poul Anderson's Dominic Flandry Series"
was first published in *Ensign Flandry*, Gregg Press, a division of
G.K. Hall and Company, Boston, 1979.

An ACE Book
Cover art by Michael Whelan
First Ace printing: January 1980

2 4 6 8 0 9 7 5 3 1
Manufactured in the United States of America

CONTENTS

TIGER BY THE TAIL

When Captain Dominic Flandry opened his eyes, he saw metal. At the same time came awareness of a thrum and quiver, almost subliminally faint but not to be mistaken for anything else in the universe. He was aboard a spacecraft running on hyperdrive.

He sat up fast. Pain stabbed him through the temples. What the blue-flaming hell? He'd gone to sleep in one of the stews of Catawrayannis, with no intention of departure from that city for weeks or months to come—or, wait, had he passed out? Memory failed. Yet he hadn't drunk much.

Realization chilled him. He was not in a ship meant for humans. The crew must be pretty manlike, to judge from the size and design of articles. He could breathe the air, though it was chilly, bore peculiar odors, and seemed a bit denser than Terran standard. The interior grav-field, while not handicapping to him, was perceptibly stronger too, laying several extra kilos on his body. Bunks, one of which he occupied, were made up with sheets of vegetable fiber and blankets woven of long bluish-gray hair. A chest which could, he supposed, double as a seat, was wooden, carved and inlaid in a style new to him; and planetary art forms were a hobby of his.

He buried face in hands and struggled to think. The headache and a vile taste in his mouth were not from liquor—at least, not from the well-chosen stuff he had been drinking in reasonable moderation. And it made no sense that he'd dropped off so early; the girl had been attractive and bouncy. Therefore—

Drugged. Oh, no! Don't tell me I've been as stupid as a hero of a holoplay. That idea is not to be borne.

Well, who would have awaited such a trick? Certainly his opposition had no reason to . . . had they? Flandry had just been out developing a further part of that structure of demimonde acquaintances and information which would eventually, by tortuous routes, bring him to those whom he sought. He had been enjoying his work as conspicuously as possible, so that no one might suspect that it *was* work. Then somehow—

He lurched to his feet and hunted blearily for his clothes. They were missing; he was naked. Damn, he'd paid three hundred credits for that outfit. He stamped across to a metal door. It wasn't automatic. In his state, he needed half a minute to figure out how the sliding latch, cast in the form of a monster's head, was operated. He flung the door open and stared down the projection cone of a blaster.

The weapon was not of any make he recognized. However, there was no doubt as to its nature. Flandry sighed, attempted to relax, and considered the guard who held it.

The being was remarkably humanoid. Certain differences of detail could quite likely be found beneath the clothes, and more basic ones beneath the skin. Among countless worlds, evolutionary coincidences are bound to happen now and then, but never evolutionary identities. Yet to the eye, crew member and captive resembled each other more than either resembled, say, a woman. *Or an alien female?* Flandry wondered. *I'll bet this is a male, and equipped pretty much like me, too.*

The stranger could almost have passed for a tall, heavily built human. Variations in bodily proportions were slight, within the normal range. To be sure, Terra had never brought forth a race with his combination of features. The skin was very white, the hair and beard tawny, but the nose rather flat, lips full, eyes oblique and violet-colored. The ears were quite foreign, pointed, motile, cowrie-convoluted. Heavy brow ridges sprouted a pair of small, jet-black horns—scarcely for combat; they might perhaps have some sensory or sexual function. On the whole, the esthetic effect was pleasing, exotic enough to excite but familiar enough to attract.

The trouble was, Flandry was not feeling pleasable. He scowled at the garb which confronted him. It consisted of a gaudily patterned kilt and tunic, cuirass and helmet of a reddish alloy, leather buskins, a murderous-looking dirk, and two shriveled right hands, hung at the belt, which had probably belonged to foes. *Barbarian!* Flandry knew.

The guard gestured him back, unslung a horn from his shoulder, and blew a howling blast. That was pure flamboyancy; anyone who could build or buy spaceships would have intercoms installed. Old

customs often lingered, though, especially when a
people acquired modern technology overnight.

Which too many have done, Flandry reflected
with grimness. *One would have been too many, and
as is—No surprise that I never heard about this
folk; it is their existence that is the nasty surprise.*

No individual could remember all the scores of
thousands of sophont species over which the Terran
Empire claimed hegemony—not to speak of those in
the domains of other starfaring civilizations, Ythrian
and Merseian and the rest. The majority were obscure, primitive by the standards of space travelers,
seldom if ever visited, their allegiance nominal. This
meant that strange things could develop among
them over centuries, unbeknownst to worlds beyond. And known space itself was the tiniest splinter
off the outer part of a spiral arm of a galaxy whose
suns numbered above a hundred billion.

Outside the Empire, knowledge faded swiftly
away. Yet there had been sporadic contact with
dwellers in the wilderness. Merchant adventurers
had searched widely about in olden days, and not
always been scrupulous about what they sold. In this
way and that, individual natives had wangled pas-
sage to advanced planets, and sometimes brought
back information of a revolutionizing sort. Often this
got passed on to other societies.

And so, here and there, cultures arose that
possessed things like starships and nuclear weapons,
and played ancient games with these new toys.
Barbarian raiders had fearfully harried about during
the Troubles. In the long run, the practice of hiring
rival barbarians as mercenaries against them only
worsened matters. After the Empire brought the

Pax, it soon established lethal discouragements of raids and attempts at conquest within its sphere. The marches lay long quiet. But now the Empire was in a bad way, it relied ever more on nonhuman hireling fighters, its grip upon the border stars was slipping . . . word got around, and latter-day buccaneers began to venture forth. . . .

Barbarians could be bought off, or played off against each other, or cowed by an occasional punitive expedition—most of the time. But if ever somebody among them formed a powerful coalition, and saw an opportunity—*vae victis!* Even if the Imperialists broke him, the harm he did first would be catastrophic. *Vae victoris!*

Flandry halted his brooding. Footfalls rang in the corridor. A minute later, a party of his captors entered the cabin, seven warriors and a chieftain.

The leader overtopped the prisoner, who was of above average height for a Terran, by a head. His eyes were pale blue, beneath a golden coronet which represented three intertwined serpentine forms. Though it would be folly to try interpreting facial expressions on such short acquaintance, this one sent a line from the remote past across Flandry's mind: "—sneer of cold command." He wore a robe of iridescent shimmerlyn, bought or looted from an Imperial world, trimmed with strips of scaly leather. A belt upheld a blaster and a slim sword. The latter might not be entirely an archaic symbol; to judge from wear on hilt and guard, it had seen use.

His gaze went up and down the nude frame before him. Flandry gave back as bland a stare as possible. At length the newcomer spoke. His Anglic was heavily accented and his voice, which was deep, had subtle overtones hinting at a not quite human conformation of teeth, palate, tongue, and throat. Nevertheless he required no vocalizer to make the sounds understandable: "You seem to be in better condition than I awaited. You are not soft, but hard."

The man shrugged. "One tries to keep in shape. It maintains capacity for drinking and lovemaking."

The alien scowled. "Have a care. Show respect. You are a prisoner, Captain Dominic Flandry."

They went through my pockets, naturally. "May I ask a respectful question? Was that girl last night paid to slip a little something extra into my drink?"

"Indeed. The Scothani are not the brainless brutes of your folklore. Few of the so-called barbarians have ever been, in fact." A stern smile. "It can be useful having your folk believe we are."

"Scothani? I don't think I've had the pleasure—"

"Hardly. We are not altogether unknown to the Imperium, but hitherto we have avoided direct contact. However, we are they from whom the Alarri fled."

Flandry harked back. He had been a boy then, but he well remembered news accounts of the fleets that swept across the marches with nuclear fire and energy sword. The Battle of Mirzan had been touch and go for a while, till a Navy task force smashed the gathered enemy strength. Yet it turned out that the Alarri were the victims of still another tribe, who had overrun their planet and laid it under tribute. Such an incident would scarcely have come to the notice of an indifferent Imperium, had not one nation of the conquered refused to surrender but, instead, boarded hordes into spacecraft and set forth in hopes of winning a new home. (They expected the Empire would buy peace from them, payment to be assistance in finding a planet they could colonize, preferably outside its borders. Terrestroid real estate is a galactic rarity. Instead, the remnants of them scattered back into the stellar wilderness. Maybe a few still survived.)

"You must have a small empire of your own by now," Flandry said.

"Aye, though not small. The gods who forged our destiny saw to it that our ancestors did not learn the secrets of power from humans, who might afterward have paid heed to us and tried to stop our growth. It was others who came to our world and started the great change."

Flandry nodded his weary head. The historical pattern was time-worn; Terra herself had been through it, over and over, long before her children departed for the stars. By way of exploration, trade, missionary effort, or whatever, a culture met another which was technologically behind it. If the latter had sufficient strength to survive the encounter, it gained knowledge of the foreigner's tricks and tactics while losing awe of him. Perhaps in the end it overcame him.

The gap between, say, a preindustrial Iron Age and an assembly of modern machines was enormous. It was not uncrossable. Basic equipment could be acquired, in exchange for natural resources or the like. Educations could be gotten. Once a class of engineers and applied scientists was in existence, progress could be made at home; if everything worked out right, it would accelerate like a landslide. After all, when you knew more or less how to build something, and had an entire, largely unplundered planet to draw on, your industrial base would soon suffice for most purposes. Presently you would have an entire planetary system to draw on.

It wasn't necessary to educate whole populations. Automated machinery did the bulk of the work. Peasants with hoes and sickles might well toil in sight of a spacefield for generations after it had come into being. In fact, the ruling class might consider extensive schooling undesirable, particularly among nationalities which its own had conquered.

New instrumentalities—old, fierce ways—

The Scothani, though, must have truly exploded forth on their interstellar career. Else Terra would not remain ignorant of them. That was suggestive of deliberate purpose with a long perspective. A prickling went along Flandry's skin. "Who were those beings that aided you?" he asked slowly. *The Merseians? They'd dearly love to see us in trouble: the worse, the dearer.*

The chieftain lifted a hand. "You are overly forward," he growled. "Have you forgotten you are alone among us, in a ship already light-years from Llynathawr and bound for Scotha itself? If you would have mercy, conduct yourself as behooves you."

Flandry assumed a humble stance. "Dare I ask why you took me, my lord?"

"You are a ranking officer of the Imperial Intelligence service. As such, you may have hostage value; but primarily we want information."

"From me? I—"

"I know." The reply was clearly disgusted. "You're typical of your kind. I've studied the Empire long enough to recognize you; I've traveled there myself, incognito, and met persons aplenty. You are another worthless younger son, given a well-paid sinecure so you can wear a bedizened uniform and play at being a fighting man."

Flandry decided to register a bit of indignation. "Sir, that isn't fair." In haste: "Not to contradict you, of course."

The barbarian laughed. It was a very human-sounding laugh, save that its heartiness was seldom heard on Terra any more. "I know you," he said. "Did you imagine I had you snatched at random, without learning something first? Your mission was to find who the ultimate leaders were of a conspiracy against the throne which had lately been uncovered. How am I aware of this? Why, you registered under your proper name at the most luxurious hotel in Catawrayannis. On a seemingly unlimited expense account, you strutted about dropping hints about your business, hints which would have been childishly dark were they not transparent. Your actual activities amounted to drinking, gambling, wenching every night and sleeping the whole day." Humor gleamed cold in the blue eyes. "Was it perhaps your intention that the Empire's enemies should be rendered helpless by mirth at the spectacle?"

Flandry cringed. "Then why was I worth kidnapping, lord?" he mumbled.

"You are bound to have some information, some of it useful. For example, details about the organization and undertakings of your corps; most of Terran Naval Intelligence is very good at secrecy. Then there are services you can perform, documents you can translate, potential allies within the Empire you can identify, perhaps liaisons you can make. Eventually you may earn your freedom, aye, and rich reward." A fist lifted. "In case you contemplate any holding back, any treachery, be sure that my torturers know their trade."

"You needn't get melodramatic," Flandry said sullenly.

The fist shot out. Flandry went to the deck with his headache gone shriekingly keen. Blood dripped from his face as he crawled to hands and knees. Above him, the voice boomed: "Little man, the first thing you will learn is how a slave addresses the crown prince of Scothania."

The Terran lurched up. The barbarian knocked him down again. Behind, hands rested on gun butts. "Does this help teach you?" inquired his owner.

Well, I dare hope he isn't a sadist, that he's merely a member of a society which values roughness and toughness. "Yes, my lord prince. Thank you."

After all, a slave in the Empire is subject to worse.

"You will be instructed what to do," said the Scothan, turned on his heel, and strode out. His guards followed, except for the sentry. The latter whipped forth his dirk and held it straight up, an obvious gesture of salute.

A couple of underlings returned his clothes to Flandry, minus the gold braid. He sighed over the soiled, ripped garments in which he had cut such a gallant figure. Conducted to a head, he cleaned himself as best he could. Its layout was not too puzzling; besides being so humanoid, his captors derived their technology ultimately from his, whether or not that had been by way of Merseia.

The blows hadn't damaged his face beyond healing. It looked back from the mirror, fair-complexioned, high in the cheekbones, straight in the nose, delicately formed lips but strong chin, sleek brown hair and a neat mustache. Sometimes he thought it was too handsome, but he'd been young when he ordered a biosculptor to reshape it for him. Maybe when he got out of this mess he should have his countenance made over to a more rugged form suitable for a man in his thirties.

The slightly dolicocephalic bone structure was his own, however, as were the eyes: large and bright, with a bare hint of slanting, their irises of that curious gray which can variously seem almost blue or green or gold. The body was natural too, and he deserved full credit for its trimness. He hated exercises, but went through a dutiful daily routine which maintained strength, coordination, and reflexes. Besides, a man in condition stood out among the flabby nobles of Terra; he'd found his figure no end of help in making his home leaves pleasant.

His cheeks were still smooth. Maybe he could promote a razor before his last dose of antibeard wore off. At the minimum, he'd need scissors if he wasn't to get all scraggly.

Well, can't stand here admiring yourself forever, old chap. Flandry did the best he could with his clothes, tilted his officer's cap at a properly rakish angle, and walked out to meet his new shipmates.

They were not such bad fellows, he soon learned. Big, lusty, gusty warriors, out for adventure and wealth and fame, they were nevertheless well disciplined, with courtesy for each other and a rough kindliness for him. They were brave, honest, loyal, capable of sentiment and even the appreciation of certain beauties in art or nature. However, they were much given to deadly rages, and scarcely an atom's worth to compassion; they might not be inherently stupid, but their interests were limited; and it would have been pleasanter if they washed more frequently.

Much of this came to Flandry just as impressions at first, though experience tended to confirm it. Few aboard the ship spoke any language he did. A couple of officers who had some Anglic—less than the prince's—told him various things, in exchange for a little satisfaction of their own curiosity. He bunked with common crew in the place where he had been confined and took his food in a mess where one stood to eat out of trenchers, sans utensils other than issue knives. Flandry, allowed none, must rely on his teeth to cut the meat and shred the vegetables. The rations had strange flavors and the cooking was uninspired, but he found everything edible and a few items tasty. Someone had thoughtfully acquired a large stock of dietary-supplement capsules for him, to supply vitamins that didn't occur on Scotha.

He was allowed to wander around pretty freely, for there was nothing he could harm and he was never out of sight. Though big, the ship was crowded, for she had been on a scouting and plundering cruise.

She was one of a dozen Cerdic had taken forth. (That was not quite the prince's name, but near enough to catch Flandry's fancy; he was a bit of a history buff.) The additional purpose was presumably to train crews. They'd descended on several worlds, not all habitable to oxygen-breathing water drinkers, and improved their warlike skills, afterward taking whatever loot they wanted. Flandry got

the impression that a couple of those planets were
under Terran suzerainty; but if so, the connection
was tenuous, and no sentient beings had been left
alive to bear witness. Cerdic was too shrewd to pro-
voke the Empire . . . yet.

He had agents on Llynathawr, which world was
the listening post for this whole Imperial sector.
They were hirelings from various starfaring races,
probably humans among them; they could well in-
clude a few Scothans, claiming to be of a subject
people who lived in a distant part of the realm.

While his flotilla orbited beyond detection, a
speedster had entered the system and made secret
landing. That wasn't hard, when border forces were
undermanned and underequipped. The spies aboard
contacted the spies in place, and brought back the
latest news to their master. Learning that a special
agent from Terra was in Catawrayannis, on an assignment of apparent importance—no matter what a
fop and fool he was—Cerdic had ordered Flandry
picked up. It would be no giveaway, for a carouser in
the wild part of town could readily come to grief and
never be seen again.

Now they were homeward bound, triumphant. It
was clear that this had been no ordinary barbarian
pirating, that Cerdic and his father Penda (another
word-play by Flandry) were no ordinary barbarian
chiefs, and that Scothania was no ordinary barbarian
nation. Could the Long Night really be drawing nigh
—in Flandry's own sacrosanct lifetime?

He shoved the thought aside. Time was lacking
for worry. Let him also dismiss fret about the job
from which he had been snatched. It would go to the
staff, who could doubtless handle it, albeit not with

the Flandry style. He had suddenly acquired a new task, whereof the first part was plain, old-fashioned survival.

After a time he was conducted to Cerdic's cabin. The place had a number of ethnic touches, such as a huge pair of tusks displayed on a bulkhead between shields and swords, animal skins on the deck, and a grotesque idol in one corner. Flandry wondered if they were there merely because they were expected. Other furniture included a desk with infotrieve and computer terminal, bookrolls and a reader for them, a holoscreen, and, yes, a number of codex volumes bearing Anglic titles. The prince occupied an Imperial-made lounger, too. Jewelry glittered across his massive breast.

"Attention!" he barked. Flandry snapped a salute and stood braced. "At ease," Cerdic said with a measure of affability. "Have you somewhat accustomed yourself to us?"

"Yes, sir," Flandry replied. He'd better.

"Your first task will be to learn Frithian, the principal language of Scotha," Cerdic directed. "As yet, few of our people speak Anglic, and many nobles and officers will want to talk to you."

"Yes, sir." It was what he would most have desired, short of his release in the course of total disaster for Scotha.

"Also, you will organize your knowledge in coherent fashion. Writing materials and a recorder will be available to you. Beware of falsification. I have traveled and lived in the Empire, remember. I will have a sense for errors and ommissions. If ever I begin to doubt you, you will be subjected to hypnoprobing."

Flandry felt an inward shiver. The instrument was bad enough when lightly employed by skilled men. In the hands of aliens, who had no proper understanding of the human psyche and would, moreover, dig deep, he'd soon have no mind left.

"I'll cooperate, sir," he promised. "Please, though, you do realize I can't produce an encyclopedia. I can't so much as think of everything I might know that would be helpful to you. I'll have to be questioned now and then, to guide my thoughts."

Cerdic gave the curious circular nod of his kind. "Understood. Different sorts of cooperation may be required of you as we learn more. If you satisfy, you shall be rewarded. In the end, working with subjugated humans on our account, you could gain considerable power."

"Sir," began Flandry in a tone of weak self-righteousness, "I could not become a—"

"Oh, aye, you could," Cerdic interrupted. "You will . . . become as thorough a traitor as your capabilities allow. I told you before, I have been in the Empire, on Terra's very self; and I have studied deeply, aided by data retrieval systems, the works of your own sociologists, and of nonhumans who have an outside view of your ways. I *know* the Empire—its self-seeking politicians and self-indulgent masses, corruption, intrigue, morality and sense of duty rotten to the heart, decline of art into craft and science into dogma, strength sapped by a despair too pervasive for you to realize what it is—aye, aye. You were a great race once, you humans; you were among the first who aspired to the stars. But that was long ago."

The accusation was oversimplified, probably dis-

ingenuous. Yet enough truth was in it to touch a
nerve. Cerdic's voice rose: "The time has waxed
ready for the young peoples, in their strength and
courage and hopefulness, to set themselves free,
burn away the decayed mass of the Empire and give
the universe something that can grow!"

Only, thought Flandry, *first comes the Long
Night. It begins with a pyrotechnic sunset across
thousands of worlds, which billions of sentient
beings will not see because they will be part of the
flames. It deepens with famine, plague, more war,
more destruction of what the centuries have built,
until at last the wild folk howl in our temples—save
where a myriad petty tyrants hold dreary court
among the shards. To say nothing of an end to good
music and high cuisine, taste in clothes and taste in
women and conversation as a fine art.*

"My lord," he ventured, "one piece of information
I must give you is that the Empire does remain, well,
formidable. For instance, it holds the Merseians at
bay and—pardon me, sir—they must be more powerful than the Scothani."

"True," Cerdic agreed. "We are not *vilimenn*—
what is an Anglic word? We are not maniacs. We
cherish no dream of overthrowing the Terrans in a
single campaign, no, nor in our own lifetimes. But
we can reave a good deal from them that they will be
unable to regain. We can press inward, step by step,
exploiting their weaknesses, finding allies not simply
among their enemies, but among their subjects.
Above all, their vices will work against them, for us
and our cause."

He leaned forward. "Yes, that is what will decide
the final outcome," he said. "We have that which

you have lost. Honesty. The Scothani are a race of honest warriors."

"No doubt, sir," Flandry admitted.

"Oh, we have our evil persons, but they are few and the custom of private challenges keeps them few. Besides, their evil is clean and open compared to yours, it is mere lawlessness or rapacity or the like. The vast bulk of the Scothani abide by our code. It would never occur to a true male of us to break an oath or desert a comrade or play false to his lord or lie on his word of honor. As for our females, they don't run loose, making eyes at every male they come across. No, they're kept properly at home until marriage, and then they know their place as mothers and houseguiders. Our youth are raised to respect the gods and the king, to fight, and to speak truth. Death is a little thing, Flandry; it comes to everyone at his hour; but honor lives forever.

"That is why we will win."

Battleships help, thought the human. And then, looking into ice-bright eyes: *He's a fanatic. But smart. That kind is apt to harm the universe most.*

Aloud, he said, "Forgive me, sir. I'm trying to understand. Isn't any stratagem a matter of lies? Your own disguised travels through the Empire—"

"One does not charge blindly against necessity," the prince responded. "Nor is one bound in any way as to what may be done with aliens. They are not of the Blood."

The good old race superiority complex, too. Oh, well.

"I tell you this," said Cerdic, "because a wisp of conscience may be left in you, making you uneasy about serving us. Think on what you have been told, see where justice dwells, and enter gladly into its house, which today stands upon Scotha. You may yet accomplish some good in a hitherto wasted life. . . . Now, report to *Kraz*—Lieutenant Eril and commence your tasks."

"Yes, sir." Flandry smeared the unction thick. "Thank you for your patience, my lord."

"Go," snapped Cerdic.

Flandry went.

At a reasonable cruising pseudospeed, the flotilla was three weeks en route to Scotha. It took Flandry about two of them to acquire an adequate command of the language. Pedagogical electronics and pharmacopoeia were unavailable, but he had a knack, which he had developed through years of study and practice; and he could work very hard when he chose.

He described, haltingly, how slow his progress was despite his best efforts. Often he complained that he hadn't followed what was said to him. A person picked up quite a bit of odd information when talkers supposed he didn't understand them. There was little of prime military significance, of course, but there was much interesting detail about organization, equipment, operations, and like—as well as general background, attitudes, beliefs, pieces of biography. . . . It all went into the neat files in Flandry's skull, to be correlated with whatever else he learned by different means.

The Scothan crew were amicable toward him, eager to hear about his fabulous civilization and to brag about their own wonderful past and future exploits. He swapped songs and dirty jokes, joined rough-and-tumble sports and did well enough to

earn some respect, even received a few confidences
from those who had troubles.

They were addicted to gambling. Flandry learned
their games, taught them a few of his, and before
journey's end had won several suits of good clothes
for alteration, plus a well-stuffed purse. He almost,
not quite, hated to take his winnings. These overgrown schoolboys had no idea what tricks were possible with cards and dice.

Day by day, he filled out the portrait of their
home. The Frithian kings had brought the nations of
Scotha under themselves a century ago, and gone onward to the stars. Certain tales suggested their tutors
had indeed been Merseians; however, no such
beings had been seen for a long time. The monarchy
was powerful, if not absolute; it was expected to pay
attention to the will of the great nobles, who had a
sort of parliament; they in turn must respect the
basic rights of free commoners, though these were
liable to various types of service as well as taxes.
Slaves had no rights, and subject peoples only what
happened to be conceded them. On the whole, the
Scothan king seemed rather stronger than the Terran
Emperor. The latter was theoretically well-nigh om-
nipotent, but in practice was hedged in by the sheer
impossibility of governing his realm in anything like
detail.

The Scothan domain was less unmanageable. It
had conquered some hundred planetary systems outright, but for the most was content to exact tribute
from these, in the form of raw materials, manufactured goods, or specialized labor. It dominated
everything else within that space. It had made client
states of several chosen societies, helping them start

their own industrial revolutions and their own en-
forced unifications of their species. Under Penda, the
coalition had grown sufficiently confident to plan
war on the Empire.

The objective was not simple plunder, albeit
wealth did beckon. Goods could be produced at
home without the risks of battle. Nor was it merely
territorial aggrandizement. That could be more safely carried on by discovering new worlds off in the
wilderness, whose inhabitants weren't able to fight
back. Nevertheless, honest toil could never in hundreds of years yield what a victory would bring in
overnight. And planets that Scothan or human could
colonize were spread thinly indeed among the suns;
long searches were necessary to find them, and then
generations of struggle and sacrifice were usually
needed to make them altogether fit. Terra had already made the investment.

Below and beyond these practical calculations
were what Flandry saw as irrationalities and recognized as the true driving forces. Scotha—Scothan society, in the form it had taken—*needed* war and conquest. The great required outlets for ambition, that
their names might match or outshine the fore-
fathers'. Lesser folk wanted a chance to better their
lot, a chance that the aristocratic, anti-commercial
order at home could not offer them without under-
mining itself. Glory was a fetish, and scant glory remained to be won in the barbarian regions. Sheer
adventurousness clamored, and that darker longing
for submergence of self which humankind had also
known, too often, too well. The needs, the drives
came together and took the shape of crusading
fervor, a sense of holy racial destiny.

Yet as Cerdic maintained, the lords of Scothania
were not demented. From Flandry's viewpoint they
were more than a little mad, but they were realistic
about it. Their strength was considerable, their plan-
ners able. They would wait for the next of the
Empire's recurrent internal crises—and Flandry had
been on Llynathawr because a new one of those
seemed to be brewing.

No matter how much might was at Terra's beck, it
was no use unless it could be brought to bear as
needed. If the best of the Navy was tied down
elsewhere, the armadas of fearless fanatics could rip
through defenses manned by time-serving mercenaries under drone officers. The Merseians might not
directly join Penda, but they would not be idle on his
behalf. The Imperial magnates would be terrified at
the prospect of having their comfortable lives interrupted by heavy demands; if a major war seemed
likely, they would snatch at any face-saving offer to
stop it. None but a few eccentrics would point out
that the dismemberment of the Empire had com-
menced and the Long Night was ineluctably on its
way.

As expected, Scotha was fully terrestroid—a trifle
bigger than the prototype, a trifle further from its
sun, its seas made turbulent by three small moons.
Seen from orbit, it had the same white-marbled blue
loveliness. Descending in a tender, Flandry wangled
permission to examine the view with instruments.
He found the continent across which the boat
slanted to be equally attractive, unlike most of his
poor raddled planet.

Modern industries, built from scratch, had not

wasted and poisoned soil, polluted air and water, scarred land with mines and highways or buried it under hideous hectares of megalopolis. No doubt some ruination had taken place, but before it had proceeded far, that sort of business moved out to space where it belonged. Meanwhile, population burgeoned, but not to unmanageability. The Frithian kings had feared that their nation might be outnumbered and overwhelmed by subject peoples of the same species, and enacted measures simple, harsh, and effective to forestall this. (For example, children were taxed at an upwardly graduated rate. Frithians, and others who were more or less Frithianized, could generally afford to pay for three or four; most couples in less advanced areas could not, but must be content with two. Contraceptive help was freely available. Infants on whom tax was not paid were taken to be sold as slaves.) Before long, space colonization began to give general relief, at first in artificial environments, later on planets in different systems.

There were approximately three billion Scothani by now, two-thirds of them off the mother globe. That did not lessen the danger, given their allies and their monstrous array of automated weapons. Nearly all of them could be mobilized. In contrast, unreckonable swarms of Imperial civilians in the target sector would be first hindrance, later hostage . . . and eventually contributory to the conqueror.

Just the same, Flandry liked what scenery he observed. The landscape was green, in delicately different shades from his home. He saw broad forests, rich plains under cultivation or grazing, picturesque old villages, steep-walled castles. Rivers and snowpeaks gleamed afar. The skies were thronged with

winged life. Now and then, a glimpse of sleek industrial buildings, proud new towers in a city, or traffic
through heaven reminded him of what had lately
been achieved.

Iuthagaar, the capital, hove in view. Once it had
been no more than a stronghold atop a small mountain which rose from a rolling valley floor. Today it
sprawled down the slopes and across kilometers
below. However foreign the architecture—lavish use
of metal, multi-staged roofs, high-lifting buildings
often fluted, enormous colonnades, wildwood parks
—Flandry found himself admiring. But on the
peak above, sprawling, gray, craggy-turreted,
emblazoned with a golden sun disc above the main
portal and topped by a hundred banners, the ancient
seat of the Frithian kings still dominated.

The tender landed at a royal spacefield. Flandry
was led off to temporary quarters. Next day (the rotation period was about nineteen hours) he was summoned before Penda.

The hall was vast and dim-lit, hung with weapons
and trophies of past wars, chill despite the fires that
blazed and crackled on a row of hearths. The dragon
throne of the king-emperor stood elevated at the
north end. Wrapped in furs, Penda sat waiting. He
had the stern manner and bleak gaze of his eldest
son, and the record indicated he was intelligent in
his fashion. It also indicated that he lacked Cerdic's
range of interests and knowledge.

The prince occupied a lower seat on his father's
right. The queen stood on the left, shivering a bit in
the damp draft. Down either wall stretched a row of
guardsmen, firelight shimmery on their helmets,
breastplates, and halberds; for business purposes

they carried blasters. Others in attendance included younger sons of the royal house, generals, councillors, visiting nobles. A few of the latter belonged to non-Scothan species and did not appear to be receiving excessive politeness. A band of musicians behind the throne twanged forth a melody. Servants scurried, fetching and carrying as they were curtly ordered.

His escorting officer named Flandry to the king. As he had been directed, the man first knelt, then, having risen, gave the salute of the Terran Navy: an effective gesture of submission. Thereafter he met Penda's eye. His position was anomalous, technically Cerdic's captured property, actually—what? And potentially?

"Let your welcome be what you earn," Penda rumbled. He proceeded to ask several fairly shrewd questions. Among them were inquiries as to what Flandry would do in various situations; immediate answers were required.

At the end, the king tugged his whitening beard and said slowly: "You are not an utter fool, you. Maybe you are not a fool at all. Were you pretending, or were you only misunderstood? We shall see. Be you turned over to General Nartheof himself, head of Intelligence, to make your report." (The Scothani did not believe in fencing their leaders off behind row after row of bureaucrats.) "You may also make suggestions, if you wish to have hope of regaining your liberty, but remember always that treachery will soon be identified and death will be the welcome end of its punishment."

"I will be honest, mighty lord," Flandry avowed.

"Is any Terran honest?" Cerdic growled.

"My lord," Flandry said with a cheerful smile, "as

long as I am paid, I serve most faithfully. I am now in your pay—willy-nilly, yes, but with some prospect of doing better than I could have in my former service."

"Argh!" exclaimed Cerdic. "I'd begun to think better of you. This makes me a little sick."

"Lord, it was your wish."

"Aye. A yeoman must needs wield a muckfork."

Flandry turned to Penda. "Mighty lord," he said, "in earnest of my intentions, may I begin at once by making a respectful proposal to your august self?"

The king grinned like a wolf. "You may."

"Mighty lord, I am a new-arrived stranger among your folk, and have scant knowledge of them or their ways. But I have lived and traveled in an Empire which rules over thousands and thousands of widely different races, and has done so for centuries. Before then, Terra had had earlier centuries of dealings with them. Grant us, I pray you, that we have learned something from experience.

"We have found it is not wise to scorn our subjects. That would gain us nothing but needless hatred. Instead, we show them whatever honor is appropriate. Meritorious individuals are even given Terran citizenship. Indeed, several entire worlds of nonhumans are included in Great Terra. Thus they have the same stake as we do in the Empire.

"Forgive me if, in my ignorance, I appear insolent. Yet my own life has given me a certain judgment about such matters. It appears to me that here are allies of yours, present on your mutual business, who are shown less than complete respect. Indeed, one or two look physically miserable." Flandry nodded toward a reptile-like being who huddled in bulky garb.

"As simple a gesture as installing radiant heating would be appreciated, perhaps more than many Scothani realize. Appreciation would breed trust and cooperativeness in higher degree than erstwhile."

He bowed and finished: "Such is my humble counsel."

Penda stroked his horns. Cerdic fairly snarled: "This is the House of the Dynasty. We observe the ways of the forebears here above all places. Shall we become soft and luxury-loving as you, we who hunt vorgari on ski?"

Flandry's glance, flitting about the chamber, caught furtive dissatisfaction on many faces. Inside, he grinned. Austerity was not the private ideal of most of these virile barbarians.

The queen spoke timidly: "Lord of my being, the captive has wisdom. What harm in being warm? I— I seem always to be cold, myself."

Flandry gave her an appreciative look. He had ascertained that Scothanian and human females were extremely similar in outward anatomy. Queen Gunli was a stunblast, with dark rippling hair, big violet eyes, daintily sculptured features, and a figure that a thin, clinging gown scarcely hid. Frithian males demanded perfect chastity of their wives, yet liked to show them off—an assertion of their own masculinity and their ability to kill any intruder.

He had picked up a trifle about her background. She was young, Penda's third; her predecessors had died at early ages, perhaps of the same weariness and grief he thought he saw in her. She was not Frithian by birth, but from a southerly country which had been more civilized. Too slow to adopt the new technology, it had been forcibly incorporated in the

world state; but on shipboard he had noticed that
personnel who hailed from it appeared to consider
themselves the cultural superiors of the Frithians,
and right about it. Greeks versus Romans. . . .

He also had a notion that Gunli held, locked away,
considerable natural liveliness. Did she curse the fate
that gave her noble blood and hence a political marriage?

For just an instant, his gaze and hers crossed.

"Be still," Cerdic told her.

Gunli's hand fell lightly on Penda's. The king
frowned. "Speak not so to your queen and step-
mother," he reproved the prince. "In truth, the
Terran's idea bears thinking about."

Flandry bowed his most ironical bow. Cocking an
eye at the lady, he caught a twinkle. She alone had
read his gesture aright.

General Nartheof made an impressive show of
blunt honesty; but a quick brain dwelt behind that
hairy countenance. He leaned back from his desk,
scratched under his leather tunic, and threw a
quizzical stare at the man who sat opposite him.

"If matters are as you claim—" he began.

"They are," said Flandry.

"Belike. Your statements do go along with what
we already know. They simply warn me that the Imperial Naval Intelligence Corps is better than mine at
what it is allowed to do. Not altogether a surprise.
Your breed did once conquer everything across four
hundred light-years or more." Nartheof lifted a finger. "However, your service is hobbled by politics;
and the fighting units it advises are staffed by venial
cowards."

Flandry said nothing, but he remembered gallantly mounted actions in his own lifetime. The haughty Scothani seemed unable to comprehend that a state as absolutely decadent as they imagined the Empire was wouldn't have endured long enough to be their rival.

"And yet," Nartheof went on thoughtfully, "your point is well taken, that if the war is prolonged, Intelligence operations will become of the first importance. Even if our victory is quick, we can expect a covert struggle with the remnant of the Empire. And the organization of this corps *is* inferior. I have the courage to admit that."

"Besides," Flandry reminded, "there are the Merseians, with ambitions of their own. Well may they help you at first, but you can be sure that later they'll turn against you. And the Ythrians may grow alarmed and decide to take measures. You need information about both those domains, and more, before you go out on the galactic stage."

"Yes, yes. Beginning with reorganization. It's ridiculous to make noble birth such a heavy factor, or a factor at all, in deciding promotions."

"And when you do advance commoners, you assume those who've done best in the ranks will make the best officers. That doesn't necessarily follow. No doubt it did, back when reckless courage and handiness with a sword counted most in battle. But now, the concept is as obsolete as . . . as your time-wasting requirement that everyone in the services learn how to use an edged weapon."

"You don't understand that certain practices are to honor our forebears," Nartheof said huffily. "You've lost all sense of race." After a moment: "Nevertheless, you're right about the need to become more, uh, rationalized before we move."

"In ten or twenty years, you might be ready," the Terran opined.

"Impossible. If nothing else, too much eagerness. I will argue for some postponement, and I will start planning how to whip my corps into better shape. Most of the bright lads are mine; and I feel I can count you in there." The general slapped his desk. "As for my fellow services, I can but try. Gods, the dunderheads that command some!" Quickly: "If you repeat that, it will go ill with you. A high-born warrior does not brook disrespect from a slave. He cannot."

Flandry gave as good an imitation of the Scothanian nod as his cervical vertebrae allowed. "Understood, sir. Yet I can serve you best, and thereby serve myself, if we can speak freely between us. Who are these less than brilliant persons?"

"*Urh-hai*, Nornagast, for one, head of the Quartermaster Corps. I've argued my gullet raw, trying to show him he's too inflexibly set up—war is full of unforeseeables, and if a naval division had its supply lines cut it would have to retreat the whole way home, for it cannot live off the country among alien planets—He listens not. And he's cousin to the king, whose life he saved once when they were young. Penda cannot dismiss him without betraying honor."

Flandry stroked his mustache. "An accident could happen to Nornagast," he murmured.

Nartheof jerked erect in his chair. "What? Did I mishear? What did you say?"

"Nothing seriously meant, sir." Flandry smiled and spread his palms. "But just for the sake of discussion, suppose—well, suppose some excellent swordsman should pick a quarrel with Nornagast. I don't doubt he has enemies. If he should unfortunately be killed in the duel, you could get to the king immediately after and have the first voice in choosing Nornagast's successor. To be sure, you would have to know beforehand that a duel was coming. This would require an arrangement with the excellent swordsman, since he'd need a guarantee against the royal wrath—oh, for example, a place to bide his time till the situation changed—"

The general's dagger flashed free. "Silence!" he roared.

"Of course, sir, if you order it." Flandry stared meekly downward and lowered his voice. "I did but speculate aloud. It strikes me as both unfair and unwise that a dolt should have power and glory when others could much better serve Scothania."

"No more of your Terran vileness." However, the knife lowered.

"Forgive me, sir. As I've repeatedly been told, mine is a low, dishonest, treacherous race. Though we did conquer widely, once."

"A warrior might go far, if only—No!" Nartheof clashed blade back in sheath. "A warrior does not bury his hands in muck."

"Certainly not. Prince Cerdic observed that a pitchfork is the proper tool for that. It doesn't mind getting dirty. Nor does he who orders its use need to soil his mind by asking how that use will proceed—" Flandry's manner grew frightened. "I *beg* your pardon, sir. I forgot myself again. May I offer amends?"

Nartheof squinted at him. "Of what sort?"

"A useful item of information I chance to possess. As you doubtless have guessed, many Imperial arsenals and munitions dumps are guarded by nothing but secrecy. Modern warfare, with its high proportion of matériel to men, doesn't cause the Navy to have enough personnel for keeping live watch on everything. And there are plenty of obscure storage places, unfindable among so many suns. I know of one not too far from here."

The Scothan grew utterly intent. His breath quickened, puffing frost-clouds into the chilly room.

"An uninhabited, barren system in the marches," Flandry continued. "The second planet has a mountain range that decks a dragon's warren of storage facilities crammed with spacecraft, weapons, auxiliary equipment, supplies—sufficient to keep a flotilla in action for months. A few ships of yours could go there, take what they chose, destroy the rest, and be gone without trace. The next periodic inspection would find no clue as to the identity of the perpetrators. Or, better yet, I could show you how to plant clues indicating it was a Merseian operation."

Nartheof gaped. "Is this truth? How do you know?"

Flandry buffed his fingernails. "You recall what my mission was to Llynathawr. Had I discovered the local admiral is in the conspiracy, which is imaginable, I was to inform a certain junior officer whose loyalty is assured, so he could take precautions."

Nartheof shook his head. "I knew the Empire was far gone," he muttered, "but I never imagined this. I find it hard to believe."

"You can easily send a few scouts to verify my story."

"Yes." Excitement quivered through the hard

voice. "I will. And notify Cerdic—"

"Or simply dispatch the expedition yourself, explaining afterward that you felt there was no time to lose. Otherwise, you know, Cerdic is bound to take charge of the raid."

"He would not like such a trick on him," said Nartheof dubiously. "The glory to be won—and glory means power—"

"Indeed. Frankly, sir, I feel you deserve more of that than you've gotten thus far. The prince could scarcely fault you for so bold and important a coup." Flandry leaned forward. "You'd gain more of the influence you need for advancing your ideas, in the service of Scothania."

"Aye. Aye. And . . . Cerdic has grown overbearing. We'd gain, were he taken down a little." Abruptly Nartheof chuckled, deep in his chest. "Aye, by Vailtam's whiskers, I'll do it!"

Then bemusement came over him. He stared long at the man before he murmured, "It'll be a stiff blow to the Empire. Directly or indirectly, it will take many human lives. Why have you told me?"

Flandry shrugged. "I've decided my best interests lie with you, sir." He put on a grave demeanor. "Though I'm afraid I'll make enemies here before all is done. I'll need a strong friend."

"You have one," declared the barbarian. "You're much too useful to be slaughtered. And—and—the gods curse you for your treachery, you soulless monster—but somehow, I cannot help liking you."

In a chamber more elegant and comfortable than the highest standards allowed—warmth, richly hued and textured hangings, incense and recorded music sweet upon the air—dice rattled across a table and came to a halt. Prince Torric swore good-naturedly as he shoved a pile of coins toward Flandry. "You have the luck of the damned with you," he laughed.

For a slave, I'm not doing too badly, reflected the man. *In fact, I'm by way of becoming well-to-do, unless my master finds out and confiscates my hoard.* "Say rather that fortune favors the weak," he purred. "The strong don't need it, highness."

"Forget titles when we're by ourselves." The young male was drunk, his cheeks flushed. Greenish wine of Scotha lay puddled near his goblet. "Yes, to the deathrealm with titles. We're friends, Dominic, good friends, not so? We've swapped many a yarn, many a song and jest. And when you straightened out those money matters for me—They could've brought disgrace on my name, you know."

"It was nothing . . . Torric. I've a head for figures, and of course a Terran education helps." Flandry regarded the coins. "I feel guilty at taking even this much from you. You do need more wealth than is yours, to maintain your proper station."

"Well, plenty waits in the Empire. I'm promised a whole planetary system to rule over."

Flandry pretended surprise. "A single system? No more, for a son of King Penda? Why, I understand males of less rank expect far larger fiefs."

"Cerdic's doing." Torric gulped from his cup, set it down with a clang, and glowered at the night in a window. "He's persuaded Father . . . any prince but him, who had any real power, might be too tempted to grasp after more . . . for only *he* is to have any claim to the supreme overlordship."

"That isn't traditional, is it? I've heard that in

olden times a new king was elected, from among the sons of the royal house, by the assembly of nobles."

As a matter of fact, that system had led to a number of civil wars. Finally it was decided that a successor should be chosen while his father still reigned. Primogeniture was usual but not legally required. Penda had practically forced the parliament to name Cerdic, with the obvious aim of establishing the precedent that the first son would always be the next king. That would be a long step toward absolute monarchy.

Torric wove his head about. He was no political sophisticate. "Thus 'twas. They wanted whoever was best."

"Is Cerdic, then?"

"He'll tell you so. Hour after hour."

"I gather you don't agree. These are dangerous times. Isn't it your duty to work for the welfare of Scothania? And who embodies that welfare more than the king?"

The prince blinked. He had forgotten, or he had never noticed, how much about himself he had let slip in the course of weeks. "Can you hear my thinking, Dominic? I wonder 'bout you—" He shook himself. "But no. I mustn't. I can't."

Flandry raised forefingers to brows. He had developed the gesture as his version of the Scothanian touching of the horns, to express surprise. "Helpless, Torric? I didn't await such words from you—you, royal warrior, descended from Saagur the Mighty, and on your mother's side from—" He let his voice trail off. The other had grown up knowing that his mother, Penda's second queen, had been higher born than the first.

"Now, now wait." Hands fumbled with goblet.

"You've been such a practical devil till now. Gone crazy, ha?"

"No, I trust not. I am simply reminding you that Cerdic's power, like that of any chieftain, rests on his supporters. The grandest of those is his father, of course. But King Penda—I mean no disrespect—the great lord will not live many more years. Cerdic is not widely liked. Someone with a lawful claim to the throne, who had spent those years quietly preparing, gathering allegiances of his own and winning them away from Cerdic—"

For a moment, shock cleared the eyes that looked into his. "Would you make a brotherslayer of me?"

"Oh, absolutely not," Flandry said. He had studied how to sound reassuring in Scothan ears. "Only an event of a kind that Terran history is full of. And for the higher good of the Race. No, I daresay Cerdic could be honorably retired to govern a planetary system. Or you, being generous, might grant him two."

"But—your sneaking ways—I, I know nothing about 'em," Torric stammered. "Don't want to. . . . I suppose you mean to dish—disaffect his faction, promise more'n he gives. . . . What's that word? Not Frithian; Ilrian." Queen Gunli was from Ilria. "*Laionas*, yes, *laionas*." Bribery. "I couldn't do that. Don't even want to hear about it."

"You wouldn't need to," Flandry replied softly. "You could leave the details to your friends. What's a male for, if he never helps a friend?"

Earl Morgaar, who held the conquered world Zanthudia in fief, was a noble of more influence than his title suggested. ("Earl" was a rough translation into Anglic.) He was also notoriously avaricious.

In a private place he maintained for his visits to Iuthagaar, he told Flandry: "Terran, your suggestion about farming out my tax-gathering has more than doubled my revenues ... until lately. Now the natives are seething. They murder my folk, they hide their goods, a number have taken up arms as guerrillas. What do they do about *that* in the Empire?"

"Surely, sir, you could crush them," the man replied.

"Aye, at vast effort and cost. And the dead pay no taxes. Ken you no better way, before my whole domain is in chaos?"

"Several, sir." Flandry sketched a few—puppet native committees, propaganda shifting the blame onto scapegoats, splashy displays of governmental concern for a select few underdogs. ... He did not add that these methods work only when skillfully administered.

"It is well," said the earl at last. His gaze probed at the man's smiling face. "You've made yourself valuable to many a lord, have you not? Like Nartheof; he's waxing mighty since he took that Imperial arsenal. And others, myself among them." He rubbed his horns. "Yet it seems much of this gain is at the expense of rival Scothani, rather than the Empire. I still wonder about Nornagast's death."

"History shows that the prospect of enormous gain always stirs up internal strife, sir," Flandry answered. "Often a strong, virtuous warrior has had to seize dominance, so that he could reunite his people against their common enemy. Think how the early Terran Emperors ended the civil wars, once they had power."

"Um-m-m—yes. It was a maxim of the forebears

that wealth corrupts. Have I not seen its truth in our
own royal court?"

"Sir," Flandry said, "we being alone, and I being
a decadent human, permit me to recall that Frithia
has seen many changes of dynasty in the past."

"What?" Morgaar sat bolt upright. "Do you imply
—No! My oath is to the king!"

"Of course, of course," the man said quickly. "I
was just thinking that not everyone is as virtuous as
you. You yourself spoke of those who are not. I fear
that good King Penda is more trustful than is wise.
Evil could well take him unawares. Enthroned, it
would soon destroy that uprightness which is the
fountainhead of Scothanian strength."

Morgaar leaned forward. His voice dropped. "Do
you imply it could become necessary to forestall—"

"Well, for the good of Scothania—"

They were discussing details within an hour. Flandry suggested that Prince Kortan was probably ap-
proachable—but one should be leery of Prince Torric, who had ambitions of his own—

Winter solstice was the occasion of religious ceremonies followed by feasting and merriment. Town
and castle blazed with light, shouted with music and
drunken laughter. Warriors and nobles swirled their
finest robes about them and boasted of the havoc
they would wreak in the Empire. On the dark side,
the number of alcoholic quarrels leading to blood-
shed was unusually high this year among the upper
classes.

There were dark corners in buildings, too. Flandry
stood in an alcove before a window and looked over
a dazzle of city lights to the mountains that reared on
the horizon, white beneath a hurtling moon. Winter-

frosty stars seemed so near that he could reach out
and pluck them from the sky. Cold breathed from
the glass pane. The sounds of revelry came to him as
if across a chasm.

A light footfall sounded beneath them. Flandry
turned and saw Gunli the queen. Her form was
shadowed, but moonlight came in to bring forth her
countenance in elfin wise. She might have been a
lovely girl of Terra, save for the little horns and—
well—

*She looks human, almost, but she isn't. I've been
able to play on these people because they're trying
to play a game that my race invented. They and we
will never truly understand each other's inward-
ness.* Flandry's lips quirked. *They do share a quaint
belief often found in our history, that the female of
the species has no talent for politics. I've a notion
Gunli could enlighten them about that, after she's
enlightened herself. In that respect, as well as in the
delectable flesh, she's human enough for all practical purposes.*

The cynicism faded before an indefinable sadness.
Damn it, he liked Gunli. They two had shared
speech, songs, memories, even mirth now and then,
throughout the past months; she was honest and
warm-hearted and—well, no matter.

"Why are you here alone, Dominic?" she asked.
Her tone was quiet. Her eyes glimmered huge in the
shifty moonlight.

"It would be imprudent for me to stay at the party," he answered wryly. "I'd cause too many fights.
Half the company hate my guts, and don't care much
for the rest of me."

She smiled. "And the other half can't do without

you." She tossed her head, her equivalent of a shrug. The dark hair sheened. "*Urh-hai*, I've come in search of solitude myself. Those savages pluck too hard on my nerves. At home—" She came to stand beside him and stared outward. He saw a glitter of tears. Scothans also wept.

"Don't cry, Gunli," he murmured. "This is the night when the sun turns, remember. A new year offers new hope."

"I can't forget the old years," she said with sudden bitterness.

Understanding touched him. He asked, softer yet: "You had somebody else once, didn't you?"

"Aye. A young knight. But he was of low degree, so they married me off to Penda, who is old and harsh. Later Jomana was killed in a raid of Cerdic's." She turned her head to regard him. "Jomana isn't what hurts, Dominic. He was dear to me, but wounds heal if we survive them. I am thinking of the other young males, and their sweethearts, wives, daughters, mothers—"

"War is what they want."

"But not what the females want. Not to wait and wait and wait for the ships to come back, never knowing whether only his sword will return. Not to rock a baby and know that a few years hence he will be a corpse on the shores of some alien planet. Not to—" She broke off and straightened her slim shoulders. "Let me not whimper. Naught can I do about it."

"You are very brave as well as beautiful, Gunli," said Flandry. "Your kind has changed fate erenow." And he sang, low, a stave he had made in the Scothan bardic form:

> *"So I see you standing,*
> *sorrowful in darkness.*
> *But the moonlight's broken*
> *by your eyes, tear-shining—*
> *moonlight in the maiden's*
> *magic net of tresses.*
> *Gods gave many gifts, but,*
> *Gunli, yours was greatest."*

All at once she was in his arms.

Sviffash of Sithafar was in a glacial rage. He paced
between the stone walls of the secret chamber, tail
lashing his bowed legs, fanged jaws biting off each
accented Frithian word.

"Like a craieex they treat me," he hissed. "I, primary one of a planet and an intelligent species, must
bow to the dirty barbarian Penda. Our ships have the
worst assignments in the fleet, our crews the last
chances at loot. Scothani on our world swagger
about among us as if we were subjugated primitives,
not civilized allies. It is unendurable!"

Flandry preserved deferential silence. He had
carefully nursed along the herpetoid's resentment
ever since he identified it, on an occasion when Sviffash had come to Iuthagaar for conference. But he
wanted the nonhuman to think everything was his
own idea.

"By the Dark Lord, were it possible, I think I'd
take us over to the Imperial side!" burst from the
scaly countenance. "Do you say they treat their subjects decently?"

"Yes, as you can verify by sending a commission of
inquiry that the Scothans need not know about.
We've learned that race prejudice is coun-
terproductive. Besides, if only because the sheer

number of peoples requires it, by and large we leave them their autonomy, except in certain matters of defense, commerce, and the like where we must have uniformity. That's to everyone's benefit. Actually, being located well outside the border, I expect Sithafar would be offered alliance rather than client status." *If the Policy Board feels it's worthwhile offering them anything*, Flandry's mind added. *I trust they'll have the wit not to make that clear until afterward.*

"My subordinates would gladly follow," said Sviffash. "They would rather sack and occupy Scothanian than Terran worlds. But they fear Penda's revenge."

"Several other leaderships feel likewise. Once a revolt began and bid fair to succeed, still more would join in. It's a matter of getting them together. You could arrange that, my lord, after I've told you who they are."

Lidless black eyes glistened in a stare. "You've been busy, Terran, have you not? Like a spinnerlegs weaving its web. Say on." Pause. "You realize, things must be so planned that, if you are caught at your work, I will be able to disown you, convincingly."

"Of course, my lord. I have a scheme prepared in detail for your scrutiny."

A tongue flickered forth and back again. "If we can—if we can—s-s-s, I myself will direct the first missile against Scotha!"

"No, my lord," Flandry said. "Scotha must be spared."

"Why?"

"Because you see, my lord, we'll have Scothan allies. They'll cooperate only on that condition. Some

of the power-seeking nobles . . . and an Ilrian na-
tionalist movement, desiring independence from
Frithia . . . which, I may tell you, has the secret help
of the queen herself. . . ."

Flandry's stare was as bleak as his voice: "It will
do you less than no good to kill me, Duke Asdagaar.
Credit me with brains. I have made my preparations.
If I die or disappear, the evidence goes straight to the
king and, by broadcast, the people."

The Scothan's hands clenched white about the
arms of his chair. Impotent fury chattered: "You devil! You slime-worm!"

Flandry wagged a finger. "Tut-tut. You are poorly
advised to call names, my dear Asdagaar. A par-
ricide, a betrayer, a breaker of oaths, a blasphemer—
Be sure that I have proof. Some of it is in writing.
More consists of the names of scattered witnesses
and accomplices, each of whom knows a little of the
entirety about you. A male without honor can await
nothing but a nasty death."

"How did you learn?" Hopelessness crept into the
duke's tone; he began to tremble.

"In various ways," Flandry said. "I've been in my
business a fair number of years, after all. For instance, I cultivated the acquaintance of your slaves
and servants. You high-born forget that the lower
classes can see and hear and draw conclusions, and
that they talk among themselves. The clues they
gave me pointed me onward."

"Uh, uh, uh." The noise was as of strangling.
"What do you want?"

"Help for certain others," Flandry replied. "You
have powerful forces at your disposal. You are the
head of your clan, which has always felt more loyal

to itself than to the throne—"

Spring breezes blew soft through the garden and woke rustling in trees. A deep odor of green life was upon it. Somewhere in twilight, a creature not unlike a bird was singing. The ancient promise of summer to come stirred in the blood.

Flandry told himself he must relax before his nerves snapped across. Matters were out of his hands now, or nearly so; the machinery he had built was in motion. The counsel was of scant use.

He had grown thin and hollow-eyed. Likewise had Gunli, though on her it heightened the loveliness. More than ever, she made him think of the elves, in myths that she had never heard.

They had gone their separate ways to meet here in this place where few came. (It was an Ilrian garden, to ease her homesickness a little.) How often had they stolen such brief whiles together? The longer times they had been able to find must be used for scheming.

Gravel scrunched beneath their feet as they walked. The path was narrow; the hands they did not link brushed hedges that had begun to flower. Flandry tried to keep his speech dry, but heard it as weary: "The spaceship got off this morning. Aethagir should have no trouble reaching Ifri. He'll have more obstacles in his way after he arrives, but he's a clever lad. He'll get my letter to Admiral Walton." A tic wakened in his cheek. "The timing's too bloody close, though. If our task force hits too soon, or too late, well, the menace to the Empire will be ended, but at what a cost!"

"I've not seen your confidence flag before," Gunli said.

"It was necessary to put on a good show, my beautiful. But the fact is, I've never juggled an empire before." Flandry drew breath. "The next several weeks will be touch and go. You'd better leave Scotha. Make an excuse; explain you need a rest, which is clear to see. Take it on Alagan or Gamlu or wherever, a safely out-of-the-way planet." He smiled with a corner of his mouth. "What point in a victory where you died? The universe would become drab."

She looked away from him. Her hand felt cold in his. "I ought to die, I who've betrayed my husband, my king."

"No, you ought to live, you who've freed your country and saved lives in the millionfold."

"But the broken oath—" Quite quietly, she started to weep.

"An oath is just a means to an end: helping people get along with each other."

"An oath is an oath. Dominic, m-my choice was to stand by Penda—or by you—"

He comforted her as well as he could. And he reflected that seldom had he felt himself so thoroughgoing a skunk.

The unaided eye could never really see a battle in space. Nothing but flashes among the stars betokened rays, warheads, incandescent vapor clouds, astronomically nearby. Farther off, across distances measured in planetary orbits, the deaths of ships were invisible.

Instruments sensed more fully, and computers integrated their data to give a running history of the combat. Admiral Thomas Walton, Imperial Terran Navy, laid down the latest printout and smiled in stark satisfaction.

"We're scrubbing them out of the sky," he said. "We've twice their strength. Besides, it's gotten pretty obvious by now that they were demoralized from the start. I don't know how else to account for their sloppiness."

"Is it known yet who they are?" wondered Chang, captain of the flagship.

"Not yet. We may salvage a piece of wreckage that'll identify them for sure, though I won't spend time searching for any. They're split into such a flinkin' lot of factions—" Walton rubbed his chin. "Judging from what data we have, their radiant of origin and similar clues, on the basis of Flandry's report I'd say it's the command of—what is that outlandish name?—Duke Markagrav. He's a royalist. However, it might be Kelry. He's in revolt against the king, though not about to join meekly with us."

Chang whistled. "Son of a bitch! The whole hegemony has just disintegrated, hasn't it? Everybody at the throat of everybody else, and hell take the hindmost. What's happened?"

Walton chuckled. "Dominic Flandry is what happened. We'll find out the details later, but his signature is on everything in sight." He leaned back and bridged his fingers. "We've a moment to chat till the next decision has to be made. I'm not free to tell you all I know about Flandry's career to date. However, since the Llynathawr business has been terminated, I can describe his *modus operandi* there. It's typical of him, insofar as anything ever is.

"I've mentioned to you that he was handling it when those barbarians kidnapped him. Needless to say, he'd done his homework, and he set up an excellent undercover operation which did eventually track down the conspirators. They'd have been

caught long before, though, if he'd stayed on hand.
Know what he was doing? He showed up with,
practically, a brass band; he put on a perfect act as a
political appointee using the case as an excuse to go
roistering, which made the plotters ease off on their
precautions; meanwhile he worked his way toward
them through the shadier characters he met.

"I've no words for how relieved I was when his
report came in and I knew his disappearance hadn't
meant he was dead. At the same time, I couldn't help
feeling sorry for the Scothanians. They'd grabbed
hold of Captain Flandry!"

Mobs howled and roiled in the streets of
Iuthagaar. Here and there, houses burned. No government remained to control horror and anger.

The remnants of Penda's troops had abandoned
the city and were in flight northward from the advancing Ilrian Liberation Army. They would be harried by Torric's irregulars, who in turn were the
fragments of a force smashed by Earl Morgaar after
Penda was slain by Asdagaar's assassins. Asdagaar
himself had died when Nartheof's fleet broke his.
The clansfolk had not fought well; it had lately become known to them what kind of male their chief
was.

But Nartheof had met death too, at the hands of
Nornagast's vengeful kin. His seizure of the throne
and attempt at restoring order had mainly worsened
the chaos. Now the royalists were scattered through
space, driven off rebellious subject planets, hunted
by their erstwhile allies, annihilated piecemeal by
the oncoming Terran armada.

Desperately, the Scothanian lords fought among

themselves and scrabbled to retrieve something from the ruin, each without thought for the rest. Some went down; some made hasty surrender to the Empire. Battle still flamed between the stars, but it was fast guttering out; the means of waging it had crumbled.

A few guards kept watch around the nearly deserted castle, waiting for the Terrans to proclaim, "Peace, ye underlings." They knew nothing else they could do but wait.

Flandry stood at a window in a high room and looked across the city. He felt no elation. Down there in the smoke, sentient beings lay dead. More would perish before the end of upheaval. The whole number would be merely in the hundreds, he guessed; the dead of the entire war were probably less than a million. Yet each of those heads had borne a cosmos within it.

To him came Gunli. Her fairness had gone bone-white, and she walked and spoke unsteadily. She had not expected Penda's murder.

She halted before him. Tapestries on the walls behind her depicted former triumphs. "Proud Scotha lies fallen, in wreck and misery," she said.

"Be happy for that," Flandry replied tonelessly.

A slim hand touched a horn. "What?"

He thought a lecture might calm her, for sure it was that she was overwrought to the edge of endurance. "Barbarian conquests never last," he said. "Barbarians have to become civilized first, before they are fit to rule a civilization.

"And Scothania had not gone through that stage. I knew almost from the beginning that it had gone straight from barbarism to decadence. Its much-vaunted honesty was its undoing. By self-righteously denying the possibility of dishonor in its own society, it left that society ignorant, uninoculated, helpless against the infection. I never believed the germ was not present. Scothans are much too humanlike. But they made the mistake of taking their hypocrisy at face value.

"Most of my work amounted just to pointing out to their key males the rewards of treachery. If they'd been truly honest, I'd have died at the first suggestion. Instead, they wanted to hear more. They found they didn't object to bribery, blackmail, betrayal, anything that seemed to be to their private advantages. Most Terrans would have seen deeper, would have wondered if the despised slave was talking to others along the same lines, would have recollected the old saying that two can play at the same game . . . and so can three, four, any number, till the game becomes unstable and somebody at last kicks the board over.

"Don't mourn for lost honor, Gunli. It never was there."

"It was in me, once." A strange light kindled in her eyes. "*I* have lost it, and though my people may become free, I am not fit to reign over them. Dominic, dishonor can only be wiped out with blood."

Unease tingled through him. "What do you mean?"

She snatched his blaster from the holster and skipped back out of reach before he could move. "Hold!" she shrilled. "Hold or I shoot!" Calmer: "You are cunning. But are you brave?"

He froze. "I think—" He paused to grope for words. Had she gone berserk? No, he believed not. But she wasn't entirely human, and she had in her the barbarian's iron code as well as the milder philosophy of her civilization. "I think I took a few risks, Gunli."

"Aye. But you never fought, fairly and openly, as a warrior should." The thinned countenance twisted in pain. Breath rasped in and out. "I act for you as well as him, Dominic. He must have his chance to avenge his father—my husband—and fallen Scotha —and you must have the chance to redeem your honor. The gods will know where justice lies."

Trial by combat, Flandry knew, *three hundred light-years and more from old Terra*.

Cerdic came through the door. He carried a sword in either hand, and laughed as he entered.

"I let him in, Dominic," Gunli cried through tears. "I had to—for Penda—but kill him, kill him!"

She ran to a window. In a convulsive movement, she threw the blaster out. The prince's ravaged visage showed surprise. She clung to the sill and sobbed, "I was afraid I might shoot you, Cerdic."

"Thanks!" he said savagely. "I may remember that when I deal with you, traitress. First—" again he cackled laughter—"I'll cut your paramour into many small pieces. For who, among the so-civilized Terrans, can wield a sword?"

Gunli staggered. "Oh, almighty gods, I never thought of that!"

She flung herself at Cerdic, nails and teeth and horns. "Get him, Dominic!" she screamed.

The prince swung a brawny arm around. She fell to the stone floor and lay half stunned.

"Now," Cerdic grinned, "choose your weapon."

Flandry came forward and took a slender shape at random. His thoughts were mostly of the queen.

Poor darling, she'd suffered more than flesh was meant to bear. May time henceforward be kinder to her.

Cerdic crossed blades with him. The Scothan's expression had gone dreamy. "I mean to take a while about this," he murmured. "Before you die, Terran, you will no longer be a male."

Steel rang. Flandry parried a slash. He point raked the prince's brow. Cerdic bellowed and stormed forward. Flandry retreated. Scothan physical strength exceeded his. The sword could be knocked out of his grasp if he wasn't careful.

His foe hewed. He was wide open for the simplest stop thrust, but Flandry preferred not to slay him. Instead, he parried again, then followed with a riposte that tore across the breast. Cerdic sprang back. Flandry made a lunge, a feint, and a glide. He took his opponent in the right forearm. Blood welled. The injury wasn't disabling, but Cerdic was shaken. Flandry executed a beat that deflected the opposing blade. With the flat of his own, he smote across knuckles. The Scothan gasped in pain, and Flandry's next blow sent his weapon spinning in midair. He stood with his enemy's point at his throat.

Flandry laughed into his stupefaction and told him: "My friend, you didn't study our decadence as thoroughly as you should have. Archaism accompanies it. *Scientific* fencing is quite popular among us."

The prince braced himself. "Then kill me and be done," he said.

"There's been too much killing. Besides, I have uses for you." The Terran cast his sword from him and cocked his fists. "However, here's one thing I've been waiting with exemplary patience for an opportunity to do."

Despite Cerdic's powerful but clumsy defense, Flandry proceeded to beat the living hell out of him.

Wind boomed around the highest tower of the castle, chill and thrusting; but save for tatters of cloud, the sky was blue with late afternoon. Golden-plumed, a few winged creatures wheeled over the deck where Flandry and Gunli stood. They had drawn cloaks about them against the blast, but she rested a hand on the parapet, and his lay across it. Below them, roofs and walls fell away toward a city where Ilrian patrols now kept the peace. Beyond, hills, fields, and woods reached green to a horizon of snowpeaks.

"What you did, girl," he said, "was nothing more or less than help save Scotha. All Scotha. Think. What would have happened if you'd gone into the Empire? Supposing you won your victory—which was always doubtful, because Terra is still mighty—but supposing you did, what would have come next? Why, the humans or the Merseians would soon have had you at civil war over the spoils. You'd have made yourselves prey for a conqueror who'd have shown small mercy. As is, the conflict did less harm, by orders of magnitude, than even your success would have; and the victors aren't vindictive."

She bowed her head. "We deserve to be subjected," she whispered.

"Oh, but you won't be," he assured her. "What gain in that for Terra, as far away as you are? Some drastic changes will be necessary, of course, to make sure no fresh danger will breed hereabouts. But the

Imperial commission that decides on them will depend heavily on *my* advice. I feel pretty sure Scotha will end as a confederation of nations under Ilrian dominance, with you the queen, and a Terran resident who keeps an eye on things but generally lets you alone." His lips brushed her cheek. "Begin thinking what you would like to see happen."

Her smile was still wan, but he saw that something of her spirit was on its way home. "I don't believe the Empire is in such a bad state," she said. "Not when it has people like you."

No, he thought, *it's worse off; but why hurt you again by explaining?*

She brought her left hand from beneath the cloak and took both his. "And what will you be doing?" she asked.

He met her gaze. Loneliness was sudden within him. How beautiful she stood there.

But what she meant could never endure. They were too foreign to each other. Best he depart soon, that the memories remain untarnished in them both. She would find someone else at last, and he—well— "I have my work," he said.

Far above them, the first of the descending Imperial ships glittered in heaven like a falling star.

THE WARRIORS FROM NOWHERE

"Crime," said Captain Dominic Flandry of the Terran Empire's Naval Intelligence Corps, "is entirely a matter of degree. If you shoot your neighbor in order to steal his property, you are a murderer and a thief, subject to enslavement. If, however, you gather a band of lusty fellows in the name of honor and glory, knock off a couple of million people, take their planet, and hit up the survivors for taxes, you are a great conqueror, a hero, a statesman, and your name goes down in the history books. Sooner or later, this inconsistency seeps into the national consciousness and produces a desire for universal peace. That in turn brings about what is known as decadence, especially among philosophers who never had to do any of the actual fighting. The Empire is in this condition, of which the early stages are the most agreeable period of a civilization to live in—somewhat analogous to a banana just starting to show brown spots. I fear, however, that by now we are just a bit overripe."

He was not jailed for his remarks because he made
them in private, sitting on the balcony of a rented
lodge on Varrak's southern continent and finishing
his usual noontime breakfast. His flamboyantly pa-
jamaed legs were cocked up on the rail. Sighting
over his coffee cup and between his feet, he saw a
mountainside drop steeply down to green sun-
flooded wilderness. That light played over a lean,
straight-boned face and a long hard body which
made him look like anything but an officer of a sated
imperium. But then, his business was a strenuous
one these days.

His current mistress offered him a cigarette and he
inhaled it into lighting. She was a stunning blonde
named Ella McIntyre, whom he had bought a few
weeks previously in Fort Lone, the planet's one city.
He had learned that she was of the old pioneer stock,
semi-aristocrats who had fallen on times so bad that
at last they had chosen by lot some of their number
to sell as "voluntary" slaves. That kind of sacrifice
was not in accordance with law or custom on Terra,
but Terra was a long way off and its tributaries necessarily had a great deal of local autonomy. Flandry
had wangled an invitation to the private auction and
decided she would be a good investment. She could
have far worse owners than himself, and when he
resold her—at a profit—he'd make sure the next one
was a decent sort too.

He sipped, wiped his mustache, and drew breath
to continue his musings. An apologetic cough
brought his head around. His valet, the only other
being in the lodge, had emerged from it. This was a
native of Shalmu, remarkably humanoid, short,
slender, with hairless green skin, prehensile tail, and

impeccable manners. Flandry had dubbed him Chives and taught him things which made him valuable in more matters than laying out a dress suit.

"Pardon me, sir," he said. His Anglic was as nearly perfect as vocal organs allowed. "Admiral Fenross is calling from the city."

Flandry swore. "Fenross! What's he doing on this planet? Tell him to—no, never mind, it's anatomically impossible." He sought the study, frowning. He wasted no love on his superior, and vice versa, but Fenross wouldn't contact a man on furlough, especially in person, unless it was urgent.

The screen held a gaunt, sharp countenance with dark-shadowed eyes. Red hair was dank with sweat. "There you are!" the admiral exclaimed. "Code 770." When Flandry had set the scrambler: "All leaves cancelled. Get busy at once." His voice broke across. "Though God knows what you or anyone can do. But it means all our heads."

Flandry took a drag of smoke that sucked in his cheeks. "What do you mean, sir?"

"The sack of Fort Lone was more than a raid—"

"What sack?"

"You mean you don't *know*?"

"Haven't tuned the telly for a week, sir. I'd better occupation." Beneath the drawl, the carefully casual manner, Flandry's skin prickled.

Fenross snarled something and said thickly, "Well, then, for your information, Captain, yesterday a barbarian force streaked in, shot out what defenses the town had, landed, looted, put the place to the torch, and were gone again in three hours from first contact. They also took about a thousand captives, mostly women. No Naval base here, you know, as thinly populated as this globe is. By the time word had gotten to the nearest patrol force and it had arrived, they were untraceable."

"You happened to be with it, sir, and have taken charge?" Flandry asked. He knew the answer; he was merely stalling while his mind regained balance and got into karate stance.

Barbarians—Beyond this Taurian sector of the Empire lay the wild stars, ungarrisoned, virtually unexplored; and among them prowled creatures who had gotten spaceships and nuclear weapons too soon. Raids and punitive expeditions had often gone back and forth across the marches. *But an assault on Varrak? Hard to believe. Predators go for fat and easy prey.*

"Of course I was, and have, you jigglebrain," Fenross snapped. "After we cleared up that last business, *I* didn't set my trajectory for the nearest vacation area. As undermanned as we are out here—Now we'll have to fight."

"I, sir?" Flandry couldn't resist saying. "That's the combat services' department, I'm told. Why pick on me?"

"You and every other man in the sector. Listen." Fenross seemed almost to lean out of the screen. "The bandits have not been identified, though mainly they look human. And . . . among the people they kidnapped is her Highness, Lady Megan of Luna, the favorite granddaughter of the Emperor himself!"

Not a muscle stirred in Flandry's visage, save to form a long, low whistle; but his belly tautened till it hurt. "Any clues at all?"

"Well, one officer did manage to lie hidden in the ruins and take a holofilm, just a few minutes' worth.

Otherwise we've only the accounts of demoralized civilians, practically worthless." Fenross paused. Obviously it hurt him to add: "Maybe it's luck that you were here. We do need you."

"I should say you do, dear chief." Modesty was not a failing of Flandry's, nor would he pass by a chance to twit his superior when he couldn't be punished for it. "All right, I'll flit directly over. Cheers."

He cut the circuit and returned to the balcony. Chives was clearing away the breakfast dishes; Ella was nervously pacing. "So long, children," the man said. "I'm on my way."

Eyes like blued silver sought him. "What has happened?" the girl asked, all at once gone calm.

Flandry gave her a smile of sorts. "I've just been handed a chance for either a triumph that may earn me a fortune, or a failure that may earn me burial in a barbarian's barnyard. If a bookmaker quotes you odds of ten to one on the latter, bet your life savings, because he's ripe for the plucking."

It was like a scene from some mythic hell, save that its kind had been enacted much too many times in history.

Against a background of shattered walls and jumping flames, men crowded, surged, shouted, laughed —big men in helmet, cuirass, kilt, some carrying archaic swords as well as modern small arms. The picture was focused on an ornamental terrace above the central plaza. There huddled a dozen young women, stripped alike of clothing and hope, weeping, shuddering, or lost in an apathy of despair. Elsewhere, others were being led off to a disc-shaped vessel, doubtless a tender to an orbiting mother ship; still others were being herded through the swarm toward the upper level. It was a hastily conducted sale. Silver, gold, gems, the plunder of the city, were tossed at a gnomish unhuman figure that squatted there and pushed each purchase downstairs to a grinning conqueror.

The film ended. Flandry looked through the transparency in the undamaged, commandeered office where he sat, out over desolation. Smoke still made an acrid haze in what had been Fort Lone. Imperial marines stood guard, a relief station dispensed food and medical help, a pair of corvettes hung in the sky and heavier battlecraft swung beyond its blueness—all of which was rather too late to do much good.

"Well," rasped Fenross, "what do you make of it?"

Flandry replayed, stopped motion, and turned the enlarger knob, till a holographic image stood big and grotesque before him. "Except for this dwarf creature," he replied, "I'd say they were all of human race."

"Of course—" The admiral sounded as if he barely stopped himself from finishing, "—idiot!" After a moment: "Could they be from some early colony out in these parts that reverted to barbarism . . . during the Troubles, perhaps? I don't believe complete records are left on every attempt at emigration and settlement made during the Breakup, but we do know quite a few were less than successful. Could such a retrograded people have worked their way back up to a point where they could start reduplicating some of the ancestral technology, before outgrowing the wild ways they'd acquired meanwhile?"

"I wonder," Flandry said. "The spacecraft in the

film is an odd design. I think there are some societies within the Merseian hegemony that employ more or less the same type, but it's not what I'd expect barbarians imitating our boats to have."

Fenross gulped. His fingernails whitened where he gripped the table edge. "If the Merseians are behind this—"

Flandry gestured at the dwarf. "Tall, dark, and handsome there may provide a clue to their origin. I don't know. That's for data retrieval in the nearest well-stocked xenological archive to tell us, and I'm afraid it is not very near at all."

He leaned back, tugged his chin, and continued low-voiced, "But I must say the pattern of this raid is strange in every respect. Varrak's well inside the border, with only a small area that's been worth colonizing, thus not an especially tempting mark. Plenty of better prospects lie closer to the Wilderness. Then too, the raiders knew exactly how to neutralize the defenses; it was done with almost unnecessary precision, scanty as they were. And, of course, the raid collared the princess. Suggests inside help, eh?"

"I thought of that, naturally," Fenross grunted. "I'm setting up a quiz of every survivor of the security force. If narco indicates anything suspicious about anybody, we'll give him the hypnoprobe."

"I suspect it's wasted effort, sir. The bandit chief is too smooth an operator to leave clues of that kind. If he had collaborators here, they left with his lads and we'll list them as 'missing, presumed killed in action.' But what's the story on her Highness?"

Fenross groaned. "She was making a tour of the marches, according to a couple of servants who escaped. Officially it was an inspection, actually it

seems to've been for thrills. How could those muck-
heads on Terra conceivably have allowed it?" His
fist struck the table, then he sighed: "Well, I've
heard she has the Emperor around her little finger."

*I suppose even the hardest old son of a bitch
must have a sentimental streak, perhaps mushier
than in most of us,* Flandry thought. *Also, his newly and forcibly acceded Majesty has so much else to
worry about, one can understand how he could be
wheedled into supposing a region was safe that
never caused him trouble before, and indeed gave
him support.*

"Anyhow," Fenross went on, "she traveled incognito, as simply a *nouveau riche* tourist, and her
staff included a crack secret service detail. No use, it
turned out. The raiders blasted their way into the
hotel where she was staying, gunned down her
guards, and made off with her and most of her attendants."

"Again," said Flandry, "they appear to have had
inside information. I'd hypothesize they got her itin-
erary beforehand, on Terra itself or early during the
trip. The looting here was a sideline and a red herring. That includes the picturesque little bit of salaci-
ty we've seen filmed. There wasn't time to sell off
any substantial fraction of an estimated thousand
prisoners, but it's the kind of thing that barbarians
are popularly supposed to do."

"I'm inclined to agree," Fenross said slowly. "I'm
also afraid, however, that some powerful people in
this sector will not. They'll demand that whole task
forces be sent to scour the Wilderness before their
own precious interests suffer attack; and they've got
the influence to have their demands met."

Flandry nodded. "Exactly," he replied. He took forth a cigarette. "What's your guess at the real motive? Ransom?"

"Probably, and I hope to God the kidnappers only want money. But—you know as well as I, barbarian kings and the like may be rough, but they're seldom stupid. I'm afraid her ransom will be concessions we can ill afford. If they are barbarians we're dealing with. If they're really, let's say, the Merseians—That hardly bears thinking about, does it?"

"I can't see the Emperor—the present one, at any rate—selling out the Empire, even to get his favorite granddaughter back."

"No . . . no. . . . But he'll be distraught when he hears, I suppose. It may go ill with officers like you and me, who were on the scene or near it." Fenross' head bobbed up and down. "Yes, I'm quite sure it will."

Flandry scowled. He was fond of living. "Somehow I doubt the operation was mounted just to get rid of you, or even of me, sir. The political purpose—"

"I haven't had a chance to wonder about that yet," Fenross snapped. "I doubtless won't get one, either. Too much else on hand. Setting up intensive studies here—probably useless, I know, but they must be carried out. Contacting commands throughout the sector. Getting an Intelligence operation mounted that'll go through the whole adjacent Wilderness, and in among the Merseians, and—" He lifted haunted eyes to meet Flandry's. "I'm an administrator, that's what I am, a bloody damned administrator, understaffed and swamped. You're the dashing, glamorous field agent, independent to the brink of insubordination, aren't you? Aren't you?

Well, don't just sit there! Get going!"

"I might do something unorthodox, sir, without checking with you first," Flandry was careful to warn. "Time could be short and you preoccupied. For the proverbial covering of my own rear end, may I have a roving commission, duly entered in the data bank? And I'll also need clearance and code for instant access to any information whatsoever."

Fenross' desperation was made plain when he mumbled, "All right, you slippery bastard, you'll have 'em, and God help us both if you misuse the authority. Now go away and start whatever you have in mind." He retained the coolness not to ask what that might be.

Flandry rose. "It might stimulate my wits if a small reward were offered, sir," he said mildly.

The lodge was as good a place as any to commence work. Like all capital ships, the dreadnaught now in orbit around Varrak bore very complete electronic files of Intelligence material pertinent to the sector of her assignment, as well as much else. The special receiver which he had brought back with him, responding to his properly identified requisition, gave him any displays he called for that were available; when he demanded printouts, those were on sheets that would crumble within the hour. In dressing gown and slippers, he sat perusing records of which many had cost lives, of which some were worth an empire. Chives kept him supplied with coffee and cigarettes.

Near dawn of the planet's thirty-one-hour day, Ella stole up behind him and laid a hand on his head. "Aren't you ever coming in to sleep, Nick?" she asked. He had encouraged her to address him famil-

iarly, but this was the first time she had yet done
so.

"Not for a while," he answered curtly, without
glancing at her. "I'll load up on stim instead, if need
be. I'm on the track of a hunch; and if it's right,
we're on mighty short rations of time."

She nodded, light sliding down unbound tresses,
and settled herself quietly onto a couch. After a while
the sun rose.

"Stars and planets and little pink asteroids," muttered Flandry all at once. "I may have an answer.
The infotrieve is a splendid invention, if you're on
the seeking rather than the hiding end of things."

She regarded him in continued silence. He got up,
moved his cramped limbs about, rumpled his seal-
brown hair. "The answer could be wrong," he said
aloud, only half to her. "If it's right, the danger is the
same, or perhaps more. Talking about sticking your
head in a lion's mouth—when the lion has halito-
sis—"

He began to pace. "Chives is a handy fellow with
a spacecraft, a gun, or a set of burglar's tools; but I
need a different kind of help as well."

"Can I give it, Nick?" Ella asked low. "I'd be glad
to. You've been good to me. I never quite expected
that."

He regarded her a moment. She rose to stand
before him, tall and lithe, descendant of those who
made a home for themselves on a hostile world and
even turned a small part of it into a bit of Terra—
"My dear," he replied, "can you shoot?"

"I used to hunt axhorns in the mountains," she
told him.

"Then . . . what'd you say if I set you free? Not
just that, but hunted up what I could of your other

kinfolk who had to be sold, and acquired them and
manumitted them and provided a bit of a grubstake?
The reward should cover that, with a trifle to spare
for my next poker game."

She had never wept before in his presence. "I, I, I
have no words."

He held her close. "The price is a considerable risk
of losing everything," he murmured. "Of death, or
torture, or degradation, or whatever horror you dare
imagine, or maybe some that you can't. We're dealing with an utterly monstrous ego. If power corrupts,
the prospect of it can do worse."

She lifted her tear-wet face to his. "You're . . .
going too . . . aren't you?" she breathed. Stepping
back, straightening: "No, don't you dare leave me
behind!"

His laugh was shaken, but he slapped her in a not
very brotherly fashion. "All right, macushla. You can
come out on the target range and prove what you
claimed about your shooting while Chives packs."

The boat Flandry chose was no match in any respect—speed, armament, comfort—for his private
speedster; but the latter was afar, and this one was
an agile fighter. In her, it was a three-day flit to Vor.
After they had rehearsed what must be done as best
they could, he spent the time amusing himself
and his companions. There might not be another
chance.

Vor had been discovered early in the age of exploration by Cynthians, but colonized by humans,
like Varrak. More terrestroid, it had become popu-
lous and wealthy, and was a natural choice of capital
for the duke who governed the Taurian Sector. Less
grandiose than Terrans, but perhaps more energetic,

its inhabitants eventually found themselves dominant in what was almost an empire within the Empire, their ruler sitting high in the councils of the
Imperium.

Flandry left Chives in charge of the boat at
Gloriana spaceport, and slipped the portmaster a
substantial bribe in case he should need cooperation.
He and Ella took a flittercab into the city and got a
penthouse in one of its better hotels. He never
stinted himself when he was on expense account, but
this time the penthouse had a sound business reason.
You could land on the roof, should a quick getaway
become necessary.

Having settled in, he phoned the ducal palace and
got through to a secretary in charge of appointments.
"This is Captain Sir Dominic Flandry of his
Majesty's Naval Intelligence Corps," he announced
to the face in the screen with a pomposity equal to its
effeminacy. "I have official business to conduct at his
Grace's earliest convenience."

"I am afraid, Sir Dominic, that his Grace is en-
gaged until—" A buzz sounded near the secretary's
elbow. "Excuse me, sir." He turned and conferred
over a sonic-shielded instrument out of the scanner
field. When he resumed the earlier conversation, he
was obsequious. "Of course, Sir Dominic. His Grace
will be pleased to see you at 1400 tomorrow."

"Good," said Flandry. "I'll bring a lollipop for
you." He switched off and laughed into Ella's
astonishment: "Usually in this business one doesn't
want fame, but sometimes the fact that one has a
certain amount of it can be used. Pretty Boy there
was being monitored, as I'd expected. He was informed that my presence is urgently desired at the
palace. No doubt the idea is to find out whether I

nourish any suspicions, and, if I do, to allay them."

Night had fallen. They had not yet turned on the lights, for the one great moon of Vor was in the wall transparency, its radiance making the roof garden outside into a sight of elven beauty. Ella also became dreamlike, quicksilver amidst shadow. But he saw how she bit her lip. "That doesn't sound good for us," she whispered.

"It sounds very much as though my notion is right. Look here." Flandry leaned back in his chair, confronted her where she hunched on a sofa, and bridged his fingers. He had been over this ground a dozen times already, but he liked to hear himself talk, and besides, it might soothe the poor, lonely, brave girl.

"The Corps is highly efficient if you point it in the right direction," he said. "In this case, the kidnapping was so designed that Fenross is pointed in a hundred different directions. He's forced to tackle the hopeless job of investigating uncounted barbarian worlds and the very Roidhunate of Merseia. But I, having a nasty suspicious mind, thought that our own space might harbor persons who wouldn't mind having the Emperor's favorite granddaughter for a house guest.

"That alien-type spaceship was a clue toward Merseia, but I didn't like it. Merseia's too far from here for it to be a likely influence on any local barbarians; and if the operation was Merseian, why such a blatant signature on it? Likewise, ordinary buccaneers would not have come to Varrak in the first place if they had any understanding of the economics of their trade, and could scarcely have garnered such accurate information in the second place.

But who then were the raiders, and who led them?

"That gnome creature gave me a hunch. He was obviously in some position of authority, or he wouldn't have been demanding loot in exchange for those girls. The pirates could simply have taken the women for themselves; it'd have made an equally effective charade. The files held no information on a race of that description, but I did find out that Duke Alfred of Tauria has a number of aliens in his household, some from regions little known or unknown.

"Let's make it a working hypothesis that those humans were also Alfred's folk, in operatic garb. What then?

"Well, my guess is that before long, word will come from what purports to be a barbarian king: he's got Princess Megan, and her ransom will be a goodly chunk of this sector. The Emperor will scarcely yield, but in his grief and outrage he'll want nothing but war. However, we're spread too thin, our internal peace is still too precarious, for him to dare bring the whole Navy to bear, or even a substantial part of it—especially when no one knows yet where the enemy lives. Duke Alfred is responsible for Tauria. He'll offer to mobilize its strength, to assume most of the burden. Mobilization *en masse* can't take place overnight, and under any other circumstances would rouse such suspicion that he'd instantly be replaced, with all his senior officers. But as matters stand, he'll be cheered on, given every possible assistance . . . and presently be ready to declare himself an independent monarch. I'm afraid that the key people in too many units will see too much gain for themselves to refuse his leadership. I'm also afraid the cost of crushing him will be too great. Probably,

after some fighting, he'll get his wish. And so the
Empire—human civilization—loses another prime
bulwark.

"At least," finished Flandry, "that's how I'd work
the swindle."

Ella shivered. "War," she said; her voice wavered.
"Cities going up in flame. Deaths in the millions.
Looting, enslaving—No!"

"Of course," he reminded her, "we need proof.
I've left my suspicions in the appropriate data bank,
in case we don't return, but saw no point in telling
Fenross just yet. He'd surely consider them fantastic;
he has an exaggerated opinion of our aristocracy.
Besides, if I'm right, the Taurian divisions of the
Corps are riddled with Alfred's agents; you don't
start a coup like this on the impulse of a moment. So
you and I are here to infiltrate right back."

She nodded, mute, and hugged herself as if caught
in a winter wind. He rose, went to her, urged her
gently to her feet, held her close and stroked her hair.
"I'm sorry," he murmured. "I needn't have repeated
all this to you, eh? It only told you once again what
an utter bastard I am, using a beautiful young girl for
a chess piece. What can I say except that I'm on the
board too, and—"

She lifted her countenance toward his. Moonlight
glimmered off tears, but somehow she smiled. "Y-y-
you're a *nice* bastard," she said.

He laughed, a bit wistfully, before he completed
his sentence: "—and we ought to have several hours
ahead of us to spend as we like. Hmmm?"

—Afterward they stood watch and watch. It was
good that they did. Between midnight and morning,
Ella shook Flandry awake. Silently, she pointed at

the optic wall. A flitter was landing on the roof.

He glided up and sought the weapons laid nearby. "Quick reaction," he said low. "I did expect his Grace would wait to receive me first. Let's hope this means he's rattled."

Ella cradled a slugthrowing rifle in her arms. Slowly moving, the moon still cast her into white, unreal relief. Her tone was steady. "Could they be innocent?"

"If so, they haven't had the courtesy to call ahead, which by itself makes me dislike them," he answered. "Here, take the rest of your gear. Come on back to the corner. Be ready to use the sofa for a shield."

Three murky forms emerged and approached the wall. Moonbeams glittered on metal in their hands. "They look like hirelings, not regular militiamen," Flandry observed. He felt quite cool, now that action was upon him. "Well, the underworld always has been a recruiting source for revolutionaries. Let's see what they do."

One man bore no gun, but a thing that Flandry soon recognized as a high-powered portable drill with a head of synthetic diamond. On his back was a tank. The bit made the lowest of whines as it went through the wall. He retracted it and brought a hose around from the tank. "Sleepy gas," Flandry said. "They want us for interrogation. But we'd never live to dine out on the experience afterward."

He and Ella had masks against the contingency, but he saw no point in donning them. Nor was he in a position to conduct a quiz himself. He gave the woman her instructions and aimed his blaster. As the nozzle of the hose came through the hole, the weap-

on cracked. A blue-white lightning bolt pierced the
wall and the intruder went down. Ella's rifle barked
next to his ear, dropping the one on the right at the
same time. They never knew which of them took the
third, a second later; both shots struck home.

The flitter did not stir. Flandry clicked his tongue.
"Nobody left at the controls," he said. "Rank
amateurism."

He went outside to make sure the three were dead
and to search for any clues. There were none to
speak of, though he strengthened his impression that
these had been civilians. Returning, he found Ella
motionless, staring down at her weapon. "I never
fired at a sophont before," she said thinly. "I never
killed a man before."

He kissed her. The lips beneath his were cold and
dry. "Don't let it bother you," he counselled. "Occupational hazard in their profession, as in mine. Remember, we're trying to head off the killing of millions of innocents." He moved toward the phone.
"It'd be in character for an officer of Intelligence not
to want the police in, and I have the authority to
order that." He punched a key. "Night manager,
please. . . . Hello. I'm afraid we've a bit of a mess
in our place. Can you have somebody come clean
up?"

The audience hall was cathedral-vaulted and ornate. Its present master had not changed it, but his
more austere personality showed in the relatively
streamlined ceremonies at court, and in the black-
uniformed guardsmen who stood ranked along the
walls. Flandry's dress garb, like the gown and veil of
the young woman who followed him, outshone the
appearance of the man on the throne.

Duke Alfred was big, his frame running to

paunchiness in middle age but still basically muscular, his blocky, gray-bearded face devoid of humor but alive with pride. His dossier had given Flandry a distinct idea that here was a dangerous person. Yet when the latter had snapped a salute and identified himself, Alfred said graciously enough: "At ease, Captain, and welcome in your own right as well as on his Majesty's service. Who is your company?"

"A token of esteem for your grace," Flandry replied. Alfred's glance dropped to the control bracelet on Ella's wrist which marked and sealed her status as property. "Ella is her name, and I've found her satisfying. Now—well, I may have to trouble you a fair amount in line of duty, and wouldn't want you to feel I was being arrogant, so—" He spread his palms and grinned his smarmiest grin.

"Well. Well, well." Alfred stroked his beard. "Let us see." Shyly, Ella lowered her veil. Appreciation kindled on his countenance. "Very good, Captain. I thank you indeed." He gestured. "Let her be well quartered." With a leer: "We'll soon get acquainted, girl, you and I."

She smiled and curtsied in half frightened, half servile fashion. She was quite an actress, as Flandry had learned when he tested her on the trip here. A gigantic, four-armed Gorzunian slave led her out, toward the harem.

"And what is your errand?" Alfred asked Flandry. "I've heard of you. You wouldn't be sent on any trifling matter."

"The details are for no ears but your Grace's and your most trusted officers'," was the reply. "However, thus far I have no details, and see no harm in confessing before this assembly that I'm on rather a fishing expedition." He went on to spin a plausible tale of Merseian agents, some of human race, at large in the outer provinces for the purpose of reviving discord, and the need to track them down. Having described the incident of the previous night, he attributed it to the machinations of the opposition, implying quite clearly that his role was partly that of decoy. The bodies were now in charge of the local Corps office, in hopes that they could be identified and thus provide a lead. Nowhere did he mention Varrak, or Ella's marksmanship.

"I've no direct knowledge of subversive activity," Alfred said after expressing appropriate shock, "but you shall certainly have every cooperation we can give you. What are your immediate needs?"

"Nothing at once, thank you, your Grace. I'll just be sniffing around. If something comes up—" Et cetera, et cetera, until dismissal.

The ducal palace was part of a castle, a fortress within an outer wall of fused stone, raised during the Troubles. By the time Flandry got to the outer gate, his spine was a-tingle. Alfred was not about to let him go freely hither and yon. There would surely be another attempt to capture him for hypnoprobing, to determine what his mission really was. When he disappeared—forever—the Merseian agents he had invented would be the obvious culprits. And this time the Duke would scarcely trust hired thugs.

Flandry checked with the commandant of Intelligence for Vor, since he knew Alfred's men would verify whether or not he did. He was unsurprised, though saddened, to hear that no progress had been made on tracking down those who dispatched his attackers. So here, at least, the dry rot had entered his own service. . . . Back in the penthouse, he changed into loose civilian dress. It concealed the weapons and kit he secured under its blouse.

In the hotel restaurant he ate a solitary supper, thinking much about Ella, and dawdled over his liqueur. Two men who had entered soon after him and taken a corner table idled too, but somewhat awkwardly. He studied them without seeming to do so. One was small and clever-looking, the other big and rangy and with a military bearing—doubtless from the household guards, out of uniform for this occasion. He would do.

At last Flandry got up and sauntered out to the ground-level street. A good many people were around, afoot, under gaudy lights and luminescent elways. (He remembered how moonbeams washed across Ella.) His shadows mingled with the crowd. He would have shaken them easily enough, but that wasn't his intention. Let him give them every break instead; they were hard-working chaps and deserved a helping hand.

He hailed a flittercab. Such vehicles were not autopiloted in Gloriana. "Know any good dives?" he asked fatuously as he climbed in. "You know, girls, dope, anything goes, but not too expensive."

"I wouldn't be much of a cabdriver if I didn't, would I, sir?" the man replied, and took off for a less respectable part of town. He landed on the twenty-fifth flange of a tall building, beneath a garish flickersign. Another taxi came down behind his.

Flandry spent a while in the bar, amused at the embarrassment of his followers, and then picked a girl, a slim creature with an insolent red mouth. She snuggled against him as they went down the corridor. A door opened for them and they passed through.

"Sorry, sister," Flandry murmured. He pulled out

his stun pistol and let her have a medium beam. As she collapsed, he eased her onto the bed. She'd be unconscious for hours. He tucked a decent sum of money into her bodice and stood waiting, weapon in hand.

It was not long before the door opened again. The two men were there. Had they bribed the madam or threatened her? In any event, this had looked like an excellent opportunity to carry out their assignment. Flandry's stunner dropped the smaller one.

The big fellow took him by surprise, pouncing like a cat. A skilled twist sent the gun clattering free against the wall. Flandry drove a knee upward. Pain lanced through him as it hit body armor. The guardsman got a hold which should have pinioned him. Flandry broke free with a trick he knew, delivered a karate chop, and added a rabbit punch. The guardsman fell.

For a moment Flandry hesitated, panting. He had no use for the short one, whom it might be safest to kill. However—He settled for giving both a calculated jolt which ought to keep them unconscious for hours. Thereafter he opened the window and stepped out onto the emergency landing. With his pocket phone he summoned another cab. It came to hover before him on its gravs, and the driver looked out into the muzzle of a blaster.

"We've three sleepers to get rid of," said Flandry cheerfully. The girl must be included, since her slack body—after she was much overdue for reappearance —would raise an alarm, as her mere absence would not. "Give a hand, friend, unless you want to add a corpse to the museum."

He had the appalled man lug his victims out into the vehicle and fly him well beyond the city. They descended on a meadow in a patch of woods. Flandry stunned the driver and laid all four out under a tree. He tucked a goodly tip in the cabbie's tunic.

Now to work! He stripped the guardsmen naked and tossed the clothes of the smaller one into the taxi. The big one he measured in detail with his identification kit, and bundled up the garb of him, complete with wallet and documents. Wildflowers grew round about, long-stemmed and white-petaled. Flandry folded all four pairs of hands on breasts and put a flower in each. *"Requiescem in pace,"* he intoned. The sleepers wouldn't wake till perhaps noon, and had a long hike to the nearest place where they could call for help. The nakedness of the guardsmen would probably cause further delay. By the time they could report in, the affair ought to be finished, one way or another.

Flandry returned in the cab. At the edge of town, he abandoned it and got a different one, which brought him to the spaceport. He was sure that a ducal agent or two would be watching his spacecraft. If so, that person saw him go aboard, presumably without seeing the bundle under his cloak. He got immediate clearance from the portmaster's office and lifted into space. His idea was that the opposition would guess he'd been scared off and was at least going to conduct his business from a safe distance. If so, splendid; he always preferred to be underestimated.

Once in orbit, he and Chives got busy disguising him. Much can be done with responsiplast on the face, contact lenses with holographic retinal patterns, false fingerprints, and the rest. Possibly more can be done by sheer theater, and Flandry had paid attention to the ways his man walked and sat and gestured. The effect wouldn't pass a close examination, but he was gambling that there wouldn't be any. When he got through, he was Lieutenant Roger Bargen of the ducal household guards.

Chives took the boat planetside again, deftly evading Traffic Control's monitors, and landed near a village some fifty kilometers from Gloriana. Dawn was not far off. Flandry walked in and caught the morning monorail to the city.

When he entered the castle, he did not report to his colonel. That would have been what he mildly termed a tactical error. It was pretty clear, though, that Bargen's assignment had been secret, none of his fellows aware of it. Therefore, if they saw him scurrying around the place, too busy for conversation, they wouldn't suppose aught was amiss. To be sure, the deception could last only a few hours; but Flandry didn't think he'd need more.

In fact, he reflected, *I bet my life I won't.*

Ella the slave, who had been Ella McIntyre and a free hillwoman of Varrak, was shocked to her guts by the harem. Incense gagged her, music scratched at her nerves, velvyl hangings in gloomy colors seemed to close in everywhere around. She prayed the Duke would not send for her that night. If he did— well, that was part of the price. However, he did not.

The inmates had a dormitory, a suite of rooms for games and relaxation, and nonhuman servants. They numbered about a score, and few of them said much to the new arrival as she prowled about; she sensed wariness in some, hostility in others, outright dread in a few. Among the worst horrors of slavery is what it does to the spirit of the enslaved.

But she had to make friends, fast. The harem,

where seclusion and secrecy were the natural order of things, was the logical place for hiding a female prisoner. Within its own walls, though, it must be the most gossippy of little worlds. She picked an alert-looking girl with wide bright eyes, wandered up to her, and smiled shyly. "Hello," she said. "I'm Ella."

The other arched her brows. "Well. How did you get here?"

"I'm a . . . a present. What's it like here? Please."

"Oh, nothing too dreadful, dear. Terribly boring most of the time." Ella shuddered at the thought of years lost thus, but smiled in meek gratitude. The other girl wanted to know everything she could tell about the outside—everything, anything—and this took several hours. Meanwhile several more women gathered to listen and comment.

Finally conversation drifted the way Ella had hoped it might. Yes, she was told, something strange had lately occurred. The entire western end of the suite was now closed off, with household troopers keeping watch. They were normal males, but television monitors kept them proper, damn it. Somebody or something new must be housed there, and speculation ran wild as to the who or the what or the why.

Ella masked her tension with an effort that only her muscles could measure. "Have you any ideas?" she asked brightly.

"Many," said her first acquaintance. "They're all wrong, I'm sure. His Grace has funny tastes. But you'll find that out, my dear."

Ella bit her lips.

That night she could not sleep. The blackness was thick and strangling. She wanted to scream and run, break free, run among the stars until she was back in

her loved, lost greenwood hills. A lifetime without
seeing the sun or feeling a wind kiss her cheeks! She
thrashed wearily about and wondered why she had
ever agreed to Flandry's proposal.

But if he lived and came to her, she could now tell
him what he needed to know. *If* he lived. And even
if he did, this was the middle of a fortress. He'd die
under hypnoprobe and she under nerve-lash. *God,
let me sleep. Only for an hour.*

In the morning, fluorotubes gave her a cold dawn.
She used the swimming pool without pleasure and
ate breakfast without tasting and wondered if she
looked as haggard as she felt.

When she left the mess, a scaled hand touched her
shoulder. She whirled about with a little shriek and
looked into a scaly, beaky countenance. Somehow it
made the question sibilant: "You are the new concubine?"

She tried to answer but her throat tightened up.

"Come." The being turned and strode off.
Numbly, she followed. The chatter in the harem
died as she went by, eyes grew wide and faces pale,
here and there a finger traced a furtive religious sign.
She was not being summoned for the master's sport.

At the end of a hall was a door, where two men
stood uniformed and armed. She thought in her fear
that they glanced at her with pity. The door opened
at the nonhuman's gestures. He waved her through.
As he also passed by, the door closed behind him.

The room beyond was small and nearly bare. It
held a chair with straps and wires and a switchboard; she recognized the electronic torture machine
which leaves no marks on the flesh. In a chair more
peculiarly shaped crouched another being that was
not human. Its small hunched body was wrapped in

gorgeous robes, and great lusterless eyes regarded her from a hairless bulge of head.

"Sit down," the creature ordered. A thin hand waved her to the electronic seat. Helpless, she obeyed. Through the stammering of her heart, she heard: "I want to discourse with you. You will do best not to lie." The voice was high and squeaky, but there was nothing ridiculous about the goblin who spoke. "For your information, I am Sarlish of Jagranath, which lies beyond the Empire, and his Grace's chief Intelligence officer. Thus you see this is no routine matter. You were brought here by a man of whom I have suspicions. Why?"

"As . . . a gift . . . sir," she whispered. Her tongue felt like a block of dried wood.

"*Timeo Danaos et dona ferentes*," remarked Sarlish surprisingly. "I did not learn of it until an hour ago, or I would have investigated sooner. You are a slave born?"

"N-no, sir. For debt—He bought me and—"

"Where are you from?"

I must not tell! "I was born on . . . on Freya—"

"Unlikely, I think. It is unfortunate that I cannot hypnoprobe you at once. That would leave you in no fit state for his Grace tonight, should you be innocent. However—" Sarlish stroked his meager chin contemplatively. "Yes. Sufficient pain will disorganize your mind until questioning will bring out inconsistencies. Should there be any, we can go on to the probe. Let us get you secured." He gestured to the other, different alien.

That being hulked forward. Ella leaped up with a yell of raw terror—and rage, rage. The creature snatched for her. She dodged and drove a kick at his midriff. He grunted and stepped back, unharmed.

She plunged for the door. As it opened, the rough hands closed on her arm. Whirling, she jabbed fingers at his eyes. He ululated and backed away.

"Ah-h-h," breathed Sarlish. He drew a stunner and took judicious aim.

"Not recommended, comrade," said a voice from the doorway.

Sarlish jumped from his seat and whirled about, to confront a blaster. The guards who lay at the newcomer's feet had quietly been stunned. "Bargen!" shrilled Sarlish, and dropped his weapon. Then, slowly: "No. Captain Flandry, is it not?"

"In person, and right in the traditional nick of time." The injured being lurched toward the Terran. Flandry slew him with a narrow beam. Sarlish scuttled forward at fantastic speed, between the man's legs, and brought him down. Ella bounded over him and caught the gnome with a flying tackle. Sarlish hissed and clawed. She struck him on the jaw with her fist, in sheer self-defense. The thin neck twisted back with a snapping noise. Sarlish kicked once and was still.

"Good show, girl!" Flandry scrambled to his feet. In a sweeping motion, he peeled off his face mask. "Too hot in this flinkin' thing. All right, did you find our princess?"

"This way." A far-off part of Ella watched, surprised, the swiftness and gladness with which she responded. She bent and took up a guardsman's blaster. "I'll show you. But can we—?"

"Not by ourselves. I got at a phone a few minutes ago and gave Chives a radio buzz. Though how he's going to locate us exactly in this warren, I don't know. Couldn't say much, you realize, necessarily using code. I simply had to assume you'd succeeded—'' Flandry swerved around a bevy of screaming girls. "Hoo-ee! No wonder the harem attendants are nonhuman!"

Ella pointed to a blank wall. "She must be behind there. No other possibility, as far as I could learn. We'll have to go around, into the next hall—"

"And get shot on the way? No, thanks!" Flandry began assembling scattered furniture into a rough barricade before the wall. "Cut our way through, will you?"

Plastic bubbled and smoked as Ella's flame attacked it. Flandry went on: "I bluffed my way into this quarter by saying I had to fetch someone. One of the ladies told me where you'd been taken. Doubtless the only reason I made it this far is that no man would dare come in unless he had orders from Alfred himself. But now there's hell to pay and no pitch hot. I only hope Chives can track us before he gets blown out of the sky." He looked along the barrel of his blaster, down the arched length of the corridor to the chamber beyond. "Hang on, here we go."

A squad of guards had burst into sight. Flandry set his weapon to needle beam. That gave maximum range, provided you had the skill to hit a target at such a distance. A man toppled. A curtain of fire raged in response. The heat of it scorched his face through the gaps in his defense. He picked off another man, and another. But the rest were zigzagging, belly-flopping, coming into wide-beam range, where a single shot could fry him. "Get that wall open, will you?" he cried.

"Done!" Ella dodged as the circle she had cut collapsed outward. Droplets of molten plastic seared her skin. The barricade burst into flame. She tumbled through the hole, heedless of its hot edges.

Flandry followed.

Beyond, a young woman crouched against the opposite wall. Terror contorted her features. She was dark and rather pretty, but a resemblance to the Imperial grandfather was in her bones. "Lady Megan?" snapped Flandry.

"Yes, yes," she whimpered. "Who are you?"

"At your service, your Highness—I hope." Flandry sent a wide beam through the hole. A man screamed forth his agony. The Terran had a moment to wonder how many brave folk—probably including Ella and himself—would be dead because a spoiled darling had wanted an excursion.

The door swung open. Ella let loose a blast. More screams followed, and horrible smoke. Flandry heaved a divan up against the door. That was cutrate protection, good only for minutes.

Sweating, blackened, blistered, his countenance turned back to the princess. "I take it you know the Duke had you kidnapped, your Highness?" he asked.

"Yes, but he wasn't going to hurt me," she wailed.

"So you think. I happen to know he intended to kill you." That was less than true, but served Flandry's purpose. In the unlikely event that he survived, Megan wouldn't get him in trouble for endangering her life. In fact, she began to babble about a reward. He hoped she would remember afterward, if there was an afterward.

He had one advantage. The Duke could not use heavy stuff without losing his hostage and, incidentally, creating a sensation throughout Gloriana. But —he passed out three gas masks.

The outer wall glowed. Blasters were cutting a fresh circle from it, big enough to let through a dozen men at a time. Doubtless they'd wear armor.

The air was thick and bitter, hot and stinking. Flandry grinned lopsidedly and laid an arm about Ella's waist. "Well, sweetheart," he said, "it was a fairly spectacular try." Her hand reached briefly up to stroke his hair.

Something bellowed. Walls and floor trembled. He heard the rumble and crash of falling masonry. A storm of gunfire awoke.

"Chives!" whooped Flandry.

"Wha-what?" gasped Megan.

"We're getting what we ordered, salade d'Alfred au Chives," burbled Flandry. "You must meet Chives, your Highness. One of nature's noblemen. He—how in this especial hell did he do it?"

A volcano growl came, and silence.

Flandry removed the divan and risked a glance into the corridor. Daylight poured through its ruined walls. The place had taken the full impact of a Naval blaster cannon, and the attacking troopers had ceased to exist. Hovering alongside was the speedster.

"Chives," said Flandry in awe, "merely swooped up to the fortress under full drive, blew his way past the defenses, and opened up on the Duke's men here."

The airlock swung wide. A green head looked out. "I would recommend haste, sir," said the Shalmuan. "The alarm is out, and they do have warcraft."

Flandry helped the women cross over. The airlock hissed shut behind them. Chives had already returned to the pilot room. The boat took off with a thunderbolt of cloven air for her wake.

Flandry sought his valet. "How did you find us?" he mumbled. "I didn't even know where the harem was myself when I called you."

"Why, sir, you must be in great need of rest and tea, if you do not see the obvious," Chives replied. "I assumed there would be some objection to the removal of her Highness and combat would ensue. Energy beams ionize the air. I employed the radiation detectors."

Flandry nodded and turned his attention to the viewscreens and instruments. A light cruiser showed against the receding brilliance of the planet. "That chap," he fretted; and then: "No. The vectors and distances . . . we're leaving him *and* his missiles behind. This can has legs. We'll make it back to Varrak all right."

"In that case, sir," Chives said, "I will turn control over to the autopilot."

He departed for the galley. Flandry sought the main cabin, where Ella strove to soothe a hysterical Megan. For a moment, as the blonde woman looked up at him, he saw utter glory.

He found a cigarette, lighted it and drew deep. "Relax," he advised, "and bathe—all of us bathe." A scowl crossed his brow. "We'll worry later about the possibility that Alfred, now he's exposed, will try to rebel anyway. He couldn't succeed, but it might prove expensive for us—give Merseia an opening, or—"

Chives appeared, a loaded tray in his hands. "I beg your pardon, sir," he said. "As I approached the castle, I monitored the bands of individually worn radio transceivers, and learned that the Duke was personally directing the assault on you. I fear I took the liberty of disintegrating his Grace. Does her Highness take sugar or lemon in her tea?"

HONORABLE ENEMIES

The door opened behind him and a voice murmured, "Good evening, Captain Flandry."

He spun about, with a reflexive grab for his stun pistol, and found himself looking at a blaster. Slowly, then, he let his empty hand fall and stood poised. His eyes searched beyond the weapon and the six talon-like fingers that held it, to the tall gaunt body and sardonic smile.

The face there was humanoid, if you overlooked countless details of shape and proportion—lean, hook-nosed, golden-skinned. There was no hair, but a feathery blue crest rose high and plumelets formed brows above the eyes. Those eyes were sheer beauty, big and luminous bronze in hue. The being wore a simple, knee-length white tunic and his clawed feet were bare. However, jewels indicating rank hung from his neck and a cloak like a gush of blood from his shoulders.

The whole Merseian group is occupied elsewhere, Flandry thought in dismay. *I've seen to that. Or supposed I had. What's gone wrong?*

He forced relaxation of a sort upon himself, and even an answering smile. The main question was how he might get out of here with a whole skin. Assessment . . . this wasn't actually a Merseian, though a member of that party. It was Aycharaych of Chereion, who had arrived only a few days ago, presumably on a mission that corresponded to Flandry's.

"Pardon the intrusion," the Terran said. "Purely professional, I assure you. No offense meant."

"And none taken," replied Aycharaych with equal urbanity. He spoke perfect Anglic, save for a touch of accent that added a kind of harsh music to it.

Nevertheless, he could easily blast the man down and later express regret that he had mistaken an ace Intelligence officer of the Terran Empire for a common burglar.

Flandry dared hope the Chereionite would not be so crass. Little was known of that race—this was the first one that the human had ever met—but they were said to have a very ancient civilization and very subtle ways. Flandry had heard stories about Aycharaych's specific operations. . . .

"You are right, Captain, I intend you no harm," the being said. Flandry started. Had his mind been read, or what? "I will be content with chiding. This attempt to search our quarters was deplorably crude, quite unworthy of you. I trust you will give us a better game in future."

Flandry gauged distances and angles. A vase on a table stood close to hand. If he could sweep it across Aycharaych's wrist—

"I would not advise that, either," said the Chereionite. He stepped aside. "You may go now. Goodnight."

The Terran moved slowly toward the door. He couldn't let himself suffer this—dismissal. It was vital that he learn what the Merseians were brewing in the way of trouble for the Empire. Yes, a karate leap and kick—

Hampered by a greater gravity than his species had evolved under, Aycharaych should not have dodged fast enough. Yet somehow he did. He wasn't there when the boot arrived. Momentum carried Flandry on past. The blaster butt cracked against the base of his skull. He fell and lay for a minute while darkness roared through him.

"You do disappoint me, Captain," said the other, most softly. "A person of your reputation should be above theatrics. Now I must bid you goodnight."

Sickly, the human got to his feet and stumbled out into the hall. Aycharaych watched, still smiling.

Long passages brought him to the suite, as capacious as a small hotel, assigned the Terran delegation. Its common room was empty, like most of the rest. A feast was going on elsewhere. Flandry mixed himself a stiff drink at the bar and settled down.

A light step and a suggestive rustle of a long shimmerlyn skirt brought his glance around. Aline Chang-Lei, the Lady Marr of Syrtis, had entered. The sight of her lifted his spirits a trifle. She was tall and slender, raven-haired and oblique-eyed and delicate of feature; the blue gown seemed to make her ivory complexion luminous. She was also one of Sol's top field agents and his teammate here.

"What's the matter?" she asked at once.

"Why are you back?" he responded. "I thought you'd be at the party, helping distract people."

She shrugged. "No further point in that, at the

present stage of it. An official function on Alfzar almost makes me long for a staid and stuffy one on Terra. I wanted a little quiet and an absence of drunks who've decided they're God's gift to womankind." Her gaze upon him sharpened. "You've failed, then. How?"

"I'd trade my air-conditioned room in hell for an answer to that." Flandry rubbed the ache at the back of his head. His wits had not yet fully recovered from the blow; he heard his voice plod through the obvious: "Look, we prevailed on the Sartaz to throw a brawl with everybody invited. We made doubly sure that every Merseian in the palace would be there. They'd trust to their robolocks to keep their place safe. They had absolutely no way of knowing we can nullify that sort of lock." The obtaining of the necessary information had been a minor triumph of his not long ago. "But what happened? No sooner was I in than Aycharaych appeared." He struggled to pronounce the name properly, but it came out sounding more Scottish than Chereionite; his vocal organs were not shaped like the other's, nor as versatile. "He was elaborately polite. Nevertheless he kept a blaster on me the whole while, anticipated my every move—would you imagine a scarecrow like him could avoid an attack and slug me? At last he sent me off wishing I had a tail to tuck between my legs."

"Oh, dear." Aline examined the bruise and stroked gentle fingers across it. Then her tone hardened: "He's bad news for certain, isn't he? What *do* we know about him? You've roved around more than most. Do you have anything to tell?"

"Nothing but what you've already heard. Apparently the Chereionites have a privileged position in the Roidhunate, not subjected like most non-Merseian races though not exactly citizens either. I've never heard of anyone who claims even to have seen their planet, or to know its location. Aycharaych appears to be quite active as a field agent—spy, saboteur, general troublemaker—but of course that's impossible to verify, precisely because he is so good at it. I'm afraid our mission is rather badly compromised, Aline."

Flandry got up and walked out onto a balcony. Both moons of Alfzar were aloft and near the full, pouring coppery light over gardens beneath that blended, kilometers away, with forest. The breeze was warm, laden with scents of flowers that had never bloomed under Sol. From afar in the vastness of the palace drifted sounds of music at the feast, on a scale and out of instruments that had never been heard on Terra.

Stars showed faint through the radiance. As he beheld them, Flandry felt daunted. Even the four million or so suns over which his Emperor claimed suzerainty were too many to know; most had never been visited more than perhaps once, if that. Too many mutually alien races; rival imperia, too, Merseia before all. . . .

Aline joined him and took his arm. "Are you letting a single failure discourage you?" she asked with careful good cheer. "Dominic Flandry, the single-handed conqueror of Scothania, brought down by that overgrown buzzard?"

"I just can't understand what happened, how he knew," the man mumbled. "The greenest cub in the Corps shouldn't have gotten caught as I was. How many of our best people has he accounted for? I'm convinced it was he who made McMurtrie disappear, three years back. Who else? Is our turn coming?"

"Oh, now!" She tried to laugh. "You know the devil himself is no better than the organization he belongs to, and Merseian Intelligence isn't that good. Were you drinking *sorgan* when you first heard about Aycharaych?"

"Drinking what?" he asked.

"Ah, I can tell you something you don't know," she said, still valiantly smiling. "Not that it's especially important. I simply happened to pick it up as a bit of gossip from one of our Alfzarian opposite numbers. It's a drug produced on a planet of this system —Cingetor? Yes. For Alfzarians it's medicinal, but in humans it has the odd property of depressing certain brain centers. The victim loses all critical sense. He believes, without question, anything you tell him."

"Hm." Flandry stroked his mustache. "Could be useful in our line of work."

"Not very. There are better ways of interrogating a prisoner, or for that matter producing a fanatic. The drug has an antidote which also confers permanent immunity. The Sartaz has forbidden its sale to his subjects who're of our species, but mainly just because it could help certain types of criminals."

"I should think our Corps would like to keep a little of it stashed away anyhow, against contingencies. And, m-m, to be sure, certain gentlemen would find it an aid to seduction."

"What are you thinking of?" she teased.

"Nothing. I don't need it," he answered smugly. The diversion had somewhat brightened his mood. "Let me put some painkiller on this bump and escort you back to the party," he suggested. "I'll fend off the amorous drunks."

"But it's so beautiful here—" she sighed. "Ah, well, if you really want to go."

The Betelgeusean System is an appropriate setting for mysteries. It has no theoretical business possessing half a dozen planets, out of forty-seven, with life upon them. After all, being considerably more massive than Sol, it was only on the main sequence for a short time, as astronomical time goes. Now it is dying, a red giant that has consumed its innermost attendants. True, the total radiation is great enough that the zone where water can be liquid includes the orbits of those six worlds. However, this condition will not prevail sufficiently long for biologies to develop, let alone intelligences.

Yet when the first Terrestrial explorers arrived, they found flourishing ecologies and a civilization whose spacecraft plied from edge to edge of the system. The Betelgeuseans had only dim traditions about ancestors who fled some catastrophe elsewhere—in slower-than-light ships, no doubt—and seeded the barrenness they found with life that transformed it. (Properly gene-engineered microorganisms could generate an oxynitrogen atmosphere in mere decades of exponential multiplication; meanwhile automated operations could produce soil in chosen areas; eventually full-sized plants and animals could be grown from cells and released; after that, life would spread of itself, being a geological force of great potency.) Perhaps the effort exhausted the pioneers, or perhaps the resource base was insufficient to maintain a high technology in that early phase. Whatever the cause, reliable records on the Betelgeusean worlds only go back for some thousands of years.

Their sun will not keep those worlds warm very much longer, and its dying gasps may well make them uninhabitable even before they start to freeze —but the span available is measured in geological rather than historical terms. It is ample for an orderly move to new homes, now that the Betelgeuseans have learned such tricks as travel at hyperdrive pseudovelocities. Meanwhile they are in no hurry about it, for they command abundant resources, with all that that implies in the way of power.

In Flandry's day, their political position was also one he often wished his own people could occupy. They had not attempted to establish an empire on the scale of Terra or Merseia, but were content to maintain hegemony over such few neighbor stars as were needed for the protection of their home. Generations of wily Sartazes had found it profitable to play potential enemies off against each other; and the great states had, in turn, found it expedient to maintain Betelgeuse as a buffer *vis-à-vis* their rivals and the peripheral barbarians.

That stability was ending, though, as tension ratcheted upward between Terra and Merseia. Squarely between the two domains, its navy commanding the most direct route and in a position to strike at the heart of either, Betelgeuse would be an invaluable ally. If Merseia could get that help, it might well be the last preparation considered necessary for all-out war. If Terra could get it, Merseia would suddenly have to make concessions.

Emissaries swarmed to the red sun, together with

spies, genteel blackmailers, purveyors of large bribes, and other such agents, whom their governments promptly disowned whenever they got caught. Official negotiations had reached the point where—Flandry claimed—clandestine activities were a major industry on the capital planet Alfzar. He and Aline had lately been dispatched to join in, he chosen primarily for his experience with nonhumans, she for her talents with her own species. Quite a few members of it had been settled here for generations, as citizens, and some of those held key positions.

And then came Aycharaych.

For the most distinguished of his foreign guests, the Sartaz gave a hunting party. That monarch evidently enjoyed watching mortal enemies forced to exchange courtesies. Doubtless this occasion did please most of the Merseians; hunting was their favorite sport. The Terrans were less happy, but could scarcely refuse.

Flandry was especially disgruntled. Though he kept in physical trim as a matter of necessity, his own favorite play was conducted in a horizontal position. Worse, he had too much else to do.

The best-laid plans of him and his colleagues were going disastrously agley. Whether Imperial, Betelgeusean, or more exotic, agent after Terran agent had come to grief. Their undertakings failed due to watchfulness, their covers were blown, their own offices were ransacked and the data banks made to yield secrets, they themselves were apt to suffer arrest, or disappearance, or unexplained demise. None among them had found the source of betrayal. Flandry's guess was generally discounted. No single being could be as effective as he thought Aycharaych must be. It just wasn't possible that the opposition could have known about so many projects, caches, contacts, hiding places—or for that matter, Flandry thought, that his rival was *never* vulnerable to any of his assassination schemes—yet, damnation, it was happening.

And now a bloody hunt!

Alfzar rotates at almost the same rate as Terra. This meant that Flandry's servant roused him at an unsanctified hour. He had no absolute prejudice against sunrise; in fact, it was quite a pretty end to an evening. To get up then was a perversion of God's gifts. Dawn here was an alien thing, too. Mist tinged blood-red drifted in dankness through the open windows of his bedroom. It smelled like wet iron. Someone was blowing a horn somewhere, doubtless with intentions of spreading cheer; but to him, local music sounded like a cat in a washing machine. Engines growled. He closed his palms around the warmth of a coffee cup and shivered.

But somebody has to prop up civilization, at least through my own lifetime, he told himself. *Consider the alternative.*

Breakfast made the universe slightly more tolerable. He dressed with some pleasure, too, in skintight green iridon, golden-hued cloak with cowl and goggles, mirrorlike boots. At his waist he secured a needle gun and the slender sword which Alfzarian custom required be worn in the royal presence. The long walk downstairs and out to a palace gate, the longer walk thence to the marshalling field, brought him fully alive.

A picturesque medley of beings moved about the

area, talking, gesturing, making ready. The Sartaz
himself was on hand—also quite humanoid to see,
short, stocky, hairless, blue-skinned, his eyes huge
and yellow in the round, blunt-faced head. He was
more plainly clad than the nobles, guards, and attendants of his race who surrounded him. The Terrans
were more or less in a cluster of their own, a great
deal less animated than the Betelgeuseans; several
seemed downright miserable. The Merseians likewise kept somewhat aloof; they had reason to feel
happy, but haughtiness prevented them from showing it in more than body language.

Flandry gave and received formal greetings all
around. Terra and Merseia were at peace, were they
not?—however many beings died and cities burned
on the marches. He kept his gray gaze sleepy, but it
missed little.

Not that there was anything new to see. The average Merseian exceeded him in height, standing a
bulky two meters in spite of the forward-leaning
posture. Also hairless, their skins were pale green
and faintly scaly in appearance, though the massive
countenances approximated the human except for an
absence of ear-flaps. A low serration ran from the
brow, down the spine, to the end of the long and
heavy tail. Form-fitting black garb, trimmed in silver, covered most of the body.

The Merseians said nothing overtly rude, but
neither did they hide their contempt. *I can understand that,* Flandry thought, as he often compulsive-
ly did. *Their civilization is young and strong, its
energies turned outward, while ours is old, sated,
decadent. All we want to do is maintain the status
quo, because we're comfortable in it. Hence we're in*

*the way of their dream of galactic overlordship. We
are the first ones they have to smash.*

*Or so they believe. And so we believe. Never
mind what the unascertainable objective truth of
the matter may be. Belief is what brings on the killing.*

Shadowy through streaming red mist, a figure approached. In unreasonable shock, Flandry recognized Aycharaych, also garbed for the chase. The
Chereionite halted before him, smiled amicably, and
said, "Good morning, Captain."

"Oh . . . yes," the man got out. "Same to you, I
suppose."

*But wait, I'm losing my manners, my suavity, I'm
letting him rattle me, and that in itself is a petty
defeat. Better I give him my petty defiance.*

"*I'm a bit surprised,*" he added. "*Wouldn't have*
thought you cared for hunting."

"Why, are we not both hunters by trade?"
Aycharaych replied. "True, as a rule I find sophonts
to be much the most interesting quarry. However,
what I have heard of the game we seek today has
made it seem sufficiently challenging. One wonders
whether the ancestral pioneers here developed them
specifically for sport."

"And then designed the rest of the local ecology to
accommodate them?" Flandry laughed. "Well,
projects have taken weirder courses than that."

The conversation became animated, ranging over
the peculiarities and mysteries of many intelligent
races. When the final horn blew its summons, Terran
and Chereionite exchanged a wryly regretful glance.
*Too bad. We were enjoying this. Too bad also that
we're on opposite sides . . . isn't it?*

Hunters swung themselves into tiny one-person airjet craft and secured the harness. Each flyer had a needle-beam energy projector in the nose. That was minimal armament against a Borthudian dragon. Flandry reflected that the Sartaz wouldn't mind if an indignant beast did away with a guest or three.

The squadron lifted in a chorus of banshee wails and streaked northward for the mountains. Breaking through the mist, pilots saw Betelgeuse as an enormous, vaguely bounded disc in a purplish sky. Presently its warmth drank up the vapors below, and landscape lay revealed in all its unearthliness. The range appeared ahead, gaunt peaks, violet-shadowed canyons, snowfields tinged bloody by the sunlight. Despite himself, Flandry thrilled.

Voices came over the radio, in the court language and occasionally, courteously, in accented Anglic or Eriau. Scouts had spotted dragons here and there. Jet after jet peeled away from the squadron to go in pursuit. Before long, Flandry found his craft alone with one other.

Then two forms rose from the ground and started winging off. His pulse accelerated, his belly muscles tightened, he brought his flyer downward in a steep dive.

Like most predators, the dragons weren't looking for trouble. Annoyed by the racket overhead, they had set off in search of peace and quiet. However, they had never had reason to acquire an instinct of fear, either. Ten scaly meters of jaws, neck, body, and tail snaked through heaven, beneath enormous leathery wings. The beasts were less leavy than they appeared, and glided more than they actually flew. Just the same, a high-energy metabolism kept such a mass aloft. Yonder teeth could rend steel.

Flandry took aim. The creature he had chosen grew monstrously in his sights. A sunbeam made an eye glare scarlet as the dragon banked to face him in battle.

He squeezed his trigger. A thin blade of lightning smote forth, to burn through scales and the vital organs beneath. Yet the monster held to its collision course. Flandry rolled out of the way. Wings buffeted air, meters from him.

He had not allowed for the tail. A sudden impact shivered his teeth together. The jet reeled and went into a spin. The dragon followed.

Flandry fought his controls and tore the craft around, upward. He barrel-rolled and confronted open jaws. His beam seared in between the fangs. The dragon stumbled in midflight. Flandry pulled away and fired into a wing, ripping it.

Another blow shuddered through him. He twisted his head about in time to see the fuselage bitten open. The second beast had come to the aid of its crippled mate.

Wind poured in, searingly cold. The dragon struck again, and this time clung. Unmanageable, the aircraft plunged groundward. Mountains reeled across Flandry's vision. *What an ending!* passed through him. *Brought down and maybe eaten by my own quarry—*

He was free. The other jet had arrived, firing with surgical precision. *All gods bless that pilot, whoever he is!* Cleanly slain, the great creature toppled Lucifer-like. Its killer whipped around to dispose of the one Flandry had wounded.

The Terran got his vehicle on an even keel. He'd

better inspect the damage, though, and give his
nerves a chance to untwist, before proceeding back.
The dragon that nearly got him had crashed on a
slope beneath a ledge big enough for a vertical landing. As he approached, he raised a hand in salute.
There lay another brave animal, done in as an act of
politics. He grounded and sat for a minute quietly
shuddering.

A whistle shrilled him back to alertness. The second aircraft was on its way down, presumably for
the pilot to see how he fared; his radio was *hors de
combat*. He opened the cockpit and climbed out to
stand on harsh yellow turf, in a gelid breeze, that he
might give proper thanks.

The vehicle set down. Its engine whined into silence, its canopy drew back, its rider got out.

Aycharaych.

Flandry's reaction was well-nigh instantaneous.
Here he stood, unrecognizable as an individual at the
distance between, in cloak and hood and goggles.
Yonder was his enemy, unsuspecting, and there
were no witnesses and any agonies of conscience
could be postponed till a convenient time—

His hand was on the butt of his needle gun when
he saw that Aycharaych's weapon was already
drawn and aimed at him. He froze. The Chereionite
approached him at an easy, steady pace, until he
could hear the quiet word: "No."

He kept both his hands well away from his person.
"Do you mean to do the honors yourself, then?" he
asked.

"Not at all, unless you absolutely force me,"
Aycharaych said. "I do wish you to take out your
gun, drop it, and step a few meters aside. Thereafter

you are free to determine if your vehicle is airworthy.
If not, I will be glad to summon assistance for you."

"You . . . are very . . . kind, sir."

"You are very useful, Captain. I perceive that you
now understand why."

Aycharaych smoothly declined to discuss the matter further.

Afternoon light streamed through a window of
Aline's room, the most private place she and Flandry
could find in the palace. Its ruddiness somehow
seemed only to bring out the pallor on her face.
"Can't be," she whispered through lips drawn tight.

"Is," Flandry replied grimly. "The only possible
answer. How he knows everything about us, everything we try and plan and—think. He can read our
minds."

"But telepathy—you know its limitations—"

Flandry nodded. "Low rate of data conveyance at
those frequencies, as well as high noise levels and
rapid degradation of the signal. Not to speak of the
coding problem. Different races have such different
brain-activity patterns that a telepath has to learn a
whole new 'language' for each. In fact, he has to do
it for every single member of a basically non-
telepathic species like ours; we don't grow up in a
shared communication mode, the way we do with
our mother tongues."

He began to pace, back and forth across the
enclosing chamber. "But Chereion's a very old
planet," he said. "Its people have the reputation
among the more superstitious Merseians of being
sorcerers. Somehow, they must be able to detect and
interpret something mental that intelligent beings

have in common universally, or almost universally. I've been wondering about—oh, a fantastic inborn ability to acquire information, store it, chase it up and down every branch of a logic tree till the meaning emerges—in hours, minutes, seconds?"

He beat fist against palm. "I am reasonably sure he can only read surface thoughts, those in the immediate awareness. Otherwise he'd have found out so much about us that the Merseians would be swaggering around on Terra by now. However, what he can do is bad enough!"

"No wonder he spared your life," Aline said drearily. "You've become the most valuable man on his side."

"And not a thing I can do about it," Flandry sighed. "I'm so helpless—we all are—that he doesn't care that we learn about him. Rather, he's no doubt made our knowledge a factor in his plans—our loss of morale at the news, for instance—

"I don't know what the range of his mind reading is. Probably just several meters: on the basis of what we know about the physical nature of the carrier waves for telepathy. But he sees me every day; and every time, he skims whatever I'm thinking of." The man's laugh jarred forth. "How do I go about *not* thinking of my work? By chanting mantras every waking moment? Better I should return home. Better we all should, perhaps, and give up on Betelgeuse."

Aline rose from her chair and came to stand before him as he halted at the window. "We'll have to get a research and development effort mounted on Terra," she said. "For some kind of helmet or whatever, that screens off transmission of thoughts."

"Of course. That doesn't help us today. Nor very much in the long run, really. Our people don't often encounter Chereionites, do they?"

She touched his arm. "Can't you avoid him while we're here?"

Flandry shrugged. "Yes, if I want to become a cipher—and you, and everybody with us. You know flinkin' well that we can't carry on a political intrigue purely by eidophone."

"What *can* we do?" Aline stood silent while Flandry took forth a cigarette and puffed it into lighting, then continued: "Whatever it is had better be fast. The Sartaz is growing cooler to Terra by the day. One can't blame him too much, considering what a series of blunders we've been making; and I hardly expect he'd believe us if we claimed that was due to Aycharaych."

Flandry blew a veil of smoke between his eyes and the alienness beyond the window through which he stared. "No doubt I shouldn't be bemoaning our situation, but spinning some elaborate counterplot," he said. "Except that I'll have to appear at this evening's banquet for the hunting party, and *he* will engage me in the most delightful conversation—"

Aline drew a quick breath. Her hand closed about his. He turned to regard her. "What is it?" he asked.

Her smile flashed for an instant, but the words came stark: "You don't really want to hear, do you?"

"Why—I suppose not," he replied, taken aback. "Though you're as vulnerable to him as anybody else."

"Yes, but I don't think I've been ransacked anywhere near as thoroughly." A tinge of bitterness: "We Terran women are expected to be subordinate,

aren't we? In practice if not in theory. Even a ranking officer does best to keep a low profile, if female.
You've been the obvious target, together with a few
other key men. I've actually seen almost nothing of
Aycharaych the whole while I've been here, and the
chances are that when I did, I wasn't concentrating
on anything too important."

She leaned close and went on in a tone gone low
and urgent: "Keep him away from me, Dominic.
Talk to him, engage his attention, give him no excuse
to come near this part of the palace. He'll realize that
that's your intention, naturally, but he won't be able
just to brush you aside . . . if you're as clever as your
reputation has it. I won't be at the banquet tonight,
since I wasn't hunting, and—yes, I'll claim illness,
ask to have a light supper brought me in this room—
Come back afterward."

His gaze intensified upon her. "Whatever you're
hatching in that lovely head," he murmured, "be
quick about it. He'll get at you soon, you know, one
way or another."

"You'd better leave now, Dominic," she said.
"Leave me to my nefarious activities."

As he departed, her look followed him, and again
she smiled.

Flandry returned from the banquet late. Wine
glowed and buzzed in his blood. He hadn't exactly
set out to get drunk, but he had wanted what relaxation he could seize . . . and found it not in the or-
giastic amusements offered, but in discourse with
Aycharaych. The talk had had nothing to do with the
conflict between them; mostly it had been about ancient history, both Terran and Merseian, and utterly

fascinating. He could almost forget that the great mind before him had no need of his speech.

Aline let him in when the scanner at her door identified him. She had muted the illumination; it flowed golden across hair, ivory sculpture of features, shimmerlyn robe. Impulsively, he kissed her, though he remembered to keep the gesture brief and light. "Good evening," he said. "How've things gone?"

"For me, mainly in thought," she answered low. "Very hard thought. Before we talk, how about a nightcap?" She gestured at a carafe and a pair of ornate goblets which had not been on her table earlier.

"No, thanks," he declined. "I've had entirely too many."

"Please," she said with a grave upward curving of lips. "For me. I need to ease off a little too."

"Well, when a lady puts it that way—" He accepted the vessel she handed him. They touched rims and drank.

The wine had a peculiar taste. If he had not taken on a considerable load already, he would have refused it after the first sip. But Aline said, "You do want it, I can see that," and he decided that he did, in spite of a sudden slight dizziness.

He sat down on the bed. She joined him. "Potent stuff, this," he muttered. "Where in the galaxy is it from?"

"Oh, no matter; it was the best the staff could promote for me on short notice, when I scarcely dared make a fuss." Aline laughed. "Good enough for government work."

"Or government idling," he said, and drank further.

"Yes, we do need to escape for a while, before we go crazy. We have tonight . . . tonight, if nothing else." As he drained his goblet and set it down, she leaned against him. "And we have love."

"What?" he asked, adolescently clumsy. The vertigo was leaving him, but he felt strange.

"No euphemism for a romp in bed, Dominic, darling," she breathed. "We love each other."

He forgot everything else as that joyous knowledge took hold of him.

Toward dawn she kissed him awake. He reached for the warmth and fragrance of her, but she sat up and told him: "No. Not yet, beloved."

A measure of sense arose, to make him sit also, leaned on a hand, and foresay, "You've news for me."

"Yes. I've wondered and wondered, and finally taken it on myself to—Well, it was supposed to be my secret, I the inconspicuous woman, till I notified our superiors here at practically the last minute. But your revelation about Aycharaych has changed everything."

He stiffened. She spoke on with a steadiness altogether unbefitting the word she gave:

"I was told before I left Terra that the Emperor and the Policy Board were considering this. Our dispatches have decided them, and I've received notice by diplomatic courier.

"A task force is in the vicinity, just outside detection range." That was no surprise in itself, though Flandry had not been informed. One tried to provide against contingencies. No doubt the Merseians had a small fleet of their own somewhere in this stellar neighborhood. "They've slipped the minor craft closer, in orbit around Betelgeuse. Those now have their orders—to get in fast, seize a beachhead, and deliver an ultimatum to the Sartaz."

"But that's impossible!" Flandry protested.

"No, it's risky, but it has a fair chance of working; and if we do nothing, Betelgeuse will go to the Merseians anyway, by default, correct? We have enough agents remaining in the defense forces here that a squadron, at least, can reach Alfzar from the outer system, undetected till too late. It'll land in the Gunazar Valley, up in the Borthudian highlands, already the night after tomorrow. Then every important place on the globe is hostage to its missiles, including especially this palace. The pill will be sweetened by such things as an offer of very substantial 'aid' if the Sartaz expels the Merseians. Admiral Fenross has been at work on the case for a long time. His best judgment is that the Sartaz will yield, furiously but still not willing to hazard all-out war."

"Will the Merseians meekly resign from the game?" Flandry wondered.

"We dare hope they will—if the coup is fast enough and complete enough to catch them off balance. It's obviously vital to keep the Betelgeuseans from suspecting anything beforehand, except for our agents among them. My job is to coordinate the actions—and inactions—of those beings, preparing for hour zero."

Flandry shook his head, as if that could dislodge bewilderment. "Why are you telling me?" he almost groaned. "Aycharaych will pluck the news right out of my skull."

"Because I can't carry out my duty alone," she explained. "I have to deal with a dozen or more officers and—well, you do *not* need to know exactly who or where. Obviously, Aycharaych will alert the Merseians, and they'll initiate some kind of counter-action."

"Such as warning the Sartaz."

"Perhaps. Though I think not; not the first thing, anyhow. They would have no proof, only Aycharaych's word, and even if he puts on a demonstration of mind reading, what is that word worth? If they do try it, we need someone on the spot to deny everything—and, of course, send out a signal to the Navy that the invasion must be cancelled. A clever man could reap advantage out of the situation, use it to discredit the Merseians or . . . or something. . . . And we've no man more clever among us than you, or better at dealing with nonhumans." She stroked his hair, brushed lips across his, and added in a whisper: "Humans, too, as I've learned."

That roused a fresh terror in him. "They'll certainly be on your trail," he said. "If they caught you, they and their damned assassins—"

"That's another thing I need your help in, seeing to it that they don't," she responded with a gallantry that twisted the heart in him. "I'm going to take a sleeping pill now that'll knock me out for the next few hours. You make sure that Aycharaych is elsewhere when I wake, and for a while afterward. I can shake any other operative, and disappear."

He nodded. "If need be, I'll attack him physically. But he'll know that, so I daresay he'll go along with the conversation I'll start. If we got into close quarters, I could break that skinny neck of his."

And fall prey to Betelgeusean justice, neither of them added.

She kissed him hard. "Thank you, dearest,

dearest," she breathed. "I'd love to make love again, but we don't dare, do we?"

"We'll try to reserve a lifetime for that, afterward," he vowed.

She took her sedative and soon was easily breathing. He looked at her for a long spell before he went in search of Aycharaych.

He found the Chereionite admiring curious blossoms in a far part of the garden, under dim red moonlight; for the sun was not yet up. The telepath's gaunt countenance bent into a smile. "Good morning, Captain," he greeted. "A little early for you, no? But then, we both have a busy time ahead of us."

He knew.

In the following pair of days, Flandry worked as he had seldom worked before. Paradoxically, there was almost nothing for him to do; but he had to keep moving about, maintain communications throughout his web of underlings, stay certain that no disaster caught him unawares. Maybe, he thought, that incessant strain was what dulled his wits and clouded his judgment; or maybe it was fear for Aline. Whatever the cause, thinking had become an effort and the intuition that separated truths from falsehoods had deserted him. For this reason alone, it was as well that events were mostly going on without him, even without his knowledge—whatever those events were.

He considered breaching security and passing the news the woman had given him on to the Terran Embassy, the special delegation, or at least certain members of the Intelligence team. But what good would that do? He'd merely increase the risk of premature disclosure to the Betelgeuseans.

Evidently the Merseians had decided against informing the Sartaz at once. Aline's estimate had been right. Yet they were not going to sit still for the operation. Aycharaych and a few of them had left in a speedster on the afternoon of the first day, giving out that they had reports to deliver at home. Flandry felt sure the reports were, in fact, going to whatever naval force the Roidhunate maintained in the offing; and its commander would have more discretion to act than an admiral of the Empire normally did.

No doubt the Merseians could smuggle some kind of combat units down onto Alfzar. The question, the really interesting question was whether they could mount an adequate effort on such short notice. Flandry guessed that they might attempt it and then, if it failed, bring in their fleet "to aid the valiant Betelgeuseans." If the Sartaz had not already capitulated to the Terrans—or even if he had, maybe —this would certainly make him a stout ally of the Roidhun.

Terra might pull the whole thing off, of course; its task force would not be far behind the initial squadron, and the Merseian chief might decide against a full-dress naval engagement. Might, might, might! The unknowns were like spiderwebs enmeshing Flandry.

He looked up Gunazar Valley on an infotrieve. It was desolate, uninhabited, the home of winds and the lair of dragons, a good site for a secret descent; but the secret no longer existed.

Flandry had the impression that only a few members of the Merseian party here had been informed, and they in confidence. They were the ones who now regarded him, when he encountered them, with hatred rather than contempt. There would have been no point, and some hazard, in telling a lot of juniors. They were as helpless as the man felt himself to be.

Aline was gone. Likewise was General Frank Bronson, the human-Betelgeusean military officer whom she had made her personal property soon after she arrived. Flandry wondered if she had converted him to an actual traitor, as Imperial agents had done to a number of personnel, or simply convinced him that the best interests of his state lay with Terra. Flandry also wondered what she was getting him to do in aid of the invasion—and how; but he shied away from that second matter in an unwonted sickness of jealousy.

The red giant crossed heaven; sank; was away; rose; crossed heaven; sank; was away—and when it rose anew, nothing had happened.

Flandry paced, chain-smoked, made a muttered litany out of every curse in any language that he had ever learned. Nothing had happened. Among the first lessons given him when he was a cadet had been: "No operation ever goes according to plan." There could easily have been some hitch, occasioning delay. But every added hour gave the Merseians more time to make ready, and to act.

On the third evening, one of his informants called him in his quarters to declare breathlessly that General Bronson was back and had requested an audience with the Sartaz—at once. Minutes later, his phone screen lit up with Aline's image. "I'm home, darling," she said. "Come on to my room."

She let him in and stood back, serious, her gaze searching him so intently that he did not at once seek to embrace her but halted and stared back. At last she said low, "You are very tired, aren't you? More than I expected. What's been going on?"

"Hardly a thing," he answered. "but I've felt rotten, and mainly I was worried about you—"

"I can do something about that," she told him with never a smile. "I must. We haven't much time. The Sartaz has agreed to let Bronson give a demonstration of 'a crucial matter' just two hours from now. We've got to set the show up, and we'll want your best advice on the psychology of it, and—But kiss me first."

He did. It lasted a while. She was the one who disengaged, went to the table, picked up a tumbler, and handed it to him. "Medicine for what ails you," she said. "Drink."

Obedient as a machine, he tossed off the dark-brown liquid. It caught at him, his head roared and spun, he lurched against the bed and fell down. "What the devil—" he gasped.

The foul sensations faded. Through him spread a kind of coolness, like a breeze of Terran springtime along his nerves and into his head. It was like the hand that Aline had laid on his brow, soothing, heartening, loving.

Clearing!

He sprang to his feet. Suddenly the preposterousness of it all loomed before him. Bumbling and weak-willed the Empire might be, and on that account scarcely likely to attempt any bold stroke; but its general staff was not incompetent, and whatever it did would be better planned than—

And he didn't love Aline. She was brave and beautiful, but he didn't love her. Yet three minutes ago, he *had*—

He looked into her eyes. Tears brimmed them as

she nodded. "Yes," she whispered, "that's how it was. I'm sorry, my dear. You'll never know how sorry I am."

A telescreen formed one wall of a conference chamber. Before it curved rows of empty seats. The place was already well occupied, however, for Bronson had taken the precaution of ranking royal guards whom he could trust along the sides—impassive blue faces above gray tunics and steel corselets, on the shoulders of which rested firearms.

The general prowled the stage, glancing at his watch every several seconds. Perspiration glistened on his skin and he reeked of it. Flandry stood relaxed, attired in court dress; when action was imminent, he could wait with panther patience. Aline seemed altogether detached, lost somewhere amidst her own thoughts.

"If this doesn't work, you know, we'll be lucky if we're hanged," Bronson said.

"You need more confidence in yourself," answered Flandry tonelessly. "Though if the scheme fails, it won't matter much whether we hang or not."

He was prevaricating there; he was most fond of living, in spite of being haunted by the ghosts of certain dreams.

A trumpet sounded, brassy between pillars and vaulted ceiling. The humans saluted and stood to attention as the Sartaz and his principal councillors entered.

He raked suspicious yellow eyes across them. "I *hope* this business is as important as you claim," he said.

Flandry took the word; that was his element. "It

is, your Majesty. It is a matter so immense that it should have been revealed to you weeks ago. Unfortunately, circumstances did not permit—as this eminent gathering will soon see—and your Majesty's loyal officer was forced to act on his own authority with what help we of Terra could give him. But if our work has gone well, the moment of revelation should also be that of salvation."

The monarch settled into a chair at the center, higher than the rest. His attenders then dared seat themselves. "What new evil have the empires wrought?" he demanded.

I don't blame him for wishing a plague on both our houses, Flandry thought, while he continued, "Your Majesty, Terra has never wished Betelgeuse anything but well. We are about to offer proof of that. If—"

An amplified voice boomed through the air: "Great Majesty, the ambassador from Merseia requests immediate audience. He maintains that it is a business whereon destiny will turn."

"No!" Bronson shouted.

The Sartaz sat motionless for half a minute before he said, "Yes. Admit his Excellency and let us hear him too."

The huge green form of Korvash the Farseeing entered in a swirl of rainbow-colored robes, a flare of gold and jewelry. Beside him was Aycharaych.

Flandry heard Bronson make a strangled noise and Aline draw a gasp. If that player got back into the game, at this precarious stage of things—Silence thickened while the newcomers went up the aisle to pay their respects.

Not thought, but instinct and impulse surged through Flandry. He sprang down off the stage. The court sword hissed from the sheath at his hip. "Stop those two!" he roared. "They would murder the Sartaz!"

Aycharaych's eyes widened. He opened his mouth to denounce what he saw in the Terran's mind—and sprang back in bare time to avoid a thrust at his body.

His own rapier whipped into his hand. In a whirr of steel, the spies met.

Korvash had drawn blade in sheer reflex. "Strike him down before he kills!" Aline cried. Guards swarmed forward.

The ambassador dropped his weapon. "This is ridiculous—" he began. A stun pistol chopped off his words. He collapsed and lay in a heap.

"That was perhaps unnecessary," the Sartaz said shrewdly. "Remove him to medical attention . . . with due care."

Flandry and Aycharaych moved across his view, viciously busy. "Get them separated!" the officer of the guards called.

"No," the Sartaz countermanded. "Let them have it out."

Aline clenched her hands together. Bronson stood appalled. Slowly, at the royal signal, the troopers resumed formation.

Flandry had thought himself a champion fencer, but Aycharaych was his match. Though the Chereionite was hampered by gravity, no human could equal his speed and precision. The blade he wielded whistled in and out and around, feinted, thrust, parried, flicked blood from his opponent's arm and shoulder; and always he smiled.

His telepathy did him little good. Fencing is a matter of reflexes more than of conscious thought.

Perhaps it gave him an extra edge, compensating for the handicap of weight.

The *Totentanz* went on. Flandry began to score in his turn. Red drops flowed down the golden visage. *I am going to wear you out, Aycharaych*, the man thought. *You'll tire before I do.* He retreated, and his enemy had no choice but to follow in hopes of a fatal opening.

Almost, he got one. Flandry's guard went awry, Aycharaych lunged, his point reached the Terran's upper arm. But then a karate kick knocked the sword spinning from his grasp, and steel was at his throat.

"Do not kill!" the Sartaz exclaimed. "We'll hear all of you out. Guards, disarm them."

"Dominic, Dominic," Aline crooned, between tears and laughter; yet she held her place on stage.

"Your Majesty," Flandry panted, "please, I beg you for your own sake, let me keep this prisoner till we've finished what we started. Time's ghastly short, and if he gets a chance, he'll spin matters out till too late. You'll soon understand."

His mind projected: *Aycharaych, if you part your lips, so help me, I'll run you through and worry about the consequences to me afterward.*

The Chereionite made the faintest of shrugs. Was there irony in it? He must have anticipated the ruler's decision:

"Very well. That would be . . . fitting."

Flandry poised more at ease. What he had said was probably not altogether a lie. No doubt the Merseians had returned with the idea of shortly springing their own surprise; they had learned— quite likely from Aycharaych, who'd tapped the mind of some aide or whoever—that Bronson and Aline were back too, realized that a Terran scheme must also be afoot, and decided it was best to act immediately, no matter how much they must improvise; meanwhile, a warning must be on its way to their troops—

"You'd better take over the demonstration," he called to Aline and Bronson. He dared not to let his attention wander for an instant from the one he confronted. At the edge of vision, he saw the general give the woman a bewildered look, and stand back as she trod forward.

"Your Majesty and nobles," she began, and self-possession welled back up within her, "we pray pardon for the haste and disorderliness of this proceeding, but feel sure you will soon realize that that was forced on us. Full explanation will be forthcoming from the Terran Imperium in due course, though you will surely also realize that it will take time to collect all the facts.

"Basically, our mission discovered that Merseia has decided to cease negotiating for an alliance which may never be granted. Instead, the Merseian plan is to compel it by arms. A small force, aided by traitors in your own ranks, has occupied the Gunazar Valley in the Borthudian range and is, at this very moment, preparing a bridgehead for invasion. With Alfzar under its weapons, the whole planetary system must yield—"

She let the uproar subside before she resumed coolly: "It was not feasible for us to pass this information on at once as we should and as we wished, for several reasons. First, it came piecemeal. Second, though it was gathered by agents we trusted, we had no documentation that would convince you. Third, Merseian agents were everywhere, and we even had reason to believe one of them could read your minds.

If they had known their plot was being revealed, they—and the Merseian strength out in space—might well have chosen to act precipitately. As representatives of Terra, we did not feel we had a right to hazard exposing the Betelgeusean worlds to a major conflict.

"Instead, we contacted General Bronson. It is no secret that he is sympathetic to us, though he remains a loyal subject of the Sartaz. We estimated that his position in your defense hierarchy was not high enough to merit much enemy attention; yet he has authority to order the actions we suggested.

"This included mounting telescopic pickups around the valley. Permit me to tune them in."

She turned a switch. An image sprang onto the screen, crags and cliffs beneath the sullen moons, stirrings and metallic gleams in the shadows beneath. The view swept around, became close, became panoramic, brightened under optical amplification. It was a view of spacecraft at rest on the ground, of armor and artillery that they had disgorged now deployed about them, of uniformed Merseians at work.

The Sartaz gave a tigerish snarl. A courtier demanded, "Can you prove this is not a counterfeit?"

"You can prove it for yourself, sir," Aline replied. "Plenty of scraps will remain. Our strategy has been simple. Before they landed, engineers in General Bronson's command planted nuclear mines. They are radio controlled." With a sense of drama that Flandry could not have bettered, she lifted, from the stage where it had lain, a red box with a switch. "The signal can be relayed from this. Perhaps your Majesty would care to start things?"

"Give me that," said the Sartaz thickly. Aline

sprang down from the stage and handed it to him, curtsying low. He flipped the switch.

Blue-white hell-flame lit the screen. It gave a vision of soil fountaining upward, landslides, a black cloud, and darkness.

"The latest explosion destroyed the last camera we had," Aline told the assembly. "Let me urge that your Majesty dispatch airborne scouts at once. They will find the proof I bespoke.

"Let me suggest further that you no longer regard Merseia as a friendly power. A detachment of the Terran Navy has been contacted and is on its way. Needless to say, it will not cross your outermost orbital radius without express permission. However, it will stand by, ready to help a Betelgeusean navy that we assume will be put on alert status.

"I believe that after Lord Korvash awakens and is permitted to send a message or two, there will be no further immediate danger from Merseia. As for the longer-range danger, that is something your Majesty must decide in your wisdom."

For the time being, deportation orders stood for every Merseian in the Betelgeusean System. What units of theirs lingered clandestinely, in hidden places on barren planets and moons and asteroids, would be of scant use—far less than their Terran counterparts.

It did not follow that Betelgeuse would conclude an alliance with the Empire. Though the Merseian ambassador had not been able, under the circumstances, to make any very effective protestations of innocence: still, the Sartaz and his advisors knew better than to believe in the disinterested benevolence of Terra. Negotiations would continue.

They might or might not lead to agreement.

That was outside Flandry's concern. Let the diplomats worry about it. He—no, Aline, and he as a helper—had done the job of their own group, which was to keep the possibility open for their side and foreclose it for the opposition.

One does not dismiss an ambassador and his staff without a certain amount of courtesy. Korvash got time to close down his affairs here in orderly fashion. On the evening before he was due to leave, Flandry invited him and Aycharaych around for drinks. The hostess was Aline, and they had the common room for the Terran delegation for a site, with nobody else present. They could have had much more than that had they asked, but settled for the most expensive liquor available.

"Matters have been somewhat too hectic for me to offer the congratulations that are your due," said the Chereionite to the man after everybody had begun to relax.

"Thank you," Flandry replied. "I don't pretend to be sportsman enough that I wish you success next time around. However, it's an amusing game that the empires underwrite for us, no?"

Inwardly he thought, and knew that the other knew he thought: *You've not lost hands down, Aycharaych. You've gotten a great deal of information from me that your side will find useful in future. But the half-life of that kind of advantage isn't usually very long, and I'll gather more when you aren't around, and I am forewarned.*

He glanced at Aline. Her demeanor was more sober than it had been when he and she impulsively planned this occasion. Was she thinking of missiles that would not strike and sentient beings that would

not die—not yet—and of the fact that Aycharaych
followed her thought?

Korvash stirred, where he squatted on a tripod of
legs and tail in the manner of his people. "I've been
overwhelmed with work myself," he growled.
"Now will you tell me exactly what it was that you
did, you Terrans?"

"Aline did it," Flandry said. "Want to tell them?"

She shook her head. "You tell them, if you wish,"
she murmured. "Please."

Flandry leaned back in his lounger, sipped from
the snifter of brandy in his grasp, and was nothing
loth to expound. "Well, then. When we realized you
could read our minds, Aycharaych, things looked
pretty hopeless. How can you possibly hide anything
from that kind of telepath, let alone deceive him?
Aline hit on the answer. First deceive yourself.

"There's an obscure drug in these parts called
sorgan. It's forbidden to humans, but that needn't
stop any competent Intelligence agent. It has the intriguing property of making its user believe whatever he's told. She fed me some without my knowledge and spun me that yarn about Terra's plan to
occupy Alfzar. I accepted it as absolute truth; you
read it out of me."

"I was puzzled," admitted the Chereionite. "It did
not seem reasonable. However, it seemed plausible
to you . . . and I am, after all, not human."

"Aline's main problem thereafter was to keep out
of your range," Flandry said. "You helped there by
haring off to get a warm reception prepared for the
Terrans, as she'd guessed you would. If you could've
stopped that invasion, then offered your act as
earnest of your altruistic love for Betelgeuse—Well,

tonight we'd've been the *personae non gratae* and you, perhaps, throwing a farewell party for us."

Korvash gusted a sigh, quite humanlike except for its volume. "Let me be honest," he said. "The decision to send for naval units, mobilize our Betelgeusean organization, act boldly, that was mine. Aycharaych counselled more caution, but I overruled him."

"Well, nobody's perfect," Flandry replied. "I have my own vices, though energy is not among them."

"This is no time for recriminations, of self or of others," Aycharaych said gently. "There will be more tomorrows. Tonight let us enjoy our truce."

The drinking lasted well on toward dawn. When finally the aliens left, Korvash offered many tipsy expressions of regard, and even of regret that the covert hostility must begin again.

Aycharaych showed no sign of changed mood. He took Aline's right hand in his bony fingers, and his eyes searched hers, even as—she remembered with an odd, half welcome sense of surrender—his mind was doing.

"Goodbye, my dear," he said, too softly for the rest to overhear. "As long as there are women like you, your race will endure."

She watched his tall form go down the corridor and her vision blurred a little. It was strange to think that her enemy knew what the man beside her did not.

HUNTERS OF THE SKY CAVE

I

It pleased Ruethen of the Long Hand to give a feast and ball at the Crystal Moon for his enemies. He knew they must come. Pride of race had slipped from Terra, while the need to appear well-bred and sophisticated had waxed correspondingly. The fact that spaceships prowled and fought, fifty light-years beyond Antares, made it all the more impossible a gaucherie to refuse an invitation from the Merseian representative. Besides, one could feel delightfully wicked and ever so delicately in danger.

Captain Sir Dominic Flandry, Imperial Naval Intelligence Corps, allowed himself a small complaint. "It's not that I refuse any being's liquor," he said, "and Ruethen has a chef for his human-type meals who'd be worth a war to get. But I thought I was on furlough."

"So you are," said Diana Vinogradoff, Right Noble Lady Guardian of the Mare Crisium. "Only I saw you first."

Flandry grinned and slid an arm about her shoulders. He felt pretty sure he was going to win his bet with Ivar del Bruno. They relaxed in the lounger and he switched off the lights.

This borrowed yacht was ridiculously frail and ornate; but a saloon which was one bubble of clear plastic, ah! Now in the sudden darkness, space leaped forth, crystal black and a wintry blaze of stars. The banded shield of Jupiter swelled even as they watched, spilling soft amber radiance into the ship. Lady Diana became a figure out of myth, altogether beautiful; her jewels glittered like raindrops on long gown and heaped tresses. Flandry stroked his neat moustache. *I don't suppose I look too hideous myself*, he thought smugly, and advanced to the attack.

"No . . . please . . . not now," Lady Diana fended him off, but in a promising way. Flandry reclined again. No hurry. The banquet and dance would take hours. Afterward, when the yacht made its leisured way home towards Terra, and champagne bubbles danced in both their heads. . . . "Why did you say that about being on furlough?" she asked, smoothing her coiffure with slim fingers. Her luminous nail polish danced about in the twilight like flying candle flames.

Flandry got a cigarette from his own shimmerite jacket and inhaled it to life. The glow picked out his face, long, narrow, with high cheekbones and gray eyes, seal-brown hair and straight nose. He sometimes thought his last biosculp had made it too handsome, and he ought to change it again. But what the devil, he wasn't on Terra often enough for the girls to get bored with his looks. Besides, his

wardrobe, which he did take pains to keep
fashionable, was expensive enough to rule out many
other vanities.

"The Nyanza business was a trifle wearing,
y'know," he said, to remind her of yet another
exploit of his on yet another exotic planet. "I came
Home for a rest. And the Merseians are such
damnably strenuous creatures. It makes me tired just
to look at one, let alone spar with him."

"You don't have to tonight, Sir Dominic," she
smiled. "Can't you lay all this feuding aside, just for
a little while, and be friends with them? I mean,
we're all beings, in spite of these silly rivalries."

"I'd love to relax with them, my lady. But you see,
they never do."

"Oh, come now! I've talked to them, often,
and—"

"They can radiate all the virile charm they need,"
said Flandry. For an instant his light tone was edged
with acid. "But destroying the Terrestrial Empire is
a full-time job."

Then, quickly, he remembered what he was
about, and picked up his usual line of banter. He
wasn't required to be an Intelligence agent all the
time. Was he? When a thousand-credit bet with his
friend was involved? Ivar del Bruno had insisted that
Lady Diana Vinogradoff would never bestow her
favors on anyone under the rank of earl. The
challenge was hard to refuse, when the target was so
intrinsically tempting, and when Flandry had good
reason to be complacent about his own abilities. It
had been a hard campaign, though, and yielding to
her whim to attend the Merseian party was only a
small fraction of the lengths to which he had gone.

But now, Flandry decided, if he played his cards

right for a few hours more, the end would be achieved. And afterwards, a thousand credits would buy a really good orgy for two at the Everest House.

Chives, valet cum pilot cum private gunman, slipped the yacht smoothly into berth at the Crystal Moon. There was no flutter of weight change, though deceleration had been swift and the internal force-field hard put to compensate. Flandry stood up, cocked his beret at a carefully rakish angle, swirled his scarlet cloak, and offered an arm to Lady Diana. They stepped through the airlock and along a transparent tube to the palace.

The woman caught a delighted gasp. "I've never seen it so close up," she whispered. "Who ever made it?"

The artificial satellite had Jupiter for background, and the Milky Way and the huge cold constellations. Glass-clear walls faced infinity, curving and tumbling like water. Planar gravity fields held faceted synthetic jewels, ruby, emerald, diamond, topaz, massing several tons each, in orbit around the central minaret. One outward thrust of bubble was left at zero gee, a conservatory where mutant ferns and orchids rippled on rhythmic breezes.

"I understand it was built for Lord Tsung-Tse about a century back," said Flandry. "His son sold it for gambling debts, and the then Merseian ambassador acquired it and had it put in orbit around Jupiter. Symbolic, eh?"

She arched questioning brows, but he thought better of explaining. His own mind ran on: *Eh, for sure. I suppose it's inevitable and so forth. Terra has been too rich far too long: we've grown old and content, no more high hazards for us. Whereas the Merseian Empire is fresh, vigorous, disciplined,*

*dedicated, et tedious cetera. Personally, I enjoy
decadence; but somebody has to hold off the Long
Night for my own lifetime, and it looks as if I'm
elected.*

Then they neared the portal, where a silver
spiderweb gate stood open. Ruethen himself greeted
them at the head of an iridescent slideramp. Such
was Merseian custom. But he bowed in Terran style
and touched horny lips to Lady Diana's hand. "A
rare pleasure, I am certain." The bass voice gave to
fluent Anglic an indescribable nonhuman accent.

She considered him. The Merseian was a true
mammal, but with more traces of reptile ancestry
than humankind: pale green skin, hairless and finely
scaled; a low spiny ridge from the head down along
the backbone to the end of a long thick tail. He was
broader than a man, and would have stood a sheer
two meters did he not walk with a forward-stooping
gait. Except for its baldness and lack of external ears,
the face was quite humanoid, even good-looking in a
heavy rough way. But the eyes beneath the
overhanging brow ridges were two small pits of jet.
Ruethen wore the austere uniform of his class, form-
fitting black with silver trim. A blaster was belted at
his hip.

Lady Diana's perfectly sculptured mouth curved
in a smile. "Do you actually know me, my lord?" she
murmured.

"Frankly, no." A barbaric bluntness. Any
nobleman of Terra would have been agile to disguise
his ignorance. "But while this log does burn upon
the altar stone, peace-holy be it among us. As my
tribe would say in the Cold Valleys."

"Of course you are an old friend of my escort," she
teased.

Ruethen cocked an eye at Flandry. And suddenly the man sensed tautness in that massive frame. Just for a moment, then Ruethen's whole body became a mask. "We have met now and then," said the Merseian dryly. "Welcome, Sir Dominic. The cloakroom slave will furnish you with a mind-screen."

"What?" Despite himself, Flandry started.

"If you want one." Ruethen bared powerful teeth at Lady Diana. "Will my unknown friend grant me a dance later?"

She lost her own coolness for a second, then nodded graciously. "That would be a . . . unique experience, my lord," she said.

It would, at that. Flandry led her on into the ballroom. His mind worried Ruethen's curious offer, like a dog with a bone. Why—?

He saw the gaunt black shape among the rainbow Terrans, and he knew. It went cold along his spine.

II

He wasted no time on excuses but almost ran to the cloakroom. His feet whispered along the crystalline floor, where Orion glittered hundreds of light-years beneath. "Mind-screen," he snapped.

The slave was a pretty girl. Merseians took pleasure in buying humans for menial jobs. "I've only a few, sir," she said. "His lordship told me to keep them for—"

"Me!" Flandry snatched the cap of wires, transistors, and power cells from her hesitant fingers. Only when it was on his head did he relax. Then he took out a fresh cigarette and steered through lilting music towards the bar. He needed a drink, badly.

Aycharaych of Chereion stood beneath high glass pillars. No one spoke to him. Mostly the humans were dancing while nonhumans of various races listened to the music. A performer from Lulluan spread heaven-blue feathers on a small stage, but few watched that rare sight. Flandry elbowed past a Merseian who had just drained a two-liter tankard. "Scotch," he said. "Straight, tall, and quick."

Lady Diana approached. She seemed uncertain whether to be indignant or intrigued. "Now I know what they mean by cavalier treatment." She pointed upward. "What *is* that thing?"

Flandry tossed off his drink. The whisky smoked down his throat, and he felt his nerves ease. "I'm told it's my face," he said.

"No, no! Stop fooling! I mean that horrible wire thing."

"Mind-screen." He held out his glass for a refill. "It heterodynes the energy radiation of the cerebral cortex in a random pattern. Makes it impossible to read what I'm thinking."

"But I thought that was impossible anyway," she said, bewildered. "I mean, unless you belong to a naturally telepathic species."

"Which man isn't," he agreed, "except for rare cases. The nontelepath develops his own private 'language,' which is gibberish to anyone who hasn't studied him for a long time as a single individual. Ergo, telepathy was never considered a particular threat in my line of work, and you've probably never heard of the mind-screen. It was developed just a few years ago. And the reason for its development is standing over there."

She followed his eyes. "Who? That tall being in the black mantle?"

"The same. I had a brush with him, and discovered to my . . . er . . . discomfiture, shall we say? . . . that he has a unique gift. Whether or not all his race does, I couldn't tell you. But within a range of a few hundred meters, Aycharaych of Chereion can read the mind of any individual of any species, whether he's ever met his victim before or not."

"But—why, then—"

"Exactly. He's *persona non grata* throughout our territory, of course, to be shot on sight. But as you know, my lady," said Flandry in a bleak tone, "we are not now in the Terrestrial Empire. Jupiter belongs to the Dispersal of Ymir."

"Oh," said Lady Diana. She colored. "A telepath!"

Flandry gave her a lopsided grin. "Aycharaych is the equivalent of a gentleman," he said. "He wouldn't tell on you. But I'd better go talk to him now." He bowed. "You are certain not to lack company. I see a dozen men converging here already."

"So there are." She smiled. "But I think Aycharaych—how *do* you pronounce it, that guttural *ch* baffles me—I think he'll be much more intriguing." She took his arm.

Flandry disengaged her. She resisted. He closed a hand on her wrist and shoved it down with no effort. Maybe his visage was a fake, he told himself once in a while, but at least his body was his own, and the dreary hours of calisthenics had some reward. "I'm sorry, my lady," he said, "but I am about to talk shop, and you're not initiated in the second oldest profession. Have fun."

Her eyes flared offended vanity. She whirled about and welcomed the Duke of Mars with far more enthusiasm than that foolish young man warranted. Flandry sighed. *I suppose I owe you a thousand credits, Ivar.* He cocked his cigarette at a defiant angle, and strolled across the ballroom.

Aycharaych smiled. His face was also closely humanoid, but in a bony, sword-nosed fashion; the angles of mouth and jaw were exaggerated into V's. It might almost have been the face of some Byzantine saint. But the skin was a pure golden hue, the brows were arches of fine blue feathers, the bald skull carried a feather crest and pointed ears. Broad chest, wasp waist, long skinny legs were hidden by the cloak. The feet, with four clawed toes and spurs on the ankles, showed bare.

Flandry felt pretty sure that intelligent life on Chereion had evolved from birds, and that the planet must be dry, with a thin cold atmosphere. He had hints that its native civilization was incredibly old, and reason to believe it was not a mere subject of Merseia. But beyond that, his knowledge emptied into darkness. He didn't even know where in the Merseian sphere the sun of Chereion lay.

Aycharaych extended a six-fingered hand. Flandry shook it. The digits were delicate within his own. For a brutal moment he thought of squeezing hard, crushing the fine bones. Aycharaych stood a bit taller than he, but Flandry was a rather big human, much broader and more solid.

"A pleasure to meet you again, Sir Dominic," said Aycharaych. His voice was low, sheer beauty to hear. Flandry looked at rust-red eyes, with a warm metallic luster, and released the hand.

"Hardly unexpected," he said. "For you, that is."

"You travel about so much," Aycharaych said. "I was sure a few men of your corps would be here tonight, but I could not be certain of your own whereabouts."

"I wish I ever was of yours," said Flandry ruefully.

"Congratulations upon your handling of *l'affaire Nyanza*. We are going to miss A'u on our side. He had a certain watery brilliance."

Flandry prevented himself from showing surprise. "I thought that aspect of the business had been hushed up," he said. "But little pitchers seem to have big ears. How long have you been in the Solar System?"

"A few weeks," said Aycharaych. "Chiefly a pleasure trip." He cocked his head. "Ah, the orchestra has begun a Strauss waltz. Very good. Though of course Johann is not to be compared to Richard, who will always be *the* Strauss."

"Oh?" Flandry's interest in ancient music was only slightly greater than his interest in committing suicide. "I wouldn't know."

"You should, my friend. Not even excepting Xingu, Strauss is the most misunderstood composer of known galactic history. Were I to be imprisoned for life with only one tape, I would choose his *Death and Transfiguration* and be satisfied."

"I'll arrange it," offered Flandry at once.

Aycharaych chuckled and took the man's arm. "Come, let us find a more peaceful spot. But I pray you, do not waste so amusing an occasion on me. I own to visiting Terra clandestinely, but that part of it was entirely for the easement of my personal curiosity. I had no intention of burgling the Imperial offices—"

"Which are equipped with Aycharaych alarms anyway."

"Telepathizing detectors? Yes, so I would assume.

I am a little too old and stiff, and your gravity a little too overpowering, to indulge in my own thefts. Nor have I the type of dashing good looks needed, I am told by all the teleplays, for cloak and dagger work. No, I merely wished to see the planet which bred such a race as yours. I walked in a few forests, inspected certain paintings, visited some chosen graves, and returned here. Whence I am about to depart, by the way. You need not get your Imperium to put pressure on the Ymirites to expel me; my courier ship leaves in twenty hours."

"For where?" asked Flandry.

"Hither and yon," said Aycharaych lightly.

Flandry felt his stomach muscles grow hard. "Syrax?" he got out.

They paused at the entrance to the null-gee conservatory. A single great sphere of water balanced like silver at its very heart, with fern jungle and a thousand purple-scarlet blooms forming a cavern around it, the stars and mighty Jupiter beyond. Later, no doubt, the younger and drunker humans would be peeling off their clothes and going for a free-fall swim in that serene globe. But now only the music dwelt here. Aycharaych kicked himself over the threshold. His cloak flowed like black wings as he arrowed across the bubble-dome. Flandry came after, in clothes that were fire and trumpeting. He needed a moment before he adjusted to weightlessness. Aycharaych, whose ancestors once whistled in Chereion's sky, appeared to have no such trouble.

The nonhuman stopped his flight by seizing a bracken frond. He looked at a violet burst of orchids and his long hawk-head inclined. "Black against the quicksilver water globe," he mused; "the universe black and cold beyond both. A beautiful arrangement, and with that touch of horror necessary to the highest art."

"Black?" Flandry glanced startled at the violet flowers. Then he clamped his lips.

But Aycharaych had already grasped the man's idea. He smiled. "*Touché*. I should not have let slip that I am colorblind in the blue wavelengths."

"But you see further into the red than I do," predicted Flandry.

"Yes. I admit, since you would infer so anyhow, my native sun is cooler and redder than yours. If you think that will help you identify it, among all the millions of stars in the Merseian sphere, accept the information with my compliments."

"The Syrax Cluster is middle Population One," said Flandry. "Not too suitable for your eyes."

Aycharaych stared at the water. Tropical fish were visible within its globe, like tiny many-colored rockets. "It does not follow I am going to Syrax," he said tonelessly. "I certainly have no personal wish to do so. Too many warcraft, too many professional officers. I do not like their mentality." He made a freefall bow. "Your own excepted, of course."

"Of course," said Flandry. "Still, if you could do something to break the deadlock out there, in Merseia's favor—"

"You flatter me," said Aycharaych. "But I fear you have not yet outgrown the romantic view of military politics. The fact is that neither side wants to make a total effort to control the Syrax stars. Merseia could use them as a valuable base, outflanking Antares and thus a spearhead poised at that entire sector of your empire. Terra wants control simply to deny us the cluster. Since neither government wishes, at present, to break the nominal state of peace, they maneuver about out there, mass naval strength, spy and snipe and hold running battles . . . but the game of all-out seizure is not worth the candle of all-out war."

"But if you could tip the scales, personally, so our boys lost out at Syrax," said Flandry, "we wouldn't counter-attack your imperial sphere. You know that. It'd invite counter-counter-attack on us. Heavens, Terra itself might be bombed! We're much too comfortable to risk such an outcome." He pulled himself up short. Why expose his own bitterness, and perhaps be arrested on Terra for sedition?

"If we possessed Syrax," said Aycharaych, "it would, with 71 per cent probability, hasten the collapse of the Terran hegemony by a hundred years, plus or minus ten. That is the verdict of our military computers—though I myself feel the faith our High Command has in them is naïve and rather touching. However, the predicted date of Terra's fall would still lie 150 years hence. So I wonder why your government cares."

Flandry shrugged. "A few of us are a bit sentimental about our planet," he answered sadly. "And then, of course, we ourselves aren't out there being shot at."

"That is the human mentality again," said Aycharaych. "Your instincts are such that you never accept dying. You, personally, down underneath everything, do you not feel death is just a little bit vulgar, not quite a gentleman?"

"Maybe. What would you call it?"

"A completion."

Their talk drifted to impersonalities. Flandry had never found anyone else whom he could so converse with. Aycharaych could be wise and learned and infinitely kind when he chose: or flick a whetted wit across the pompous face of empire. To speak with him, touching now and then on the immortal questions, was almost like a confessional—for he was not human and did not judge human deeds, yet he seemed to understand the wishes at their root.

At last Flandry made a reluctant excuse to get away. *Nu*, he told himself, *business is business*. Since Lady Diana was studiously ignoring him, he enticed a redhaired bit of fluff into an offside room, told her he would be back in ten minutes, and slipped through a rear corridor. Perhaps any Merseian who saw him disappear wouldn't expect him to return for an hour or two; might not recognize the girl when she got bored waiting and found her own way to the ballroom again. One human looked much like another to the untrained nonhuman eye, and there were at least a thousand guests by now.

It was a flimsy camouflage for his exit, but the best he could think of.

Flandry re-entered the yacht and roused Chives. "Home," he said. "Full acceleration. Or secondary drive, if you think you can handle it within the System in this clumsy gold-plated hulk."

"Yes, sir. I can."

At faster-than-light, he'd be at Terra in minutes, rather than hours. Excellent! It might actually be possible to arrange for Aycharaych's completion.

More than half of Flandry hoped the attempt would fail.

III

It happened to be day over North America, where Vice Admiral Fenross had his offices. Not that that mattered; they were like as not to work around the clock in Intelligence, or else Flandry could have gotten his superior out of bed. He would, in fact, have preferred to do so.

As matters worked out, however, he created a satisfactory commotion. He saved an hour by having Chives dive the yacht illegally through all traffic lanes above Admiralty Center. With a coverall over his party clothes, he dove from the airlock and rode a grav repulsor down to the 40th flange of the Intelligence tower. While the yacht was being stopped by a sky monitor, Flandry was arguing with a marine on guard duty. He looked down the muzzle of a blaster and said: "You know me, Sergeant. Let me by. Urgent."

"I guess I do know your face, sir," the marine answered. "But faces can be changed and nobody gets by me without a pass. Just stand there while I buzzes a patrol."

Flandry considered making a jump for it. But the Imperial Marines were on to every kick of judo he knew. Hell take it, an hour wasted on identification —Wait. Memory clicked into place. "You're Mohandas Parkinson," said Flandry. "You have four darling children, your wife is unreasonably monogamous, and you were playing Go at Madame Cepheid's last month."

Sergeant Parkinson's gun wavered. "Huh?" he said. Then, loudly, "I do' know whatcher talking about!"

"Madame Cepheid's Go board is twenty meters square," said Flandry, "and the pieces are live girls. In the course of a game—Does that ring a bell, sergeant? I was there too, watching, and I'm sure your wife would be delighted to hear you are still capable of such truly epic—"

"Get on your way, you . . . blackmailer!" choked Parkinson. He gulped and added, "Sir."

Captain Flandry grinned, patted him on his helmet, holstered his weapon for him, and went quickly inside.

Unlike most, Fenross had no beautiful receptionist in his outer office. A robovoice asked the newcomer's business. "Hero," he said blandly. The robot said Admiral Fenross was occupied with a most disturbing new development. Flandry said he was also, and got admission.

Hollow-cheeked and shaky, Fenross looked across his desk. His eyes were not too bloodshot to show a flick of hatred. "Oh," he said. "You. Well, Captain, what interrupts your little tête-à-tête with your Merseian friends?"

Flandry sat down and took out a cigarette. He was not surprised that Fenross had set spies on him, but the fact was irritating nonetheless. *How the devil did this feud ever get started?* he wondered. *Is it only that I took that girl . . . what was her name, anyway? Marjorie? Margaret? . . . was it only that I once took her from him when we were cadets together? Why, I did it for a joke. She wasn't very good-looking in spite of everything biosculp could do.*

"I've news too hot for any com circuit," he said. "I just now—"

"You're on furlough," snapped Fenross. "You've got no business here."

"What? Look, it was Aycharaych! Himself! At the Crystal Moon!"

A muscle twitched in Fenross' cheek. "I can't hear an unofficial report," he said. "All ruin is exploding beyond Aldebaran. If you think you've done something brilliant, file an account in the regular channels."

"But—for God's sake!" Flandry sprang to his feet. "Admiral Fenross, sir, whatever the hell you want me to call you, he's leaving the Solar System in a matter of hours. Courier boat. We can't touch him in Ymirite space, but if we waylaid him on his way out —He'll be tricky, the ambush might not work, but name of a little green pig, if we can get Aycharaych it'll be better than destroying a Merseian fleet!"

Fenross reached out a hand which trembled ever so faintly, took a small pillbox and shook a tablet loose. "Haven't slept in forty hours," he muttered. "And you off on that yacht. . . . I can't take cognizance, Captain. Not under the circumstances." He glanced up again. Slyness glistened in his eyes. "Of course," he said, "if you want to cancel your own leave—"

Flandry stood a moment, rigid, staring at the desk-bound man who hated him. Memory trickled back: *After I broke off with her, yes, the girl did go a bit wild. She was killed in an accident on Venus, wasn't she . . . drunken party flying over the Saw . . . yes, I seem to've heard about it. And Fenross has never even looked at another woman.*

He sighed. "Sir, I am reporting myself back on active duty."

Fenross nodded. "File that with the robot as you leave. Now I've got work for you."

"But Aycharaych—"

"We'll handle him. I've got a more suitable assignment in mind." Fenross grinned, tossed down his pill and followed it with a cup of water from the desk fountain. "After all, a dashing field agent ought to dash, don't you think?"

Could it be just the fact that he's gotten more rank but I've had more fun? wondered Flandry. *Who knows? Does he himself?* He sat down again, refusing to show expression.

Fenross drummed the desk top and stared at a blank wall. His uniform was as severe as regulations permitted—Flandry's went in the opposite direction —but it still formed an unnecessarily gorgeous base for his tortured red head. "This is under the strictest secrecy," he began in a rapid, toneless voice. "I have no idea how long we can suppress the news, though. One of our colonies is under siege. Deep within the Imperial sphere."

Flandry was forced to whistle. "Where? Who?"

"Ever heard of Vixen? Well, I never had either before this. It's a human-settled planet of an F6 star about a hundred light-years from Sol, somewhat north and clockwise of Aldebaran. Oddball world, but moderately successful as colonies go. You know that region is poor in systems of interest to humans, and very little explored. In effect, Vixen sits in the middle of a desert. Or does it? You'll wonder when I tell you that a space fleet appeared several weeks ago and demanded that it yield to occupation. The ships were of exotic type, and the race crewing them can't be identified. But some, at least, spoke pretty good Anglic."

Flandry sat dead still. His mind threw up facts, so familiar as to be ridiculous, and yet they must now be considered again. The thing which had happened was without precedent.

An interstellar domain can have no definite borders; stars are scattered too thinly, their types too intermingled. And there are too many of them. In very crude approximation, the Terrestrial Empire was a sphere of some 400 light-years diameter, centered on Sol, and contained an estimated four million stars. But of these less than half had even been visited. A bare 100,000 were directly concerned with the Imperium, a few multiples of that number might have some shadowy contact and owe a theoretical allegiance. Consider a single planet; realize that it is a *world*, as big and varied and strange as this Terra ever was, with as many conflicting elements of race and language and culture among its natives; estimate how much government even one planet requires, and see how quickly a reign over many becomes impossibly huge. Then consider, too, how small a percentage of stars are of any use to a given species (too hot, too cold, too turbulent, too many companions) and, of those, how few will have even one planet where that species is reasonably safe. The Empire becomes tenuous indeed. And its inconceivable extent is still the merest speck on one outlying part of one spiral arm of one galaxy; among a hundred billion or more great suns, those known to any single world are the barest, tiniest handful.

However—attack that far within the sphere? No! Individual ships could sneak between the stars easily enough. But a war fleet could never come a hundred light-years inward from the farthest Imperial bases. The instantaneous "wake" of disturbed space-time, surging from so many vessels, would be certain of detection somewhere along the line. Therefore—

"Those ships were built within our sphere," said Flandry slowly. "And not too many parsecs from Vixen."

Fenross sneered. "Your genius dazzles me. As a matter of fact, though, they might have come further than usual, undetected, because so much of the Navy is out at Syrax now. Our interior posts are stripped, some completely deserted. I'll agree the enemy must base within several parsecs of Vixen. But that doesn't mean they live there. Their base might be a space station, a rogue planet, or something else we'll never find; they could have sent their fleet to it a ship at a time, over a period of months."

Flandry shook his head. "Supply lines. Having occupied Vixen, they'll need to maintain their garrison till it's self-sufficient. No, they have a home somewhere in the Imperial sphere, surely in the same quadrant. Which includes only about a million stars! Say, roughly, 100,000 possibilities, some never even catalogued. How many years would it take how many ships to check out 100,000 systems?"

"Yeh. And what would be happening meanwhile?"

"What has?"

"The Vixenites put up a fight. There's a small naval base on their planet, unmanned at present, but enough of the civilian population knew how to make use of its arsenal. They got couriers away, of course, and Aldebaran Station sent what little help it could. When last heard from, Vixen was under siege. We're dispatching a task force, but it'll take time to get there. That wretched Syrax business ties our hands. Reports indicate the aliens haven't overwhelming strength; we could send enough ships to make mesons of them. But if we withdrew that many from Syrax, they'd come back to find Merseia entrenched in the Cluster."

"Tie-in?" wondered Flandry.

"Who knows? I've got an idea, though, and your assignment will be to investigate it." Fenross leaned over the desk. His sunken eyes probed at Flandry's. "We're all too ready to think of Merseia when anything goes wrong," he said bleakly. "But after all, they live a long ways off. There's another alien power right next door . . . and as closely interwoven with Merseia as it is with us."

"You mean Ymir?" Flandry snorted. "Come now, dear chief, you're letting your xenophobia run away with you."

"Consider," said Fenross. "Somebody, or something, helped those aliens at Vixen build a modern war fleet. They couldn't have done it alone: we'd have known it if they'd begun exploring stellar space, and knowledge has to precede conquest. Somebody, very familiar with our situation, has briefed the aliens on our language, weapons, territorial layout—the works. Somebody, I'm sure, told them when to attack: right now, when nearly our whole strength is at Syrax. *Who?* There's one item. The aliens use a helium-pressure power system like the Ymirites. That's unmistakable on the detectors. Helium-pressure is all right, but it's not as convenient as the hydrogen-heavy atom cycle; not if you live under terrestroid conditions, and the aliens very definitely do. The ships, their shape I mean, also have a subtly Ymirite touch. I'll show you pictures that have arrived with the reports. Those ships look as if they'd been designed by some engineer more used to working with hydro-lithium than steel."

"You mean the Ymirites are behind the aliens? But—"

"But nothing. There's an Ymirite planet in the Vixen system too. Who knows how many stars those crawlers have colonized . . . stars we never even heard about? Who knows how many client races they might lord it over? And they travel blithely back and forth, across our sphere and Merseia's and—

Suppose they are secretly in cahoots with Merseia. What better way to smuggle Merseian agents into our systems? We don't stop Ymirite ships. We aren't able to! But any of them could carry a force-bubble with terrestroid conditions inside. . . . I've felt for years we've been too childishly trustful of Ymir. It's past time we investigated them in detail. It may already be too late!"

Flandry stubbed out his cigarette. "But what interest have they got in all this?" he asked mildly. "What could any oxygen-breathing race have that they'd covet—or bribe them with?"

"That I don't know," said Fenross. "I could be dead wrong. But I want it looked into. You're going back to Jupiter, Captain. At once."

"What?"

"We're chronically undermanned in this miserable stepchild of the service," said Fenross. "Now, worse than ever. You'll have to go alone. Snoop around as much as you can. Take all the time you need. But don't come back without a report that'll give some indication—one way or another!"

Or come back dead, thought Flandry. He looked into the twitching face across the desk and knew that was what Fenross wanted.

IV

He got Chives out of arrest and debated with himself whether to sneak back to Ruethen's party. It was still going on. But no. Aycharaych would never have mentioned his own departure without assuming Flandry would notify headquarters. It might be his idea of a joke—it might be a straightforward challenge, for Aycharaych was just the sort who'd enjoy seeing if he could elude an ambush—most likely, the whole thing was deliberate, for some darkling purpose. In any event, a junior Intelligence officer or two could better keep tabs on the Chereionite than Flandry, who was prominent. Having made arrangements for that, the man took Chives to his private flitter.

Though voluptuous enough inside, the *Hooligan* was a combat boat, with guns and speed. Even on primary, sub-light drive, it could reach Jupiter in so few hours that Flandry would have little enough time to think what he would do. He set the autopilot and bade Chives bring a drink. "A stiff one," he added.

"Yes, sir. Do you wish your whites laid out, or do you prefer a working suit?"

Flandry considered his rumpled elegance and sighed. Chives had spent an hour dressing him—for nothing. "Plain gray zip-suit," he said. "Also sackcloth and ashes."

"Very good, sir." The valet poured whisky over ice. He was from Shalmu, quite humanoid except for bald emerald skin, prehensile tail, one-point-four meter height, and details of ear, hand, and foot. Flandry had bought him some years back, named him Chives, and taught him any number of useful arts. Lately the being had politely refused manumission. ("If I may make so bold as to say it, sir, I am afraid my tribal customs would now have a lack of interest for me matched only by their deplorable lack of propriety.")

Flandry brooded over his drink awhile. "What do you know about Ymir?" he asked.

"Ymir is the arbitrary human name, sir, for the chief planet of a realm—if I may use that word advisedly—coterminous with the Terrestrial Empire, the Merseian, and doubtless a considerable part of the galaxy beyond."

"Don't be so bloody literal-minded," said Flandry. "Especially when I'm being rhetorical. I mean, what do you know about their ways of living, thinking, believing, hoping? What do they find beautiful and what is too horrible to tolerate? Good galloping gods, what do they even use for a government? They call themselves the Dispersal when they talk Anglic—but is that a translation or a mere tag? How can we tell? What do you and I have in common with a being that lives at a hundred below zero, breathing hydrogen at a pressure which makes our ocean beds look like vacuum, drinking liquid methane and using allotropic ice to make his tools?

"We were ready enough to cede Jupiter to them: Jupiter-type planets throughout our realm. They had terrestroid planets to offer in exchange. Why, that swap doubled the volume of our sphere. And we traded a certain amount of scientific information with them, high-pressure physics for low-pressure, oxygen metabolisms versus hydrogen . . . but disappointingly little, when you get down to it. They'd been in interstellar space longer than we had. (And how did they learn atomics under Ymirite air pressure? Me don't ask it!) They'd already observed our kind of life throughout . . . how much of the galaxy? We couldn't offer them a thing of importance, except the right to colonize some more planets in peace. They've never shown as much interest in our wars—the wars of the oxygen breathers on the pygmy planets—as you and I would have in a fight between two ant armies. Why should they care? You could drop Terra or Merseia into Jupiter and it'd hardly

make a decent splash. For a hundred years, now, the
Ymirites have scarcely said a word to us. Or to
Merseia, from all indications. Till now.

"And yet I glanced at the pictures taken out near
Vixen, just before we left. And Fenross, may he fry,
is right. Those blunt ships were made on a planet
similar to Terra, but they have Ymirite lines . . . the
way the first Terran automobiles had the motor in
front, because that was where the horse used to
be. . . . It could be coincidence, I suppose. Or a red
herring. Or—I don't know. How am I supposed to
find out, one man on a planet with ten times the
radius of Terra? Judas!" He drained his glass and
held it out again.

Chives refilled, then went back to the clothes
locker. "A white scarf or a blue?" he mused. "Hm,
yes, I do believe the white, sir."

The flitter plunged onward. Flandry needed a
soberjolt by the time he had landed on Ganymede.

There was an established procedure for such a visit. It hadn't been used for decades, Flandry had to
look it up, but the robot station still waited patiently
between rough mountains. He presented his creden-
tials, radio contact was made with the primary
planet, unknown messages travelled over its surface.
A reply was quick: yes, Captain, the governor can
receive you. A spaceship is on its way, and will be at
your disposal.

Flandry looked out at the stony desolation of
Ganymede. It was not long before a squat, shimmer-
ing shape had made grav-beam descent. A tube
wormed from its lock to the flitter's. Flandry sighed
"Let's go," he said, and strolled across. Chives
trotted after with a burden of weapons, tools, and
instruments—none of which was likely to be much

use. There was a queasy moment under Ganymede's natural gravity, then they had entered the Terra-conditioned bubble.

It looked like any third-class passenger cabin, except for the outmoded furnishings and a bank of large viewscreens. Hard to believe that this was only the material inner lining of a binding-force field: that that same energy, cousin to that which held the atomic nucleus together, was all which kept this room from being crushed beneath intolerable pressure. Or, at the moment, kept the rest of the spaceship from exploding outward. The bulk of the vessel was an alloy of water, lithium, and metallic hydrogen, stable only under Jovian surface conditions.

Flandry let Chives close the airlock while he turned on the screens. They gave him a full outside view. One remained blank, a communicator, the other showed the pilot's cabin.

An artificial voice, ludicrously sweet in the style of a century ago, said: "Greeting, Terran. My name, as nearly as it may be rendered in sonic equivalents, is Horx. I am your guide and interpreter while you remain on Jupiter."

Flandry looked into the screen. The Ymirite didn't quite register on his mind. His eyes weren't trained to those shapes and proportions, seen by that weirdly shifting red-blue-brassy light. (Which wasn't the real thing, even, but an electronic translation. A human looking straight into the thick Jovian air would only see darkness.) "Hello, Horx," he said to the great black multi-legged shape with the peculiarly tendrilled heads. He wet his lips, which seemed a bit dry. "I, er, expect you haven't had such an assignment before in your life."

"I did several times, a hundred or so Terra-years ago," said Horx casually. He didn't seem to move, to touch any controls, but Ganymede receded in the viewscreens and raw space blazed forth. "Since then I have been doing other work." Hesitation. Or was it? At last: "Recently, though, I have conducted several missions to our surface."

"What?" choked Flandry.

"Merseian," said Horx. "You may enquire of the governor if you wish." He said nothing else the whole trip.

Jupiter, already big in the screen, became half of heaven. Flandry saw blots march across its glowing many-colored face, darknesses which were storms that could have swallowed all Terra. Then the sight was lost, he was dropping through the atmosphere. Still the step-up screens tried loyally to show him something: he saw clouds of ammonia crystals, a thousand kilometers long, streaked with strange blues and greens that were free radicals; he saw lightning leap across a purple sky, and the distant yellow flare of sodium explosions. As he descended, he could even feel, very dimly, the quiver of the ship under enormous winds, and hear the muffled shriek and thunder of the air.

They circled the night side, still descending, and Flandry saw a methane ocean, beating waves flattened by pressure and gravity against a cliff of black allotropic ice, which crumbled and was lifted again even as he watched. He saw an endless plain where things half trees and half animals—except that they were neither, in any Terrestrial sense—lashed snaky fronds after ribbon-shaped flyers a hundred meters in length. He saw bubbles stream past on a red wind, and they were lovely in their myriad colors and they sang in thin crystal voices which somehow penetrated the ship. But they couldn't be true bubbles at this pressure. Could they?

A city came into view, just beyond the dawn line. If it was a city. It was, at least, a unified structure of immense extent, intricate with grottos and arabesques, built low throughout but somehow graceful and gracious. On Flandry's screen its color was polished blue. Here and there sparks and threads of white energy would briefly flash. They hurt his eyes. There were many Ymirites about, flying on their own wings or riding in shell-shaped power gliders. You wouldn't think of Jupiter as a planet where anything could fly, until you remembered the air density; then you realized it was more a case of swimming.

The spaceship came to a halt, hovering on its repulsor field. Horx said: "Governor Thua."

Another Ymirite squatted suddenly in the outside communication screen. He held something which smoked and flickered from shape to shape. The impersonally melodious robot voice said for him, under the eternal snarling of a wind which would have blown down any city men could build: "Welcome. What is your desire?"

The old records had told Flandry to expect brusqueness. It was not discourtesy; what could a human and an Ymirite make small talk about? The man puffed a cigarette to nervous life and said: "I am here on an investigative mission for my government." Either these beings were or were not already aware of the Vixen situation; if not, then they weren't allies of Merseia and would presumably not tell. Or if they did, what the devil difference? Flandry explained.

Thua said at once, "You seem to have very small grounds for suspecting us. A mere similarity of appearances and nuclear technology is logically insufficient."

"I know," said Flandry. "It could be a fake."

"It could even be that one or a few Ymirite individuals have offered advice to the entities which instigated this attack," said Thua. You couldn't judge from the pseudo-voice, but he seemed neither offended nor sympathetic: just monumentally uninterested. "The Dispersal has been nonstimulate as regards individuals for many cycles. However, I cannot imagine what motive an Ymirite would have for exerting himself on behalf of oxygen breathers. There is no insight to be gained from such acts, and certainly no material profit."

"An aberrated individual?" suggested Flandry with little hope. "Like a man poking an anthill—an abode of lesser animals—merely to pass the time?"

"Ymirites do not aberrate in such fashion," said Thua stiffly.

"I understand there've been recent Merseian visits here."

"I was about to mention that. I am doing all I can to assure both empires of Ymir's strict neutrality. It would be a nuisance if either attacked us and forced us to exterminate their species."

Which is the biggest brag since that fisherman who caught the equator, thought Flandry, *or else is sober truth.* He said aloud, choosing his words one by one: "What, then, were the Merseians doing here?"

"They wished to make some scientific observations of the Jovian surface," said Thua. "Horx guided them, like you. Let him describe their activities."

The pilot stirred in his chamber, spreading black wings. "We simply cruised about a few times. They had optical instruments, and took various spectroscopic readings. They said it was for research in solid-state physics."

"Curiouser and curiouser," said Flandry. He stroked his moustache. "They have as many jovoid planets in their sphere as we do. The detailed report on Jovian conditions which the first Ymirite settlers made to Terra, under the treaty, has never been secret. No, I just don't believe that research yarn."

"It did seem dubious," agreed Thua, "but I do not pretend to understand every vagary of the alien mind. It was easier to oblige them than argue about it."

Chives cleared his throat and said unexpectedly: "If I may take the liberty of a question, sir, were all these recent visitors of the Merseian species?"

Thua's disgust could hardly be mistaken: "Do you expect me to register insignificant differences between one such race and another?"

Flandry sighed. "It looks like deadlock, doesn't it?" he said.

"I can think of no way to give you positive assurance that Ymir is not concerned, except my word," said Thua. "However, if you wish you may cruise about this planet at random and see if you observe anything out of the ordinary." His screen went blank.

"Big fat chance!" muttered Flandry. "Give me a drink, Chives."

"Will you follow the governor's proposal?" asked Horx.

"Reckon so." Flandry flopped into a chair. "Give us the standard guided tour. I've never been on

Jupiter, and might as well have something to show for my time."

The city fell behind, astonishingly fast. Flandry sipped the whisky Chives had gotten from the supplies they had along, and watched the awesome landscape with half an eye. Too bad he was feeling so sour; this really was an experience such as is granted few men. But he had wasted hours on a mission which any second-year cadet could have handled . . . while guns were gathered at Syrax and Vixen stood alone against all hell . . . or even while Lady Diana danced with other men and Ivar del Bruno waited grinning to collect his bet. Flandry said an improper word. "What a nice subtle bed of coals for Fenross to rake me over," he added. "The man has a genius for it." He gulped his drink and called for another.

"We're rising, sir," said Chives much later.

Flandry saw mountains which trembled and droned, blue mists that whirled about their metallic peaks, and then the Jovian ground was lost in darkness. The sky began to turn blood color. "What are we heading for now?" he asked. He checked a map. "Oh, yes, I see."

"I venture to suggest to the pilot, sir, that our speed may be a trifle excessive," said Chives.

Flandry heard the wind outside rise to a scream, with subsonic undertones that shivered in his marrow. Red fog flew roiled and tattered past his eyes. Beyond, he saw crimson clouds the height of a Terrestrial sierra, with lightning leaping in their bellies. The light from the screens washed like a dull fire into the cabin.

"Yes," he muttered. "Slow down, Horx. There'll be another one along in a minute, as the story has it—"

And then he saw the pilot rise up in his chamber,
fling open a door, and depart. An instant afterward
Flandry saw Horx beat wings against the spaceship's
furious slipstream; then the Ymirite was whirled
from view. And then Chives saw the thing which
hung in the sky before them, and yelled. He threw
his tail around Flandry's waist while he clung with
hands and legs to a bunk stanchion.

And then the world exploded into thunder and
night.

V

Flandry awoke. He spent centuries wishing he
hadn't. A blurred green shape said: "Your aneurine,
sir."

"Go 'way," mumbled Flandry. "What was I
drinking?"

"Pardon my taking the liberty, sir," said Chives.
He pinned the man's wrists down with his tail, held
Flandry's nose with one hand and poured the drug
down his mouth with the other. "There, now, we
are feeling much better, aren't we?"

"Remind me to shoot you, slowly." Flandry
gagged for a while. The medicine took hold and he
sat up. His brain cleared and he looked at the screen
bank.

Only one of the viewers still functioned. It showed
thick, drifting redness, shot through with blues and
blacks. A steady rough growling, like the breakup of
a polar ice pack, blasted its way through the ultimate
rigidity of the force bubble—God, what must the
noise be like outside? The cabin was tilted. Slumped
in its lower corner, Flandry began to glide across the
floor again; the ship was still being rolled about. The
internal gravity field had saved their lives by

cushioning the worst shock, but then it had gone dead. He felt the natural pull of Jupiter upon him, and every cell was weary from its own weight.

He focused on a twisted bunkframe. "Did I do that with my own little head?"

"We struck with great force, sir," Chives told him. "I permitted myself to bandage your scalp. However, a shot of growth hormone will heal the cuts in a few hours, sir, if we escape the present dilemma."

Flandry lurched to his feet. His bones seemed to be dragging him back downward. He felt the cabin walls tremble and heard them groan. The force bubble had held, which meant that its generator and the main power plant had survived the crash. Not unexpectedly; a ship like this was built on the "fail safe" principle. But there was no access whatsoever from this cabin to the pilot room—unless you were an Ymirite. It made no difference whether the ship was still flyable or not. Human and Shalmuan were stuck here till they starved. Or, more likely, till the atomic-power plant quit working, under some or other of the buffers this ship was receiving.

Well, when the force-field collapsed and Jovian air pressure flattened the cabin, it would be a merciful death.

"The hell with that noise," said Flandry. "I don't want to die so fast I can't feel it. I want to see death coming, and make the stupid thing fight for every centimeter of me."

Chives gazed into the sinister crimson which filled the last electronic window. His slight frame stooped, shaking in the knees; he was even less adapted to Jovian weight than Flandry. "Where are we, sir?" he husked. "I was thinking primarily about what to make for lunch, just before the collision, and—"

"The Red Spot area," said Flandry. "Or, rather, the fringe of it. We must be on an outlying berg, or whatever the deuce they're called."

"Our guide appears to have abandoned us, sir."

"Hell, he got us into this mess. On purpose! I know for a fact there's at least one Ymirite working for the enemy—whoever the enemy is. But the information won't be much use if we become a pair of grease spots."

The ship shuddered and canted. Flandry grabbed a stanchion for support, eased himself down on the bunk, and said, very quickly, for destruction roared around him:

"You've seen the Red Spot from space, Chives. It's been known for a long time, even before space travel, that it's a . . . a mass of aerial pack ice. Lord, what a fantastic place to die! What happens is that at a certain height in the Jovian atmosphere, the pressure allows a red crystalline form of ice—not the white stuff we splash whisky onto, or the black allotrope down at the surface, or the super-dense variety in the mantle around the Jovian core. Here the pressure is right for red ice, and the air density is identical, so it floats. An initial formation created favorable conditions for the formation of more . . . so it accumulated in this one region, much as polar caps build up on cozier type planets. Some years a lot of it melts away—changes phase—the Red Spot looks paler from outside. Other years you get a heavy pile-up, and Jupiter seems to have a moving wound. But always, Chives, the Red Spot is a pack of flying glaciers, stretching broader than all Terra. And we've been crashed on one of them!"

"Then our present situation can scarcely be accidental, sir," nodded Chives imperturbably. "I daresay, with all the safety precautions built into this ship, Horx thought this would be the only way to destroy us without leaving evidence. He can claim a stray berg was tossed in our path, or some such tale." Chives sniffed. "Not sportsmanlike at all, sir. Just what one would expect of a . . . a native."

The cabin yawed. Flandry caught himself before he fell out of the bunk. At this gravity, to stumble across the room would be to break a leg. Thunders rolled. White vapors hissed up against crimson in the surviving screen.

"I'm not on to these scientific esoterica," said Flandry. His chest pumped, struggling to supply oxygen for muscles toiling under nearly three times their normal weight. Each rib felt as if cast in lead. "But I'd guess what is happening is this. We maintain a temperature in here which for Jupiter is crazily high. So we're radiating heat, which makes the ice go soft and—We're slowly sinking into the berg." He shrugged and got out a cigarette.

"Is that wise, sir?" asked Chives.

"The oxygen recyclers are still working," said Flandry. "It's not at all stuffy in here. Air is the least of our worries." His coolness cracked over, he smote a fist on the wall and said between his teeth: "It's this being helpless! We can't go out of the cabin, we can't do a thing but sit here and take it!"

"I wonder, sir." Slowly, his thin face sagging with gravity, Chives pulled himself to the pack of equipment. He pawed through it. "No, sir. I regret to say I took no radio. It seemed we could communicate through the pilot." He paused. "Even if we did find a way to signal, I daresay any Ymirite who received our call would merely interpret it as random static."

Flandry stood up, somehow. "What do we have?"

A tiny excitement shivered along his nerves. Outside, Jupiter boomed at him.

"Various detectors, sir, to check for installations. A pair of spacesuits. Sidearms. Your burglar kit, though I confess uncertainty what value it would have here. A microrecorder. A—"

"*Wait a minute!*"

Flandry sprang towards his valet. The floor rocked beneath him. He staggered towards the far wall. Chives shot out his tail and helped brake the man. Shaking, Flandry eased himself down and went on all fours to the corner where the Shalmuan squatted.

He didn't even stop to gibe at his own absent-mindedness. His heart thuttered. "Wait a minute, Chives," he said. "We've got an airlock over there. Since the force-bubble necessarily reinforces its structure, it must still be intact; and its machinery can open the valves even against this outside pressure. Of course, we can't go through ourselves. Our space armor would be squashed flat. But we can get at the mechanism of the lock. It also, by logical necessity, has to be part of the Terra-conditioned system. We can use the tools we have here to make a simple automatic cycle. First the outer valve opens. Then it shuts, the Jovian air is exhausted from the chamber and Terrestrial air replaces same. Then the valve opens again . . . and so on. Do you see?"

"No, sir," said Chives. A deadly physical exhaustion filmed his yellow eyes. "My brain feels so thick . . . I regret—"

"A signal!" yelled Flandry. "We flush oxygen out into a hydrogen-cum-methane atmosphere. We supply an electric spark in the lock chamber to ignite the mixture. Whoosh! A flare! Feeble and blue enough —but not by Jovian standards. Any Ymirite anywhere within tens of kilometers is bound to see it as brilliant as we see a magnesium torch. And it'll repeat. A steady cycle, every four or five minutes. If the Ymirites aren't made of concrete, they'll be curious enough to investigate . . . and when they find the wreck on this berg, they'll guess our need and—"

His voice trailed off. Chives said dully, "Can we spare the oxygen, sir?"

"We'll have to," said Flandry. "We'll sacrifice as much as we can stand, and then halt the cycle. If nothing has happened after several hours, we'll expend half of what's left in one last fireworks." He took an ultimate pull on his cigarette, ground it out with great care, and fought back to his feet. "Come on, let's get going. What have we to lose?"

The floor shook. It banged and crashed outside. A fog of free radicals drifted green past the window, and the red iceberg spun in Jupiter's endless gale.

Flandry glanced at Chives. "You have one fault, laddy," he said, forcing a smile to his lips. "You aren't a beautiful woman." And then, after a moment, sighing: "However, it's just as well. Under the circumstances."

VI

—And in that well-worn nick of time, which goes to prove that the gods, understandably, love me, help arrived. An Ymirite party spotted our flare. Having poked around, they went off, bringing back another force-bubble ship to which we transferred our nearly suffocated carcasses. No, Junior, I don't know what the Ymirites were doing in the Red Spot area. It must be a dank cold place for them too. But I had guessed they would be sure to maintain some *kind of monitors, scientific stations, or what have you around there, just as we monitor the weather-breeding regions of Terra.*

Governor Thua didn't bother to apologize. He didn't even notice my valet's indignant demand that the miscreant Horx be forthwith administered a red-ice shaft, except to say that future visitors would be given a different guide (how can they tell?) and that this business was none of his doing and he wouldn't waste any Ymirite's time with investigations or punishment or any further action at all. He pointed out the treaty provision, that he wasn't bound to admit us, and that any visits would always be at the visitor's own risk.

The fact that some Ymirites did rescue us proves that the conspiracy, if any, does not involve their whole race. But how highly placed the hostile individuals are in their government (if they have anything corresponding to government as we know it) —I haven't the groggiest.

Above summary for convenience only. Transcript of all conversation, which was taped as per ungentlemanly orders, attached.

Yes, Junior, you may leave the room.

Flandry switched off the recorder. He could trust the confidential secretary, who would make a formal report out of his dictation, to clean it up. Though he wished she wouldn't.

He leaned back, cocked feet on desk, trickled smoke through his nostrils, and looked out the clear wall of his office. Admiralty Center gleamed, slim faerie spires in soft colors, reaching for the bright springtime sky of Terra. You couldn't mount guard across 400 light-years without millions of ships; and that meant millions of policy makers, scientists, engineers, strategists, tacticians, coordinators, clerks . . . and they had families, which needed food, clothing, houses, schools, amusements . . . so the heart of the Imperial Navy became a city in its own right. *Damn company town*, thought Flandry. And yet, when the bombs finally roared out of space, when the barbarians howled among smashed buildings and the smoke of burning books hid dead men in tattered bright uniforms—when the Long Night came, as it would, a century or a millennium hence, what difference?—something of beauty and gallantry would have departed the universe.

To hell with it. Let civilization hang together long enough for Dominic Flandry to taste a few more vintages, ride a few more horses, kiss a lot more girls and sing another ballad or two. That would suffice. At least, it was all he dared hope for.

The intercom chimed. "Admiral Fenross wants to see you immediately, sir."

"Now he tells me," grunted Flandry. "I wanted to see him yesterday, when I got back."

"He was busy then, sir," said the robot, as glibly as if it had a conscious mind. "His lordship the Earl of Sidrath is visiting Terra, and wished to be conducted through the operations center."

Flandry rose, adjusted his peacock-blue tunic, admired the crease of his gold-frogged white trousers, and covered his sleek hair with a jewel-banded officer's cap. "Of course," he said, "Admiral Fenross couldn't possibly delegate the tour to an aide."

"The Earl of Sidrath is related to Grand Admiral the Duke of Asia," the robot reminded him.

Flandry sang beneath his breath, *"Brown is the color of my true love's nose,"* and went out the door. After a series of slideways and gravshafts, he reached Fenross' office.

The admiral nodded his close-cropped head beyond the desk. "There you are." His tone implied Flandry had stopped for a beer on the way. "Sit down. Your preliminary verbal report on the Jovian mission has been communicated to me. Is that really all you could find out?"

Flandry smiled. "You told me to get an indication, one way or another, of the Ymirite attitude, sir," he purred. "That's what I got: an indication, one way or another."

Fenross gnawed his lip. "All right, all right. I should have known, I guess. Your forte never was working with an organization, and we're going to need a special project, a very large project, to learn the truth about Ymir."

Flandry sat up straight. "Don't," he said sharply. "What?"

"Don't waste men that way. Sheer arithmetic will defeat them. Jupiter alone has the area of a hundred Terras. The population must be more or less proportional. How are our men going to percolate around, confined to the two or three spaceships that Thua has available for them? Assuming Thua doesn't simply refuse to admit any further oxygen-breathing nuisances. How are they going to question, bribe, eavesdrop, get a single piece of information? It's a truism that the typical Intelligence job consists of gathering a million unimportant little facts and fitting them together into one big fact. We've few enough agents as is, spread ghastly thin. Don't tie them up in an impossible job. Let them keep working on Merseia, where they've a chance of accomplishing something!"

"And if Ymir suddenly turns on us?" snapped Fenross.

"Then we roll with the punch. Or we die." Flandry shrugged and winced; his muscles were still sore from the pounding they had taken. "But haven't you thought, sir, this whole business may well be a Merseian stunt—to divert our attention from them, right at this crisis? It's exactly the sort of bear trap Aycharaych loves to set."

"That may be," admitted Fenross. "But Merseia lies beyond Syrax; Jupiter is next door. I've been given to understand that his Imperial Majesty is alarmed enough to desire—" He shrugged too, making it the immemorial gesture of a baffled underling.

"Who dropped that hint?" drawled Flandry. "Surely not the Earl of Sidrath, whom you were showing the sights yesterday while the news came in that Vixen had fallen?"

"Shut up!" Almost, it was a scream. A jag of pain went over Fenross' hollowed countenance. He reached for a pill. "If I didn't oblige the peerage," he said thickly, "I'd be begging my bread in Underground and someone would be in this office who'd never tell them no."

Flandry paused. He started a fresh cigarette with unnecessary concentration. *I suppose I am being unjust to him*, he thought. *Poor devil. It can't be much fun being Fenross.*

Still, he reflected, Aycharaych had left the Solar System so smoothly that the space ambush had never even detected his boat. Twenty-odd hours ago, a battered scoutship had limped in to tell the Imperium that Vixen had perforce surrendered to its nameless besiegers, who had landed *en masse* after reducing the defenses. The last dispatch from Syrax described clashes which had cost the Terrans more ships than the Merseians. Jupiter blazed a mystery in the evening sky. Rumor said that after his human guests had left, Ruethen and his staff had rolled out huge barrels of bitter ale and caroused like trolls for many hours; they must have known some reason to be merry.

You couldn't blame Fenross much. But would the whole long climb of man, from jungle to stars, fall back in destruction—and no single person even deserve to have his knuckles rapped for it?

"What about the reinforcements that were being sent to Vixen?" asked Flandry.

"They're still on their way." Fenross gulped his pill and relaxed a trifle. "What information we have, about enemy strength and so on, suggests that another standoff will develop. The aliens won't be strong enough to kick our force out of the system—"

"Not with Tom Walton in command. I hear he is." A very small warmth trickled into Flandry's soul.

"Yes. At the same time, now the enemy is established on Vixen, there's no obvious way to get them off without total blasting—which would sterilize the planet. Of course, Walton can try to cut their supply lines and starve them out; but once they get their occupation organized, Vixen itself will supply them. Or he can try to find out where they come from, and counter-attack their home. Or perhaps he can negotiate something. I don't know. The Emperor himself gave Admiral Walton what amounts to carte blanche."

It must have been one of his Majesty's off days, decided Flandry. *Actually doing the sensible thing.*

"Our great handicap is that our opponents know all about us and we know almost nothing about them," went on Fenross. "I'm afraid the primary effort of our Intelligence must be diverted towards Jupiter for the time being. But someone has to gather information at Vixen too, about the aliens." His voice jerked to a halt.

Flandry filled his lungs with smoke, held it a moment, and let it out in a slowflood. "Eek," he said tonelessly.

"Yes. That's your next assignment."

"But . . . me, alone, to Vixen? Surely Walton's force carries a bunch of people."

"Of course. They'll do what they can. But parallel operations are standard espionage procedure, as even you must know. Furthermore, the Vixenites made the dramatic rather than the logical gesture. After their planet had capitulated, they got one boat out, with one person aboard. The boat didn't try to reach any Terrestrial ship within the system. That was wise, because the tiny force Aldebaran had sent was already broken in battle and reduced to sneak raids. But neither did the Vixenite boat go to Aldebaran itself. No, it came straight here, and the pilot expected a personal audience with the Emperor."

"And didn't get it," foretold Flandry. "His Majesty is much too busy gardening to waste time on a mere commoner representing a mere planet."

"Gardening?" Fenross blinked.

"I'm told his Majesty cultivates beautiful pansies," murmured Flandry.

Fenross gulped and said in great haste: "Well, no, of course not. I mean, I myself interviewed the pilot, and read the report carried along. Not too much information, though helpful. However, while Walton has a few Vixenite refugees along as guides and advisors, this pilot is the only one who's seen the aliens close up, on the ground, digging in and trading rifle shots with humans; has experienced several days of occupation before getting away. Copies of the report can be sent after Walton. But that first-hand knowledge of enemy behavior, regulations, all the little unpredictable details . . . that may also prove essential."

"Yes," said Flandry. "If a spy is to be smuggled back on to Vixen's surface. Namely me."

Fenross allowed himself a prim little smile. "That's what I had in mind."

Flandry nodded, unsurprised. Fenross would never give up trying to get him killed. Though in all truth, Dominic Flandry doubtless had more chance of pulling such a stunt and getting back unpunctured than anyone else.

He said idly: "The decision to head straight for Sol wasn't illogical. If the pilot had gone to Aldebaran, then Aldebaran would have sent us a courier reporting the matter and asking for orders. A roundabout route. This way, we got the news days quicker. No, that Vixenite has a level head on his shoulders."

"Hers," corrected Fenross.

"Huh?" Flandry sat bolt upright.

"She'll explain any details," said Fenross. "I'll arrange an open requisition for you: draw what equipment you think you'll need. And if you survive, remember, I'll want every millo's worth accounted for. Now get out and get busy! I've got work to do."

VII

The *Hooligan* snaked out of Terran sky, ran for a time on primary drive at an acceleration which it strained the internal grav-field to compensate for, and, having reached a safe distance from Sol, sprang over into secondary. Briefly the viewscreens went wild with Doppler effect and aberration. Then their circuits adapted to the rate at which the vessel pulsed in and out of normal space-time-energy levels; they annulled the optics of pseudo-speed, and Flandry looked again upon cold many-starred night as if he were at rest.

He left Chives in the turret to make final course adjustments and strolled down to the saloon. "All clear," he smiled. "Estimated time to Vixen, thirteen standard days."

"What?" The girl, Catherine Kittredge, half rose from the luxuriously cushioned bench. "But it took me a month the other way, an' I had the fastest racer on our planet."

"I've tinkered with this one," said Flandry, "Or, rather, found experts to do so." He sat down near her, crossing long legs and leaning an elbow on the mahogany table which the bench half-circled. "Give me a screwdriver and I'll make any firearm in the cosmos sit up and speak. But space drives have an anatomy I can only call whimsical."

He was trying to put her at ease. Poor kid, she had seen her home assailed, halfway in from the Imperial marches that were supposed to bear all the wars; she had seen friends and kinfolk slain in battle with un-human unknowns, and heard the boots of an occupying enemy racket in once-familiar streets; she had fled to Terra like a child to its mother, and been cold-ly interviewed in an office and straightway bundled back on to a spaceship, with one tailed alien and one suave stranger. Doubtless an official had told her she was a brave little girl and now it was her duty to return as a spy and quite likely be killed. And mean-while rhododendrons bloomed like cool fire in Terra's parks, and the laughing youth of Terra's aristocracy flew past on their way to some newly opened pleasure house.

No wonder Catherine Kittredge's eyes were wide and bewildered.

They were her best feature, Flandry decided: large, set far apart, a gold-flecked hazel under long lashes and thick dark brows. Her hair would have been nice too, a blonde helmet, if she had not cut it off just below the ears. Otherwise she was nothing much to look at—a broad, snub-nosed, faintly freckled countenance, generous mouth and good chin. As nearly as one could tell through a shapeless gray coverall, she was of medium height and on the stocky side. She spoke Anglic with a soft regional accent that sounded good in her low voice; but all her mannerisms were provincial, fifty years out of date. Flandry wondered a little desperately what they could talk about.

Well, there was business enough. He flicked buttons for autoservice. "What are you drinking?" he asked. "We've anything within reason, and a few things out of reason, on board."

She blushed. "Nothin', thank you," she mumbled.

"Nothing at all? Come, now. Daiquiri? Wine? Beer? Buttermilk, for heaven's sake?"

"Hm?" She raised a fleeting glance. He discovered Vixen had no dairy industry, cattle couldn't survive there, and dialed ice cream for her. He himself slugged down a large gin-and-bitters. He was going to need alcohol—two weeks alone in space with Little Miss Orphan!

She was pleased enough by discovering ice cream to relax a trifle. Flandry offered a cigarette, was refused, and started one for himself. "You'll have plenty of time to brief me en route," he said, "so don't feel obliged to answer questions now, if it distresses you."

Catherine Kittredge looked beyond him, out the

viewscreen and into the frosty sprawl of Andromeda. Her lips twitched downward, ever so faintly. But she replied with a steadiness he liked: "Why not? 'Twon't bother me more'n sittin' an' broodin'."

"Good girl. Tell me, how did you happen to carry the message?"

"My brother was our official courier. You know how 'tis on planets like ours, without much population or money: whoever's got the best spaceship gets a subsidy an' carries any special dispatches. I helped him. We used to go off jauntin' for days at a time, an'—No," she broke off. Her fists closed. "I *won't* bawl. The aliens forced a landin'. Hank went off with our groun' forces. He didn't come back. Sev'ral days after the surrender, when things began to settle down a little, I got the news he'd been killed in action. A few of us decided the Imperium had better be given what information we could supply. Since I knew Hank's ship best, they tol' me to go."

"I see." Flandry determined to keep this as dry as possible, for her sake. "I've a copy of the report your people made up, of course, but you had all the way to Sol to study it, so you must know more about it than anyone else off Vixen. Just to give me a rough preliminary idea, I understand some of the invaders knew Anglic and there was a certain amount of long-range parleying. What did they call themselves?"

"Does that matter?" she asked listlessly.

"Not in the faintest, at the present stage of things, except that it's such a weary cliché to speak of Planet X."

She smiled, a tiny bit. "They called themselves the Ardazirho, an' we gathered the *ho* was a collective endin'. So we figure their planet is named Ardazir. Though I can't come near pronouncin' it right."

Flandry took a stereopic from the pocket of his iridescent shirt. It had been snapped from hiding, during the ground battle. Against a background of ruined human homes crouched a single enemy soldier. Warrior? Acolyte? Unit? Armed, at least, and a killer of men.

Preconceptions always got in the way. Flandry's first startled thought had been *Wolf!* Now he realized that of course the Ardazirho was not lupine, didn't even look notably wolfish. Yet the impression lingered. He was not surprised when Catherine Kittredge said the aliens had gone howling into battle.

They were described as man-size bipeds, but digitigrade, which gave their feet almost the appearance of a dog's walking on its hind legs. The shoulders and arms were very humanoid, except that the thumbs were on the opposite side of the hands from mankind's. The head, arrogantly held on a powerful neck, was long and narrow for an intelligent animal, with a low forehead, most of the brain space behind the pointed ears. A black-nosed muzzle, not as sharp as a wolf's and yet somehow like it, jutted out of the face. Its lips were pulled back in a snarl, showing bluntly pointed fangs which suggested a flesh-eater turned omnivore. The eyes were oval, close set, and gray as sleet. Short thick fur covered the entire body, turning to a ruff at the throat; it was rusty red.

"Is this a uniform?" asked Flandry.

The girl leaned close to see. The pictured Ardazirho wore a sort of kilt, in checkerboard squares of various hues. Flandry winced at some of the combinations: rose next to scarlet, a glaring crimson offensively between two delicate yellows. "Barbarians indeed," he muttered. "I hope Chives can stand the shock." Otherwise the being was

dressed in boots of flexible leather and a harness
from which hung various pouches and equipment.
He was armed with what was obviously a magnetronic rifle, and had a wicked-looking knife at his
belt.

"I'm not sure," said the girl. "Either they don't
use uniforms at all, or they have such a variety that
we've not made any sense of it. Some might be
dressed more or less like him, others in a kind o' tunic
an' burnoose, others in breastplates an' fancy plumed
helmets."

"Him," pounced Flandry. "They're all male,
then?"

"Yes, sir, seems that way. The groun' fightin'
lasted long enough for our biologists to dissect an'
analyze a few o' their dead. Accordin' to the report,
they're placental mammals. It's clear they're from a
more or less terrestroid planet, probably with a
somewhat stronger gravity. The eye structure suggests their sun is bright, type A5 or thereabouts. That
means they should feel pretty much at home in our
badlands." Catherine Kittredge shrugged sadly.
"Figure that's why they picked us to start on."

"They might have been conquering for some
time," said Flandry. "A hot star like an A5 is no use
to humans; and I imagine the F-type like yours is
about as cool as they care for. They may well have
built up a little coterminous kingdom, a number of B,
A, and F suns out in your quadrant, where we don't
even have a complete astronomical mapping—let
alone having explored much . . . Hm. Didn't you get
a chance to interrogate any live prisoners?"

"Yes. 'Twasn't much use. Durin' the fightin', one
of our regiments did encircle a unit o' theirs an'
knock it out with stun beams. When two o' them

woke up an' saw they were captured, they died."

"Preconditioning," nodded Flandry. "Go on."

"The rest didn't speak any Anglic, 'cept one who'd picked up a little bit. They questioned him." The girl winced. "I don't figure 'twas very nice. The report says towards the end his heart kept stoppin' an' they'd revive it, but at last he died for good . . . Anyway, it seems a fair bet he was tellin' the truth. An' he didn't know where his home star was. He could understan' our coordinate system, an' translate it into the one they used. But that was zeroed arbitrarily on S Doradus, an' he didn't have any idea about the coordinates of Ardazir."

"Memory blank." Flandry scowled. "Probably given to all the enlisted ranks. Such officers as must retain full information are conditioned to die on capture. What a merry monarch they've got." He twisted his moustache between nervous fingers. "You know, though, this suggests their home is vulnerable. Maybe we should concentrate on discovering where it is."

The girl dropped her eyes. She lost a little color. "Do you think we can, my lord?" she whispered. "Or are we just goin' to die too?"

"If the mission involves procedures illegal or immoral, I should have no trouble." Flandry grinned at her. "You can do whatever honorable work is necessary. Between us, why, God help Ardazir. Incidentally, I don't rate a title."

"But they called you Sir Dominic."

"A knighthood is not a patent of nobility. I'm afraid my relationship to the peerage involves a bar sinister. You see, one day my father wandered into this sinister bar, and—" Flandry rambled on, skirting the risqué, until he heard her laugh. Then he laughed back and said: "Good girl! What do they call you at home? Kit, I'll swear. Very well, we're off to the wars, you the Kit and I the caboodle. Now let's scream for Chives to lay out caviar and cheeses. Afterwards I'll show you to your stateroom." Her face turned hot, and he added, "Its door locks on the inside."

"Thank you," she said, so low he could scarcely hear it. Smoky lashes fluttered on her cheeks. "When I was told to come—with you—I mean, I didn't know—"

"My dear girl," said Flandry, "credit me with enough experience to identify a holstered needle gun among more attractive curves beneath that coverall."

VIII

There was always something unreal about a long trip through space. Here, for a time, you were alone in the universe. No radio could outpace you and be received, even if unimaginable distance would not soon have drowned it in silence. No other signal existed, except another spaceship, and how would it find you unless your feeble drive-pulsations were by the merest chance detected? A whole fleet might travel many parsecs before some naval base sensed its wake with instruments; your one mote of a craft could hurtle to the ends of creation and never be heard. There was nothing to be seen, no landscape, no weather, simply the enormous endless pageantry of changing constellations, now and then a cold nebular gleam between flashing suns, the curdled silver of the Milky Way and the clotted stars near Sagittarius. Yet you in your shell were warm, dry, breathing sweet recycled air; on a luxury vessel like the *Hooligan*, you might listen to recorded Lysarcian bells, sip Namorian maoth and taste Terran grapes.

Flandry worked himself even less mercifully than he did Chives and Kit. It was the hard, dull grind which must underlie all their hopes: study, rehearsal, analysis of data, planning and discarding and planning again, until brains could do no more and thinking creaked to a halt. But then recreation became pure necessity—and they were two humans with one unobtrusive servant, cruising among the stars.

Flandry discovered that Kit could give him a workout, when they played handball down in the hold. And her stubborn chess game defeated his swashbuckling tactics most of the time. She had a puckish humor when she wasn't remembering her planet. Flandry would not soon forget her thumbnail impression of Vice Admiral Fenross: "A mind like a mousetrap, only he ought to let some o' those poor little mice go." She could play the lorr, her fingers dancing over its twelve primary strings with that touch which brings out the full ringing resonance of the secondaries; she seemed to know all the ballads from the old brave days when men were first hewing their home out of Vixen's wildness, and they were good to hear.

Flandry grew slowly aware that she was the opposite of bad-looking. She just hadn't been sculpted into the monotonously aristocratic appearance of Terra's high-born ladies. The face, half boyish, was her own, the body full and supple where it counted. He swore dismally to himself and went on a more rigorous calisthenic program.

Slowly the stars formed new patterns. There came a time when Aldebaran stood like red flame, the

brightest object in all heaven. And then the needle-
point of Vixen's sun, the star named Cerulia,
glistened keen and blue ahead. And Flandry turned
from the viewscreen and said quietly: "Two more
days to go. I think we'll have captain's dinner tonight."

"Very good, sir," said Chives. "I took it upon myself to bring along some live Maine lobster. And I
trust the Liebfraumilch '51 will be satisfactory?"

"That's the advantage of having a Shalmuan for
your batman," remarked Flandry to Kit. "Their race
has more sensitive palates than ours. They can't go
wrong on vintages."

She smiled, but her eyes were troubled.

Flandry retired to his own cabin and an argument.
He wanted to wear a peach-colored tunic with his
white slacks; Chives insisted that the dark blue, with
a gold sash, was more suitable. Chives won, naturally. The man wandered into the saloon, which was
already laid out for a feast, and poured himself an
apéritif. Music sighed from the recorder, nothing
great but sweet to hear.

A football came lightly behind him. He turned and
nearly dropped his glass. Kit was entering in a sheer
black dinner gown; one veil the color of fire
flickered from her waistline. A filigree tiara crowned
shining hair, and a bracelet of Old Martian silver
coiled massive on her wrist.

"Great hopping electrons," gasped Flandry.
"Don't *do* such things without warning! Where did
the paintbrush come from to lay on the glamour that
thick?"

Kit chuckled and pirouetted. "Chives," she said.
"Who else? He's a darlin'. He brought the jew'lry
along, an' he's been makin' the dress at odd moments this whole trip."

Flandry shook his head and clicked his tongue. "If Chives would accept manumission, he could set himself up in business, equipping lady spies to seduce poor officers like me. He'd own the galaxy in ten years."

Kit blushed and said hastily: "Did he select the tape too? I always have loved Mendelssohn's Violin Concerto."

"Oh, is that what it is? Nice music for a sentimental occasion, anyway. My department is more the administration of drinks. I prescribe this before dinner: Ansan aurea. Essentially, it's a light dry vermouth, but for once a non-Terran soil has improved the flavor of a Terran plant."

She hesitated. "I don't—I never—"

"Well, high time you began." He did not glance at the viewscreen, where Cerulia shone like steel, but they both knew there might not be many hours left for them to savor existence. She took the glass, sipped, and sighed.

"Thank you, Dominic. I've been missin' out on such a lot."

They seated themselves. "We'll have to make that up, after this affair is over," said Flandry. A darkening passed through him, just long enough to make him add: "However, I suspect that on the whole you've done better in life than I."

"What do you mean?" Her eyes, above the glass, reflected the wine's hue and became almost golden.

"Oh . . . hard to say." His mouth twisted ruefully upward. "I've no romantic illusions about the frontier. I've seen too much of it. I'd a good deal rather loll in bed sipping my morning chocolate than bounce into the fields before dawn to cultivate the grotch or scag the thimbs or whatever dreary technicalities it is that pioneers undergo. And yet, well, I've no illusions about my own class either, or my own way of life. You frontier people are the healthy ones. You'll be around—most of you—long after the Empire is a fireside legend. I envy you that."

He broke off. "Pardon me. I'm afraid spiritual jaundice is an occupational disease in my job."

"Which I'm still not sure what it—Oh, dear." Kit chuckled. "Does alcohol act that fast? But really, Dominic, I wish you'd talk a little about your work. All you've said is, you're in Naval Intelligence. I'd like to know what you do."

"Why?" he asked.

She flushed and blurted: "To know you better."

Flandry saw her confusion and moved to hide it from them both: "There's not a lot to tell. I'm a field agent, which means I go out and peek through windows instead of sitting in an office reading the reports of window peekers. Thanks to the circumstance that my immediate superior doesn't like me, I spend most of my working time away from Terra, on what amounts to a roving commission. Good old Fenross. If he was ever replaced by some kindly father-type who dealt justly with all subordinates, I'd dry up and blow away."

"I think that's revoltin'." Anger flashed in her voice.

"What? The discrimination? But my dear lass, what is any civilization but an elaborate structure of special privileges? I've learned to make my way around among them. Good frogs, d'you think I *want* a nice secure desk job with a guaranteed pension?"

"But still, Dominic—a man like you, riskin' his life again an' again, sent almost alone against all Ardazir . . . because someone doesn't like you!" Her face still burned, and there was a glimmer of tears in the hazel eyes.

"Hard to imagine how that could be," said Flandry with calculated smugness. He added, lightly and almost automatically: "But after all, think what an outrageous special privilege your personal heredity represents: so much beauty, charm, and intelligence lavished on one little girl."

She grew mute, but faintly she trembled. With a convulsive gesture, she tossed off her glass.

Easy, boy, thought Flandry. A not unpleasurable alertness came to life. *Emotional scenes are the last thing we want out here.* "Which brings up the general topic of you," he said in his chattiest tone. "A subject well worth discussing over the egg flower soup which I see Chives bringing in . . . or any other course, for that matter. Let's see, you were a weather engineer's assistant for a living, isn't that right? Sounds like fun, in an earnest high-booted way." *And might prove useful,* added that part of him which never took a vacation.

She nodded, as anxious as he to escape what they had skirted. They took pleasure in the meal, and talked of many things. Flandry confirmed his impression that Kit was not an unsophisticated peasant. She didn't know the latest delicious gossip about you-know-who and that actor. But she had measured the seasons of her strange violent planet; she could assemble a machine so men could trust their lives to it; she had hunted and sported, seen birth and death; the intrigues of her small city were as subtle as any around the Imperial throne. Withal, she had the innocence of most frontier folk—or call it optimism, or honor, or courage—at any rate, she had not begun to despair of the human race.

But because he found himself in good company, and this was a special occasion, he kept both their glasses filled. After a while he lost track of how many times he had poured.

When Chives cleared the table and set out coffee and liqueur, Kit reached eagerly for her cup. "I need this," she said, not quite clearly, " 'Fraid I had too much to drink."

"That was the general idea," said Flandry. He accepted a cigar from Chives. The Shalmuan went noiselessly out. Flandry looked across the table. Kit sat with her back to the broad viewscreen, so that the stars were jewels clustered around her tiara.

"I don't believe it," she said after a moment.

"You're probably right," said Flandry. "What don't you believe?"

"What you were sayin' . . . 'bout the Empire bein' doomed."

"It's better not to believe that," he said gently.

"Not because o' Terra," she said. She leaned forward. The light was soft on her bare young shoulders. "The little bit I saw there was a hard blow. But Dominic, as long's the Empire has men like, like you —we'll take on the whole universe an' win."

"Blessings," said Flandry in haste.

"No." Her eyes were the least bit hazed, but they locked steadily with his. She smiled, more in tenderness than mirth. "You won't wriggle off the hook with a joke this time, Dominic. You gave me too much to drink, you see, an'—I mean it. A planet with you on its side has still got hope enough."

Flandry sipped his liqueur. Suddenly the alcohol touched his own brain with its pale fires, and he thought, *Why not be honest with her? She can take it. Maybe she even deserves it.*

"No, Kit," he said. "I know my class from the inside out, because it is my class and I probably wouldn't choose another even if some miracle made me able to. But we're hollow, and corrupt, and death has marked us for its own. In the last analysis, however we disguise it, however strenuous and hazardous and even lofty our amusements are, the only reason we can find for living is to have fun. And I'm afraid that isn't reason enough."

"But it is!" she cried.

"You think so," he said, "because you're lucky enough to belong to a society which still has important jobs uncompleted. But we aristocrats of Terra, we enjoy life instead of enjoying what we're doing . . . and there's a cosmos of difference.

"The measure of our damnation is that every one of us with any intelligence—and there are some—every one sees the Long Night coming. We've grown too wise; we've studied a little psycho-dynamics, or perhaps only read a lot of history, and we can see that Manuel's Empire was not a glorious resurgence. It was the Indian summer of Terran civilization. (But you've never seen Indian summer, I suppose. A pity: no planet has anything more beautiful and full of old magics.) Now even that short season is past. Autumn is far along; the nights are cold and the leaves are fallen and the last escaping birds call through a sky which has lost all color. And yet, we who see winter coming can also see it won't be here till after our lifetimes . . . so we shiver a bit, and swear a bit, and go back to playing with a few bright dead leaves."

He stopped. Silence grew around them. And then, from the intercom, music began again, a low orchestral piece which spoke to deep places of their awareness.

"Excuse me," said Flandry. "I really shouldn't

have wished my sour pessimism on you."

Her smile this time held a ghost of pity. "An' o' course 'twouldn't be debonair to show your real feelin's, or try to find words for them."

"*Touché!*" He cocked his head. "Think we could dance to that?"

"The music? Hardly. The *Liebestod* is background for somethin' else. I wonder if Chives knew."

"Hm?" Flandry looked surprised at the girl.

"I don't mind at all," she whispered. "Chives is a darlin'."

Suddenly he understood.

But the stars were chill behind her. Flandry thought of guns and dark fortresses waiting for them both. He thought of knightly honor, which would not take advantage of the helplessness which is youth—and then, with a little sadness, he decided that practical considerations were what really turned the balance for him.

He raised the cigar to his mouth and said softly, "Better drink your coffee before it gets cold, lass."

With that the moment was safely over. He thought he saw disappointed gratitude in Kit's hurried glance, but wasn't sure. She turned around, gazing at the stars merely to avoid facing him for the next few seconds.

Her breath sighed outward. She sat looking at Cerulia for a whole minute. Then she stared down at her hands and said tonelessly: "Figure you're right 'bout the Empire. But then what's to become o' Vixen?"

"We'll liberate it, and squeeze a fat indemnity out of Ardazir," said Flandry as if there were no doubt.

"Uh-uh." She shook her head. Bitterness began to edge her voice. "Not if 'tisn't convenient. Your Navy might decide to fight the war out where 'tis. An'

then my whole planet, my people, the little girl next
door an' her kitten, trees an' flowers an' birds, why,
'twill just be radioactive ash blowin' over dead gray
hills. Or maybe the Imperium will decide to com-
promise, an' let Ardazir keep Vixen. Why not?
What's one planet to the Empire? A swap might, as
you say, buy them peace in their own lifetimes. A
few million human bein's, that's nothin', write them
off in red ink." She shook her head again in a dazed
way. "Why are we goin' there, you an' I? What are
we workin' for? Whatever we do can come to
nothin', from one stroke of a pen in some bored
bureaucrat's hand. Can't it?"

"Yes," said Flandry.

IX

Cerulia, being a main-sequence star, did not need
vastly more mass than Sol to shine more fiercely. Vix-
en, the fourth planet out, circled its primary in one
and a half standard years, along such an orbit that it
received, on the average, about as much radiation as
Terra.

"The catch lies in that word 'average'," murmured
Flandry.

He floated in the turret with Chives, hands on the
control panel and body weightless in a cocoon of pilot harness. To port, the viewscreens were dimmed,
lest the harsh blue sun burn out his eyes. Elsewhere,
distorted constellations sprawled stark against night.
Flandry picked out the Jupiter-type planet called
Ogre by the humans of Vixen: a bright yellow glow,
its larger moons visible like sparks. And what were
its Ymirite colonists thinking?

"Ogre's made enough trouble for Vixen all by
itself," complained Flandry. "Its settlers ought to be

content with that and not go plotting with Ardazir. If they are, I mean." He turned to Chives. "How's Kit taking this free-fall plunge?"

"I regret to say Miss Kittredge did not look very comfortable, sir," answered the Shalmuan. "But she said she was."

Flandry clicked his tongue. Since the advent of gravity control, there had been little need for civilians ever to undergo weightlessness; hence Kit, susceptible to it, didn't have the training that would have helped. Well, she'd be a lot sicker if an Ardazirho missile homed on the *Hooligan*. Nobody ever died of space nausea: no such luck!

Ardazir would undoubtedly have mounted tight guard over conquered Vixen. Flandry's detectors were confirming this. The space around the planet quivered with primary-drive vibrations, patrolling warcraft, and there must be a network of orbital robot monitors to boot. A standard approach was certain to be spotted. There was another way to land, though, if you were enough of a pilot and had enough luck. Flandry had decided to go ahead with it, rather than contact Walton's task force. He couldn't do much there except report himself in . . . and then proceed to Vixen anyway, with still more likelihood of detection and destruction.

Engines cold, the *Hooligan* plunged at top meteoric velocity straight towards her goal. Any automaton was sure to register her as a siderite, and ignore her. Only visual observation would strip that disguise off; and space is so vast that even with the closest blockade, there was hardly a chance of passing that close to an unwarned enemy. Escape from the surface would be harder, but this present stunt was foolproof. Until you hit atmosphere!

Flandry watched Vixen swelling in the forward viewscreens. To one side Cerulia burned, ominously big. The planet's northern dayside was like a slice of incandescence; polarizing telescopes showed bare mountains, stony deserts, rivers gone wild with melted snows. In the southern hemisphere, the continents were still green and brown, the oceans deeply blue, like polished cobalt. But cloud banded that half of the world, storms marched roaring over hundreds of kilometers, lightning flared through rain. The equator was hidden under a nearly solid belt of cloud and gale. The northern aurora was cold flame; the south pole, less brilliant, still shook great banners of light into heaven. A single small moon, 100,000 kilometers from the surface, looked pale against that luminance.

The spaceship seemed tomb silent when Flandry switched his attention back to it. He said, just to make a noise, "And this passes for a terrestroid, humanly habitable planet. What real estate agents they must have had in the pioneer days!"

"I understand that southern Cerulia IV is not unsalubrious most of the year, sir," said Chives. "It is only now, in fact, that the northern part becomes lethal."

Flandry nodded. Vixen was the goat of circumstance: huge Ogre had exactly four times the period, and thus over millions of years resonance had multiplied perturbation and brought the eccentricity of Vixen's orbit close to one-half. The planet's axial inclination was 24°, and northern midsummer fell nearly at periastron. Thus, every eighteen months, Cerulia scorched that hemisphere with fourfold the radiation Terra got from Sol. This section of the orbit was hastily completed, and most of Vixen's year was spent in cooler regions. "But I daresay the Ardazirho timed their invasion for right now," said Flandry. "If they're from an A-type star, the northern weather shouldn't be too hard on them."

He put out his final cigarette. The planet filled the bow screen. Robot mechanisms could do a lot, but now there must also be live piloting . . . or a streak in Vixen's sky and a crater blasted from its rock.

At the *Hooligan*'s speed, she crossed the tenuous upper air layers and hit stratosphere in a matter of seconds. It was like a giant's fist. Flandry's harness groaned as his body hurtled forward. There was no outside noise, yet, but the flitter herself shrieked in metallic pain. The screens became one lurid fire, air heated to incandescence.

Flandry's arm trembled with weight. He slammed it down on the drive switches. Chives' slight form could not stir under these pressures, but the green tail darted, button to dial to vernier. Engines bellowed as they fought to shed velocity. The vessel glowed red; but her metal was crystallized to endure more than furnace heat. Thunder banged around her, within her. Flandry felt his ribs shoved towards his lungs, as direction shifted. Still he could only see flame outside. But his blurring eyes read instruments. He knew the vessel had levelled off, struck denser atmosphere, skipped like a stone, and was now rounding the planet in monstrous shuddering bounces.

First then did he have time to reactivate the internal compensators. A steady one gee poured its benediction through him. He drew uneven breath into an aching chest. "For this we get *paid*?" he mumbled.

While Chives took over, and the thermostat

brought the turret near an endurable temperature,
Flandry unbuckled and went below to Kit's stateroom. She lay unstirring in harness, a trickle of blood
from the snub nose. He injected her with stimulol.
Her eyes fluttered open. Briefly, she looked so young
and helpless that he must glance away. "Sorry to jolt
you back to consciousness in this fashion," he said.
"It's bad practice. But right now, we need a guide."

"O' course." She preceded him to the turret. He
sat down and she leaned over his shoulder, frowning
at the viewscreens. The *Hooligan* burrowed into atmosphere on a steep downward slant. The roar of
cloven air boomed through the hull. Mountains rose
jagged on a night horizon. "That's the Ridge," said
Kit. "Head yonder, over Moonstone Pass." On the
other side, a shadowed valley gleamed with rivers,
under stars and a trace of aurora. "There's the Shaw,
an' the King's Way cuttin' through. Land anywhere
near, 'tisn't likely the boat will be found."

The Shaw belied its name; it was a virgin forest,
40,000 square kilometers of tall trees. Flandry set his
craft down so gently that not a twig was broken, cut
the engines and leaned back. "Thus far," he
breathed gustily, "we is did it, chillun!"

"Sir," said Chives, "may I once again take the liberty of suggesting that if you and the young lady go
off alone, without me, you need a psychiatrist."

"And may I once again tell you where to stick your
head," answered Flandry. "I'll have trouble enough
passing myself off as a Vixenite, without you along.
You stay with the boat and keep ready to fight. Or,
more probably, to scramble out of here like an egg."

He stood up. "We'd better start now, Kit," he
added. "That drug won't hold you up for very many
hours."

Both humans were already dressed in the soft
green coveralls Chives had made according to Kit's
description of professional hunters. That would also
explain Flandry's little radio transceiver, knife and
rifle; his accent might pass for that of a man lately
moved here from the Avian Islands. It was a thin
enough diguise . . . but the Ardazirho wouldn't have
an eye for fine details. The main thing was to reach
Kit's home city, Garth, undetected. Once based
there, Flandry could assess the situation and start
making trouble.

Chives wrung his hands, but bowed his master
obediently out the airlock. It was midwinter, but also
periastron; only long nights and frequent rains
marked the season in this hemisphere. The forest
floor was thick and soft underfoot. Scant light came
through the leaves, but here and there on the high
trunks glowed yellow phosphorescent fungi, enough
to see by. The air was warm, full of strange green
scents. Out in the darkness there went soft whis-
tlings, callings, croakings, patterings, once a scream
which cut off in a gurgle, the sounds of a foreign
wilderness.

It was two hours' hike to the King's Way. Flandry
and Kit fell into the rhythm of it and spoke little. But
when they finally came out on the broad starlit rib-
bon of road, her hand stole into his. "Shall we walk
on?" she asked.

"Not if Garth is fifty kilometers to go," said Flandry. He sat down by the road's edge. She lowered
herself into the curve of his arm.

"Are you cold?" he asked, feeling her shiver.

" 'Fraid," she admitted.

His lips brushed hers. She responded shyly, un-
practiced. It beat hiking. Or did it? *I never liked hors*

d'oeuvres alone for a meal, thought Flandry, and drew her close.

Light gleamed far down the highway. A faint growl waxed. Kit disengaged herself. "Saved by the bell," murmured Flandry, "but don't stop to wonder which of us was." She laughed, a small and trembling sound beneath unearthly constellations.

Flandry got up and extended his arm. The vehicle ground to a halt: a ten-car truck. The driver leaned out. "Boun' for Garth?" he called.

"That's right." Flandry helped Kit into the cab and followed. The truck started again, its train rumbling for 200 meters behind.

"Goin' to turn in your gun, are you?" asked the driver. He was a burly bitter-faced man. One arm carried the traces of a recent blaster wound.

"Figure so," Kit replied. "My husban' an' I been trekkin' in the Ridge this last three months. We heard 'bout the invasion an' started back, but floods held us up—rains, you know—an' our radio's given some trouble too. So we aren't sure o' what's been happenin'."

"Enough." The driver spat out of the window. He glanced sharply at them. "But what the gamma would anybody be doin' in the mountains this time o' year?"

Kit began to stammer. Flandry said smoothly, "Keep it confidential please, but this is when the cone-tailed radcat comes off the harl. It's dangerous, yes, but we've filled six caches of grummage."

"Hm . . . uh . . . yeh. Sure. Well, when you reach Garth, better not carry your gun yourself to the wolf headquarters. They'll most likely shoot you first an' ask your intentions later. Lay it down somewhere an' go ask one o' them would he please be so kind as to come take it away from you."

"I hate to give up this rifle," said Flandry.

The driver shrugged. "Keep it, then, if you want to take the risk. But not aroun' me. I fought at Burnt Hill, an' played dead all night while those howlin' devils hunted the remnants of our troop. Then I got home somehow, an' that's enough. I got a wife an' children to keep." He jerked his thumb backward. "Load o' rare earth ore this trip. The wolves'll take it, an' Hobden's mill will turn it into fire-control elements for 'em, an' they'll shoot some more at the Empire's ships. Sure, call me a quislin'—an' then wait till you've seen your friends run screamin' down your street with a pack o' batsnakes flappin' an' snappin' at them an' the wolves boundin' behind laughin'. Ask yourself if you want to go through that, for an Empire that's given us up already."

"Has it?" asked Flandry. "I understood from one 'cast that there were reinforcements coming."

"Sure. They're here. One o' my chums has a pretty good radio an' sort o' followed the space battle when Walton's force arrived, by receivin' stray messages. It petered out pretty quick, though. What can Walton do, unless he attacks this planet, where the wolves are now based, where they're already makin' their own supplies an' munitions? An' if he does that—" The headlight reflections shimmered off sweat on the man's face. "No more Vixen. Just a cinder. You pray God, chum, that the Terrans don't try to blast Ardazir off Vixen."

"What's happening, then, in space?" asked Flandry.

He didn't expect a coherent reply. To the civilian, as to the average fighter, war is one huge murky chaos. It was a pure gift when the driver said: "My chum caught radio 'casts beamed at us from the Terran fleet. The wolves tried to jam it, of course, but I heard, an' figure 'tis mostly truth. Because 'tis bad enough! There was a lot o' guff about keepin' up our courage, an' sabotagin' the enemy, an'—" The driver rasped an obscenity. "Sorry, ma'm. But wait till you see what 'tis really like aroun' Garth an' you'll know how I feel about *that* idea. Admiral Walton says his fleet's seized some asteroid bases an' theirs isn't tryin' to get him off 'em. Stalemate, you see, till the wolves have built up enough strength. Which they're doin', fast. The reason the admiral can't throw everything he's got against them in space is that he has to watch Ogre too. Seems there's reason to suspect Ymir might be in cahoots with Ardazir. The Ymirites aren't sayin'. You know what they're like."

Flandry nodded. "Yes. 'If you will not accept our word that we are neutral, there is no obvious way to let you convince yourselves, since the whole Terran Empire could not investigate a fraction of Dispersal territory. Accordingly, we shall not waste our time discussing the question.' "

"That's it, chum. You've got the very tone. They might be honest, sure. Or they might be waitin' for the minute Walton eases up his watch on 'em, to jump him."

Flandry glanced out. The stars flashed impersonally, not caring that a few motes of flesh named them provinces for a few centuries. He saw that part of this planet's sky had no stars, a hole into forever. Kit had told him it was called the Hatch. But that was only a nearby dark nebula, not even a big one. The clear white spark of Rigel was more sinister, blazing from the heart of Merseia's realm. And what of Ogre, tawny above the tree?

"What do you think will happen?" Kit's voice

could scarcely be heard through the engine grumble.

"I don't even dare guess," said the driver. "Maybe Walton'll negotiate something—might leave us here, to become wolf-cattle, or might arrange to evacuate us an' we can become beggars on Terra. Or he might fight in space . . . but even if he doesn't attack their forts here on Vixen, we'll all be hostages to Ardazir, won't we? Or the Ymirites might . . . No, ma'm, I'm just drivin' my truck an' drawin' my pay an' feedin' my family. Shorter rations every week, it seems. Figure there's nothin' else any one person can do. Is there?"

Kit began to cry, a soft hopeless sobbing on Flandry's shoulder. He laid an arm around her and they sat thus all the way to Garth.

X

Night again, after a short hot winter day of thunderstorms. Flandry and Emil Bryce stood in the pit blackness of an alley, watching a nearly invisible street. Rain sluiced over their cloaks. A fold in Flandry's hood was letting water trickle in, his tunic was soaked, but he dared not move. At any moment now, the Ardazirho would come by.

The rain roared slow and heavy, down over the high-peaked roofs of Garth, through blacked-out streets and gurgling into the storm drains. All wind had stopped, but now and then lightning glared. There was a brief white view of pavement that shimmered wet, half-timbered houses with blind shutters crowded side by side, a skeletal transmitter tower for one of the robotic weather-monitor stations strewn over the planet. Then night clamped back down, and thunder went banging through enormous hollow spaces.

Emil Bryce had not moved for half an hour. But he really was a hunter by trade, thought Flandry. The Terran felt an unreasonable resentment of Bryce's guild. Damn them, it wasn't fair, in that trade they stood waiting for prey since they were boys—and *he* had to start cold. No, hot. It steamed beneath his rain cape.

Feet resounded on the walk. They did not have a human rhythm. And they did not smack the ground first with a boot-heel, but clicked metal-shod toes along the pavement. A flashbeam bobbed, slashing darkness with a light too blue and sharp for human comfort. Watery reflections touched Bryce's broad red face. His mouth alone moved, and Flandry could read fear upon it. *Wolves!*

But Bryce's dart gun slithered from under this cloak. Flandry eased steel knucks onto one hand. With the other, he gestured Bryce back. He, Flandry, must go first, pick out the precise enemy he wanted—in darkness, in rain, and all their faces non-human. Nor would uniforms help; the Ardazirho bore such a wild variety of dress.

But . . . Flandry was trained. It had been worth a rifle, to have an excuse for entering local invader headquarters. Their garrison in Garth was not large: a few hundred, for a city of a quarter million. But modern heavy weapons redressed that, robotanks, repeating cannon, the flat announcement that any town where a human uprising actually succeeded would be missiled. (The glassy crater which had been Marsburg proved it.) The Garth garrison was there chiefly to man observation posts and anti-spacecraft defenses in the vicinity; but they also collected firearms, directed factories to produce for their army, prowled in search of any citizens with spirit left to fight. Therefore, Flandry told himself, their chief officer must have a fair amount of knowledge—and the chief officer spoke Anglic, and Flandry had gotten a good look at him while surrendering the rifle, and Flandry was trained to tell faces apart, even nonhuman faces—

And now Clanmaster Temulak, as he had called himself, was going off duty, from headquarters to barracks. Bryce and others had been watching the Ardazirho for weeks. They had told Flandry that the invaders went on foot, in small armed parties, whenever practicable. Nobody knew quite why. Maybe they preferred the intimacy with odors and sounds which a vehicle denied; it was known they had better noses than man. Or perhaps they relished the challenge: more than once, humans had attacked such a group, been beaten off and hunted down and torn to pieces. Civilians had no chance against body armor, blast-weapons, and reflexes trained for combat.

But I'm not a civilian, Flandry told himself, *and Bryce has some rather special skills*.

The quarry passed by. Scattered flashbeam light etched the ruffled, muzzled heads against flowing dimness. There were five. Flandry identified Temulak, helmeted and corseleted, near the middle. He glided out of the alley, behind them.

The Ardazirho whipped about. How keen were their ears? Flandry kept going. One red-furred alien hand dropped towards a holstered blaster. Flandry smashed his steel-knuckled fist at Temulak's face. The enemy bobbed his head, the knucks clanged off the helmet. And light metal sheathed his belly, no blow would have effect there. The blaster came out. Flandry chopped down his left palm, edge on, with savage precision. He thought he felt wristbones crack beneath it. Temulak's gun glattered to the pavement. The Ardazirho threw back his head and howled, ululating noise hurled into the rain. And HQ only half a kilometer away, barracks no further in the opposite direction—

Flandry threw a karate kick to the jaw. The officer staggered back. But he was quick, twisting about to seize the man's ankle before it withdrew. They went down together. Temulak's right hand still hung useless, but his left snatched for Flandry's throat. The Terran glimpsed fingernails reinforced with sharp steel plectra. He threw up an arm to keep his larynx from being torn. Temulak howled again. Flandry chopped at the hairy neck. The Ardazirho ducked and sank teeth into Flandry's wrist. Anguish went like flame along the nerves. But now Temulak was crouched before him. Flandry slammed down a rabbit punch. Temulak slumped. Flandry got on his back and throttled him.

Looking up, gasping, the man saw shadows leap and yell in the glow of the dropped flashlight. There had been no way to simply needle Temulak. He was wanted alive, and Flandry didn't know what anaesthetics might be fatal to an Ardazirho. But Bryce had only to kill the guards, as noiselessly as possible. His airgun spat cyanide darts, quick death for any oxygen breather. And his skilled aim sent those darts into exposed flesh, not uselessly breaking on armor. Two sprawled in the street. Another had somehow jumped for Bryce's throat. The hunter brought up one boot. It clanged on a breastplate, but sheer force sent the alien lurching backward. Bryce shot him. By then the last one had freed his blaster. It crashed and blazed through rain. Bryce had already dropped. The ion bolt sizzled where he had been. Bryce fired, missed, rolled away from another blast, fired again and missed. Now howling could be heard down the street, as a pack of invaders rallied to come and help.

Flandry reached across Temulak's gaunt body, picked up the Clanmaster's gun, and waited. He was nearly blind in this night. The other Ardazirho's blaster flamed once more. Flandry fired where it showed. The alien screamed, once, and thudded to the street. Scorched hair and meat smoked sickly in the wet air.

"Out o' here!" gasped Bryce. He sprang erect. "They're comin'! An' they'll track us by scent—"

"I came prepared for *that*," said Flandry. A brief hard grin peeled his teeth. He let Bryce pick up Temulak while he got a flat plastibottle from his tunic. He turned a pressure nozzle and sprayed a liter of gasoline around the area. "If their noses are any good for several minutes after this, I give up. Let's go."

Bryce led the way, through the alley to the next street, down a block of horribly open paving, then hand-over-hand across a garden wall. No private human vehicles could move after dark without being shot at from the air, but it wasn't far to the underground hideout. In fact, too close, thought Flandry. But then, who on Vixen had any experience with such operations? Kit had looked up those friends in Garth who smuggled her out, and they had led Flandry straight to their bitter little organization. It expedited matters this time, yes, but suppose the Ardazirho had supplied a ringer? Or . . . it was only a matter of time before they started questioning humans in detail, under drugs and duress. Then you needed cells, changing passwords, widely scattered boltholes, or your underground was done for.

Flandry stumbled through drenched flowerbeds. He helped Bryce carry Temulak down into the hurricane cellar: standard for every house in Garth. A tunnel had been dug from this one; its door, at least, was well concealed. Flandry and Bryce groped for several hundred meters to the other end. They emerged beneath a house whose address they should not have been permitted to know.

Judith Hurst turned about with a small shriek when the cellar door opened. Then dim light picked out Bryce's heavy form, and Temulak still limp in the hunter's arms. Flandry came behind, shedding his cape with a relieved whistle. "Oh," gasped Judith. "You got him!"

Bryce's eyes went around the circle of them. A dozen men stood with taut brown faces in the light of a single small fluoro. Their shadows fell monstrous in the corners and across the window shutters. Knives and forbidden guns gleamed at their belts. Kit was the only person seated, still slumped in the dull sadness of stimulol reaction.

"Damn near didn't," grunted Bryce. "Couldn't have, without the captain here. Sir Dominic, I apologize for some things I'd been thinkin' lately 'bout Terra."

"An' I." Judith Hurst trod forward, taking both the Navy man's hands. She was among the few women in the underground, and Flandry thought it a crime to risk such looks being shot up. She was tall, with long auburn hair and skin like cream; her eyes were sleepy brown in a full, pouting face; her figure strained at shorts and bolero. "I never thought I'd see you again," she said. "But you've come back with the first real success this war's had for us."

"Two swallows do not make a drinking bout," warned Flandry. He gave her his courtliest bow. "Speaking of which, I could use something liquid, and cannot imagine a more ornamental cupbearer. But first, let's deal with friend Temulak. This way, isn't it?"

As he passed Kit, her exhausted eyes turned up to him. Slow tears coursed down her face. "Oh, Dominic, you're alive," she whispered. "That makes everything else seem like nothin'." She rose to wobbly legs. He threw her a preoccupied smile and continued on past, his brain choked with technicalities.

Given a proper biopsych lab, he could have learned how to get truth out of Temulak with drugs and electronics. But now he just didn't have enough data on the species. He would have to fall back on certain widely applicable, if not universal, rules of psychology.

At his orders, an offside room in the cellar had been provided with a comfortable bed. He stripped Temulak and tied him down, firmly, but using soft bonds which wouldn't chafe. The prisoner began to stir. By the time Flandry was through and Temulak immobile, the gray alien eyes were open and the muzzle wrinkled back over white teeth. A growl rumbled in Temulak's throat.

"Feeling better?" asked the man unctuously.

"Not as well as I shall when we pull you down in the street." The Anglic was thickly accented, but fluent, and it bore a haughtiness like steel.

"I shudder." Flandry kindled a cigarette. "Well, comrade, if you want to answer some questions now, it will save trouble all around. I presume, since you're alive, you've been blanked of your home sun's coordinates. But you retain clues." He blew a thoughtful smoke ring. "And, to be sure, there are the things you obviously do know, since your rank requires it. Oh, all sorts of things, dear heart, which my side is just dying to find out." He chuckled. "I don't mean that literally. Any dying will be done by you."

Temulak stiffened. "If you think I would remain alive, at the price of betraying the *orbekh*—"

"Nothing so clear-cut."

The red fur bristled, but Temulak snarled: "Nor will pain in any degree compel me. And I do not believe you understand the psycho-physiology of my race well enough to undertake total reconditioning."

"No," admitted Flandry, "not yet. However, I haven't time for reconditioning in any event, and torture is so strenuous . . . besides offering no guarantee that when you talk, you won't fib. No, no, my friend, you'll want to spill to me pretty soon. Whenever you've had enough, just call and I'll come hear you out."

He nodded to Dr. Reineke. The physician wheeled forth the equipment he had abstracted from Garth General Hospital at Flandry's request. A blindfolding hood went over Temulak's eyes, sound-deadening wax filled his ears and plugged his nose, a machine supplied him with intravenous nourishment and another removed body wastes. They left him immobile and, except for the soft constant pressure of bonds and bed, sealed into a darkness like death. No sense impressions could reach him from outside. It was painless, it did no permanent harm, but the mind is not intended for such isolation. When there is nothing by which it may orient itself, it rapidly loses all knowledge of time; an hour seems like a day, and later like a week or a year. Space and material reality vanish. Hallucinations come, and the will begins to crumble. Most particularly is this true when the victim is among enemies, tensed to feel the whip or knife which his own ferocious culture would surely use.

Flandry closed the door. "Keep a guard," he said. "When he begins to holler, let me know." He peeled off his tunic. "From whom can I beg something dry to wear?"

Judith gave his torso a long look. "I thought all Terrans were flabby, Sir Dominic," she purred. "I was wrong about that too."

His eyes raked her. "And you, my dear, make it abundantly plain that Vixenites are anything but," he leered.

She took his arm. "What do you plan to do next?"

"Scratch around. Observe. Whip this maquisard outfit into something efficient. There are so many stunts to teach you. To name just one, any time you've no other amusement, you can halt work at a war factory for half a day with an anonymous telecall warning that a time bomb's been planted and the staff had better get out. Then there's all the rest of your planet to organize. I don't know how many days I'll have, but there's enough work to fill a year of 'em." Flandry stretched luxuriously, "Right now, though, I want that drink I spoke of."

"Here you are, sir." Bryce held out a flask.

Judith flicked a scowl at him. "Is that white mule all you can offer the captain?" she cried. Her hair glowed along her back as she turned to smile again at Flandry. "I know you'll think I'm terribly forward, but I have two bottles o' real Bourgogne at my house. 'Tis only a few blocks from here, an' I know a safe way to go."

Oh-oh! Flandry licked his mental chops. "Delighted," he said.

"I'd invite the rest o' you," said Judith sweetly, "but 'tisn't enough to go aroun', an' Sir Dominic deserves it the most. Nothin's too good for him, that's what I think. Just nothin' at all."

"Agreed," said Flandry. He bowed good night and went out with her.

Kit stared after them a moment. As he closed the door, he heard her burst into weeping.

XI

Three of Vixen's 22-hour rotation periods went by, and part of a fourth, before the message came that Temulak had broken. Flandry whistled. "It's about time! If they're all as tough as that—"

Judith clung to him. "Do you have to go right now, darlin'?" she murmured. "You've been away so much . . . out prowlin', spyin', an' the streets still full o' packs huntin' for whoever attacked that squad —I'm terrified for you."

Her look was more inviting than anxious. Flandry kissed her absent-mindedly. "We're patriots and all that sort of rot," he said. "I could not love you so much, dear, et cetera. Now do let go." He was out the door before she could speak further.

The way between her house and the underground's went mostly from garden to garden, but there was a stretch of public thoroughfare. Flandry put hands in pockets and sauntered along under rustling feather palms as if he had neither cares nor haste. The other humans about, afoot or in groundcars, were subdued, the pinch of hunger and shabbiness already upon them. Once a party of

Ardazirho whirred past on motor unicycles; their sharp red muzzles clove the air like prows, and they left a wake of frightened silence behind them. The winter sun burned low to northwest, big and dazzling white in a pale sky, among hurried stormclouds.

When Flandry let himself into the cellar, only Emil Bryce and Kit Kittredge were there. The hunter lounged on guard. From the closed door behind him came howling and sobbing. "He babbled he'd talk," said Bryce. "But can you trust what he says?"

"Interrogation is a science too," answered Flandry. "If Temulak is enough like a human to break under isolation, he won't be able to invent consistent lies fast enough when I start throwing questions at him. Did you get that recorder I wanted?"

"Here." Kit picked it up. She looked very small and alone in all the shadows. Sleeplessness had reddened her eyes. She brought the machine to Flandry, who met her several meters from Bryce. She leaned towards him on tiptoe and whispered shakily: "What will you do now?"

Flandry studied her. He had gotten to know her well on the journey here, he thought. But that was under just one set of conditions—and how well does one human ever know another, in spite of all pretentious psychology? Since capturing the Ardazirho, he had only seen her on a single brief visit to this cellar. They had had a few moments alone, but nothing very personal was said. There had been no time for it. He saw how she trembled.

"I'm going to quiz brother Temulak," he told her. "And afterwards I could use some dinner and a stiff drink."

"With Judith Hurst?" It startled him, how ferociously she spat it out.

"Depends," he said in a careful tone.

"Dominic—" She hugged herself, forlornly, to stop shivering. Her gaze blurred, seeing his. "Don't. Please don't make me do . . . what I don't want—"

"We'll see." He started towards the inner door. Kit began to cry, hopelessly this time.

Bryce got up. "Why, what all's the matter?" he asked.

"She's overtired." Flandry opened the door.

"Worse'n that." The hunter looked from him to the girl and back again. Resentment smouldered in his growl: "Maybe it's none o' my business—"

"It isn't." Flandry stepped through, closing the door behind him.

Temulak lay shuddering and gasping. Flandry set up the recorder and unplugged the Ardazirho's ears. "Did you want to speak to me?" he asked mildly.

"Let me go!" shrieked Temulak. "Let me go, I say! *Zamara shammish ni ulan!*" He opened his mouth and howled. It was so much like a beast that a crawling went along Flandry's spine.

"We'll see, after you've cooperated." The man sat down.

"I never thought . . . you gray people . . . gray hearts—" Temulak whimpered. He dribbled between his fangs.

"Good night, then," said Flandry. "Sweet dreams."

"No! No, let me see! Let me smell! I will . . . *zamara, zamara*—"

Flandry began to interrogate.

It took time. The basic principle was to keep hitting, snap out a question, yank forth the answer, toss the next question, pounce on the smallest discrepancies, always strike and strike and strike with never a second's pause for the victim to think. Without a partner, Flandry was soon tired. He kept going, on cigarettes and nerves; after the first hour, he lost count of time.

In the end, having a full tape, he relaxed a moment. The air was nearly solid with smoke. Sweat felt sticky under his clothes. He puffed yet another cigarette and noticed impersonally the shakiness of his hand. But Temulak whined and twitched, beaten close to mindlessness by sheer psychic exhaustion.

The picture so far was only a bare outline, thought Flandry in a dull far-off way. How much could be told in one night of an entire world, its greatness and rich variety, its many peoples and all their histories? How much, to this day, do we really know about Terra? But the tape held information worth entire ships.

Somewhere there was a sun, brighter even than Cerulia, and a planet called Ardazir by its principal nation. ("Nation" was the Anglic word; Flandry had an impression that "clan alliance" or "pack aggregate" might more closely translate *orbekh*.) Interplanetary travel had been independently achieved by that country. Then, some fifteen standard years ago, gravitics, superlight pseudo-speeds, the whole apparatus of the modern galaxy, had burst upon Ardazir. The war lords (chiefs, speakers, pack leaders?) of Urdahu, the dominant *orbekh*, had promptly used these to complete the subjugation of their own world. Then they turned outward. Their hungers ravened into a dozen backward systems, looting and enslaving; engineers followed, organizing the conquered planets for further war.

And now the attack on the human empire had begun. The lords of Urdahu assured their followers that Ardazir had allies, mighty denizens of worlds so

alien that there could never be any fear of attack—
though these aliens had long been annoyed by humankind, and found in Ardazir an instrument to destroy and replace the Terran Empire . . . Temulak
had not enquired more deeply, had not thought
much about it at all. The Ardazirho seemed, by nature, somewhat more reckless and fatalistic than
men, and somewhat less curious. If circumstances
had provided a chance for adventure, glory, and
wealth, that was enough. Precautions could be left
in care of the *orbekh*'s wise old females.

Flandry smoked in a thick silence. If Ymir were,
indeed, behind Ardazir—it would be natural for
Ymir to cooperate temporarily with Merseia, whip-
sawing Terra between the Syrax and Vixen crises.
Maybe Merseia was next on Ymir's list. Thereafter
Ardazir would hardly prove troublesome to wreck.

But what grudge could Ymir have against oxygen
breathers, or even against Terra alone? There had
been some small friction, yes, inevitably—but nothing serious, surely the monsters rubbed each other
more raw than . . . *And yet Horx did his level best
to kill me. Why? What could he have been hired
with? What material thing from a terrestroid planet
would not collapse in his hands on Jupiter? What
reason would he have, except orders from his own
governor, who was carrying out a policy hatched on
Ymir itself . . . ?*

Flandry clenched a fist. There was an answer to
that question, but not one he dared rely on without
further proof. He bent his mind back towards prac-
ticalities. Mostly the tape held such details: the
number of Ardazirho ships and troops in this system,
recognition signals, military dispositions across Vix-
en, the layout of forts and especially of the great

headquarters den; the total population of Ardazir, resources, industry, army and navy . . . Temulak was
not in on many state secrets, but he had enough indications to give Flandry gooseflesh. Two million or
so warriors occupied Vixen; a hundred million were
still at home or on the already conquered planets,
where war matériel was being rapidly stockpiled; officers had all been informed that there were plenty of other vulnerable Imperial outposts, human
colonies or the home worlds of Terran-allied species . . . Yes, Ardazir was surely planning to strike
elsewhere within the Empire, and soon. Another one
or two such blows, and the Imperial Navy *must* surrender Syrax to Merseia, turn inward and defend the
mother planet. At which point—

Not true that an army marches on its stomach,
thought Flandry. *It needs information even more
than food. Marches on its head. Which, no doubt,
is why the Imperial High Command has so many
flat-heads*.

He chuckled. Bad as it was, the joke strengthened
him. And he was going to need strength.

"Will you let me see?" asked Temulak in a small,
broken voice.

"I will deprive you no longer of my beauty," said
Flandry. He unhooded the rufous head and drew his
wax plugs from the nose. Temulak blinked dazedly
into smoke and one dull light. Flandry uncoupled the
machines which had kept him alive. "You'll remain
our guest, of course," he said. "If it turns out you
prevaricated, back you go in the dark closet."

Temulak bristled. His teeth snapped together,
missing the man's arm by a centimeter.

"Naughty!" Flandry stepped back. "For that, you
can stay tied up for a while."

Temulak snarled from the cot: "You gray-skinned hairléss worm, if you think your *valkuza's* tricks will save you from the Black People—I myself will rip out your gullet and strangle you with your own bowels!"

"And foreclose my mortgage," said Flandry. He went out, closing the door behind him.

Bryce and Kit started. They had fallen asleep in their chairs. The hunter rubbed his eyes. "God o' the galaxy, you been at it a long time!" he exclaimed.

"Here." Flandry tossed him the tape spool. "This has to reach Admiral Walton's fleet. It's necessary, if not quite sufficient, for your liberation. Can do?"

"The enemy would pick up radio," said Bryce doubtfully. "We still got a few spaceships hid, but Kit's was the fastest. An' since then, too, the wolf space guard's been tightened till it creaks."

Flandry sighed. "I was afraid of that." He scribbled on a sheet of paper. "Here's a rough map to show you where my personal flitter is. D'you know this tune?" He whistled. "No? That proves you've a clean mind. Well, learn it." He rehearsed the Vixenite till he was satisfied. "Good. Approach the flitter whistling that, and Chives won't shoot you without investigation. Give him this note. It says for him to take the tape to Walton. If anything can run that blockade without collecting a missile, it's Chives in the *Hooligan*."

Kit suppressed a gasp. "But then you, Dominic— no escape—"

Flandry shrugged. "I'm much too tired to care about aught except a nice soft bed."

Bryce, sticking the spool under his tunic, grinned: "Whose?"

Kit stood as if struck.

Flandry nodded slightly at her. "That's the way of

it." He glanced at his chrono. "Close to local midnight. Shove off, Bryce, lad. But stop by and tell Dr. Reineke to shift his apparatus and the prisoner elsewhere. It's always best to keep moving around, when you're being searched for. And nobody, except the pill peddler and whoever helps him, is to know where they stash Temulak next. All clear?"

"Dominic—" Kit closed her fists till the knuckles stood white. She stared down at the floor; he could only see her short bright hair.

He said gently: "I have to sleep or collapse, lass. I'll meet you at noon by the Rocket Fountain. I think we've a few private things to discuss."

She turned and fled upstairs.

Flandry departed too. The night sky was aflicker with aurora; he thought he could hear its ionic hiss in the city's blacked-out silence. Once he scrambled to a rooftop and waited for an Ardazirho patrol to go by. Wan blue light glimmered off their metal and their teeth.

Judith made him welcome. "I've been so worried, darlin'—"

He considered her a while. Weariness dragged at him. But she had put out a late supper, with wine and a cold game bird, as she knew he liked it; and her hair glowed red by candlelight. Sleep be damned, Flandry decided. He might be permanently asleep tomorrow.

He did nap for a few morning hours, and went out before noon. Explorers' Plaza had been a gay scene once, where folk sat leisurely in the surrounding gardens, sipping coffee and listening to harp trees in the wind and watching life stream past. Now it was empty. The metal fountain itself, in the form of an ancient space rocket, still jetted many-colored heatless fires from its tail; but they seemed pale under the gloomy winter sky.

Flandry took out a cigarette, sat down on the fountain rim and waited. A few preliminary raindrops kissed his half lifted face.

A military truck careened out of a deserted street and ground to a halt. Three Ardazirho leaped from the cab. Kit was with them. She pointed at Flandry. Lightning blinked immediately overhead, and sudden thunder swamped her words. But the tone was vindictive.

"Halt, human!"

It must have been the only Anglic phrase any of the three invaders knew. They bayed it again and yet again as Flandry sprang to the plaza. He ducked and began to run, zigzagging.

No shots were fired. An Ardazirho yelped glee and opened the truck body. Wings snapped leathery. Flandry threw a glance behind. A score of meterlong snake bodies were streaming upward from the truck. They saw him, whistled and stooped.

Flandry ran. His heart began to pump, the wildness of irrational uncontrollable terror. The batsnakes reached him. He heard teeth click together behind his nape. A lean body coiled on his right arm. He jerked the limb up, frantic. Wings resisted him. Fangs needled into his flesh. The rest of the pack whirled and dived and whipped him with their tails.

He started to run again. The three Ardazirho followed, long bounds which took them over the ground faster than a man could speed. They howled, and there was laughter in their howling. The street was empty, resounding under boots. Shuttered windows looked down without seeing. Doors were closed and locked.

Flandry stopped. He spun around. His right arm was still cumbered. The left dived beneath his tunic. His needler came out. He aimed at the nearest of the laughing ruddy devils. A batsnake threw itself on his gun hand. It bit with trained precision, into the fingers. Flandry let the weapon fall. He snatched after the snake—to wring just one of their damned necks—!

It writhed free. Its reptile-like jaws grinned at him. Then the Ardazirho closed in.

XII

Most of the year, Vixen's northern half was simply desert, swamp, or prairie, where a quick vegetative life sprang up and animals that had been estivating crept from their burrows. The arctic even knew snow, when winter-long night had fallen. But in summer the snows melted to wild rivers, the rivers overflowed and became lakes, the lakes baked dry. Storms raged about the equator and into the southern hemisphere, as water precipitated again in cooler parts. Except for small seas dreary amidst salt flats, the north blistered arid. Fires broke loose, the pampas became barren again in a few red days. Under such erosive conditions, this land had no mountains. Most of it was plain, where dust and ash scoured on a furnace wind. In some places rose gnarled ranges, lifeless hills, twisted crags, arroyos carved by flash floods into huge earth scars.

The Ardazirho had established their headquarters in such a region, a little below the artic circle. Thousands of lethal kilometers made it safe from human ground attack, the broken country was camouflage and protection from spaceships. Not that they tried to conceal their fortress absolutely. That would have been impossible. But it burrowed deep into the range and offered few specific targets.

Here and there Flandry saw a warship sitting insolently in the open, a missile emplacement, a detector station, a lookout tower black and lean against the blinding sky. Outer walls twisted through gullies and over naked ridges; Ardazirho sentries paced them, untroubled by dry cruel heat, blue-white hellglare, pouring ultraviolet radiation. But mostly, the fortress went inside the hills, long vaulted tunnels where boots clashed and voices echoed from room to den-like room. Construction had followed standard dig-in methods; prodigal use of atomic energy to fuse the living rock into desired patterns, then swift robotic installation of the necessary mechanisms. But the layout was rougher, more tortuous, less private, than man or Merseian would have liked. The ancestral Ardazirho had laired in caves and hunted in packs.

Flandry was hustled into a small room equipped as a laboratory. A pair of warriors clamped him in place. A grizzled technician began to prepare instruments.

Often, in the next day or two, Flandry screamed. He couldn't help it. Electronic learning should not go that fast. But finally, sick and shaking, he could growl the Urdahu language. Indeed, he thought, the Ardazirho had been thoroughly briefed. They understood the human nervous system so well that they could stamp a new linguistic pattern on it in mere hours, and not drive the owner insane.

Not quite.

Flandry was led down endless booming halls. Their brilliant bluish fluorescence hurt his eyes; he must needs squint. Even so, he watched what passed. It might be a truckload of ammunition, driven at crazy speed by a warrior who yelped curses at foot traffic. Or it might be a roomful of naked red-furred shapes: sprawled in snarling, quarrelsome fellowship; gambling with tetrahedral dice for stakes up to a year's slavery; watching a wrestling match which employed teeth and nails; testing nerve by standing up in turn against a wall while the rest threw axes. Or it might be a sort of chapel, where a single scarred fighter wallowed in pungent leaves before a great burning wheel. Or it might be a mess hall and a troop lying on fur rugs, bolting raw meat and howling in chorus with one who danced on a monstrous drumhead.

The man came at last to an office. This was also an artificial cave, thick straw on the floor, gloom in the corners, a thin stream of water running down a groove in one wall. A big Ardazirho lay prone on a hairy dais, lifted on both elbows to a slanting desktop. He wore only a skirt of leather strips, a crooked knife, and a very modern blaster. But the telescreen and intercom before him were also new, and Flandry's guards touched their black noses in his presence.

"Go," he said in the Urdahu. "Wait outside." The guards obeyed. He nodded at Flandry. "Be seated, if you wish."

The human lowered himself. He was still weak from what he had undergone, filthy, ill-fed, and ragged. Automatically he smoothed back his hair, and thanked human laziness for its invention of long-lasting antibeard enzyme. He needed such morale factors.

His aching muscles grew tight. Things were in motion again.

"I am Svantozik of the Janneer Ya," said the rough voice. "I am told that you are Captain Dominic Flandry of Terran Naval Intelligence. You may consider my status approximately the same."

"As one colleague to another," husked Flandry, "will you give me a drink?"

"By all means." Svantozik gestured to the artesian stream.

Flandry threw him a reproachful look, but needed other things too badly to elaborate. "It would be a kindly deed, and one meriting my gratitude, if you provided me at once with dark lenses and cigarettes." The last word was perforce Anglic. He managed a grin. "Later I will tell you what further courtesies ought to be customary."

Svantozik barked laughter. "I expected your eyes would suffer," he said. "Here." He reached in the desk and tossed over a pair of green polarite goggles, doubtless taken off a Vixenite casualty. Flandry put them on and whistled relief. "Tobacco is forbidden," added Svantozik. "Only a species with half-dead scent organs could endure it."

"Oh, well. There was no harm in asking." Flandry hugged his knees and leaned back against the cave wall.

"None. Now, I wish to congratulate you on your daring exploits." Svantozik's smile looked alarming enough, but it seemed friendly. "We searched for your vessel, but it must have escaped the planet."

"Thanks," said Flandry, quite sincerely. "I was afraid you would have gotten there in time to blast it." He cocked his head. "In return . . . see here, my friend [literally: croucher-in-my-blind], when dealing with my species, it is usually better to discourage them. You should have claimed you had caught my boat before it could escape, manufacturing false evidence if necessary to convince me. That would make me much more liable to yield my will to yours."

"Oh, indeed?" Svantozik pricked up his ears. "Now among the Black People, the effect would be just opposite. Good news tends to relax us, make us grateful and amenable to its bearer. Bad tidings raise the quotient of defiance."

"Well, of course it is not that simple," said Flandry. "In breaking down the resistance of a man, the commonest technique is to chivvy him for a protracted time, and then halt the process, speak kindly to him—preferably, get someone else to do that."

"Ah." Svantozik drooped lids over his cold eyes. "Are you not being unwise in telling me this—if it is true?"

"It is textbook truth," said Flandry, "as I am sure whatever race has instructed you in the facts about Terra's Empire will confirm. I am revealing no secret. But as you must be aware, textbooks have little value in practical matters. There is always the subtlety of the individual, which eludes anything except direct intuition based on wide, intimate experience. And you, being nonhuman, cannot ever have such an experience of men."

"True." The long head nodded. "In fact, I remember now reading somewhat of the human trait you mention . . . but there was so much else to learn, prior to the Great Hunt we are now on, that it had slipped my memory. So you tantalize me with a fact I could use—if I were on your side!" A sudden deep chuckle cracked in the ruffed throat. "I like you, Captain, the Sky Cave eat me if I do not."

Flandry smiled back. "We could have fun. But what are your intentions towards me now?"

"To learn what I can. For example, whether or not you were concerned in the murder of four warriors in Garth and the abduction of a fifth, not long ago. The informant who led us to you has used hysterics —real or simulated—to escape detailed questioning so far. Since the captured Ardazirho was a Clanmaster, and therefore possessed of valuable information, I suspect you had a hand in this."

"I swear upon the Golden Ass of Apuleius I did not."

"What is that?"

"One of our most revered books."

"The Powers only hunt at night," quoted Svantozik. "In other words, oaths are cheap. I personally do not wish to hurt you unduly, being skeptical of the value of torture anyhow. And I know that officers like you are immunized to the so-called truth sera. Therefore, reconditioning would be necessary: a long, tedious process, the answers stale when finally you wanted to give them, and you of little further value to us or yourself." He shrugged. "But I am going back to Ardazir before long, to report and wait reassignment. I know who will succeed me here: an officer quite anxious to practice some of the techniques which we have been told are effective on Terrans. I recommend you cooperate with me instead."

This must be one of their crack field operatives, thought Flandry, growing cold. *He did the basic Intelligence work on Vixen. Now, with Vixen in hand, he'll be sent to do the same job when the next Terran planet is attacked. Which will be soon!*

Flandry slumped. "Very well," he said in a dull tone. "I captured Temulak."

"Ha!" Svantozik crouched all-fours on the dais. The fur stood up along his spine, the iron-colored eyes burned. "Where is he now?"

"I do not know. As a precaution, I had him moved elsewhere, and did not inquire the place."

"Wise," Svantozik relaxed. "What did you get from him?"

"Nothing. He did not crack."

Svantozik stared at Flandry. "I doubt that," he said. "Not that I scorn Temulak—a brave one—but you are an extraordinary specimen of a civilization older and more learned than mine. It would be strange if you had not—"

Flandry sat up straight. His laughter barked harsh. "Extraordinary?" he cried bitterly. "I suppose so . . . the way I allowed myself to be caught like a cub!"

" 'No ground is free of possible pits,' " murmured Svantozik. He brooded a while. Presently: "Why did the female betray you? She went to our head-quarters, declared you were a Terran agent, and led our warriors to your meeting place. What had she to gain?"

"I don't know," groaned Flandry. "What difference does it make? She is wholly yours now, you know. The very fact she aided you once gives you the power to make her do it again—lest you denounce her to her own people." Svantozik nodded, grinning. "What do her original motives matter?" The man sagged back and picked at the straw.

"I am interested," said Svantozik. "Perhaps the same process may work again, on other humans."

"No." Flandry shook his head in a stunned way. "This was personal. I suppose she thought I had be-trayed her first— Why am I telling you this?"

"I have been informed that you Terrans often have strong feelings about individuals of the opposite sex," said Svantozik. "I was told it will occasionally drive you to desperate, meaningless acts."

Flandry passed a tired hand across his brow. "Forget it," he mumbled. "Just be kind to her. You can do that much, can you not?"

"As a matter of fact—" Svantozik broke off. He sat for a moment, staring at emptiness.

"*Great unborn planets!*" he whispered.

"What?" Flandry didn't look up.

"No matter," said Svantozik hastily. "Ah, am I right in assuming there was a reciprocal affection on your part?"

"It is no concern of yours!" Flandry sat up and shouted it. "I will hear no more! Say what else you will, but keep your filthy snout out of my own life!"

"So," breathed Svantozik. "Yes-s-s-s. . . . . Well, then, let us discuss other things."

He hammered at Flandry a while, not with quite the ruthlessness the human had shown Temulak. Indeed, he revealed a kind of chivalry: there was respect, fellow feeling, even an acrid liking in him for this man whose soul he hunted. Once or twice Flandry managed to divert the conversation—they spoke briefly of alcoholic drinks and riding animals; they traded some improper jokes, similar in both cultures.

Nevertheless, Svantozik hunted. It was a rough few hours.

At last Flandry was taken away. He was too worn to notice very much, but the route did seem devious. He was finally pushed into a room, not unlike Svantozik's office, save that it had human-type furniture and illumination. The door clashed behind him.

Kit stood waiting.

XIII

For a moment he thought she would scream. Then, very quickly, her eyes closed. She opened them again. They remained dry, as if all her tears had been spent. She took a step toward him.

"Oh, God, Kit," he croaked.

Her arms closed about his neck. He held her to him. His own gaze flickered around the room, until it found a small human-made box with a few controls which he recognized. He nodded to himself, ever so faintly, and drew an uneven breath. But he was still uncertain.

"Dominic, darlin'—" Kit's mouth sought his.

He stumbled to the bunk, sat down and covered his face. "Don't," he whispered. "I can't take much more."

The girl sat down beside him. She laid her head on his shoulder. He felt how she trembled. But the words came in glorious anticlimax: "That debuggin' unit is perfectly good, Dominic."

He wanted to lean back and shout with sudden uproarious mirth. He wanted to kick his heels and thumb his nose and turn handsprings across the cell. But he held himself in, letting only a rip of laughter come from lips which he hid against her cheek.

He had more than half expected Svantozik to provide a bugscrambler. Only with the sure knowledge that any listening devices were being negated by electronic and sound-wave interference, would even a cadet of Intelligence relax and speak freely. He suspected, though, that a hidden lens was conveying a silent image. They could talk, but both of them must continue to pantomime.

"How's it been, Kit?" he asked. "Rough?"

She nodded, not play-acting her misery at all. "But I haven't had to give any names," she gulped. "Not yet."

"Let's hope you don't," said Flandry.

He had told her in the hurricane cellar—how many centuries ago? ... "This is picayune stuff. I'm not doing what any competent undercover agent couldn't: what a score of Walton's men will be trying as soon as they can be smuggled here. I've something crazier in mind. Quite likely it'll kill us, but then again it might strike a blow worth whole fleets. Are you game, kid? It means the risk of death, or torture, or life-long slavery on a foreign planet. What you'll find worst, though, is the risk of having to sell out your own comrades, name them to the enemy, so he will keep confidence in you. Are you brave enough to sacrifice twenty lives for a world? I believe you are—but it's as cruel a thing as I could ask of any living creature."

"They brought me straight here," said Kit, holding him. "I don't think they know quite what to make o' me. A few minutes ago, one o' them came hotfootin' here with the scrambler an' orders for me to treat you ..." a slow flush went over her face, ". . . kindly. To get information from you, if I could, by any means that seemed usable."

Flandry waved a fist in melodramatic despair, while out of a contorted face his tone came levelly: "I expected something like this. I led Svantozik, the local snooper-in-chief, to think that gentle treatment from one of my own species, after a hard grilling from him, might break me down. Especially if you were the one in question. Svantozik isn't stupid at all, but he's dealing with an alien race, us, whose psychology he knows mainly from sketchy second-hand accounts. I've an advantage: the Ardazirho are new to me, but I've spent a lifetime dealing with all shapes and sizes of other species. Already I see what the Ardazirho have in common with several peoples whom I horn-swoggled in the past."

The girl bit her lip to hold it steady. She looked around the stone-walled room, and he knew she thought of kilometers of tunnel, ramparts and guns, wolfish hunters, and the desert beyond where men could not live. Her words fell thin and frightened: "What are we goin' to do now, Dominic? You never told me what you planned."

"Because I didn't know," he replied. "Once here, I'd have to play by ear. Fortunately, my confidence in my own ability to land on my feet approaches pure conceit, or would if I had any faults. We're not doing badly, Kit. I've learned their principal language, and you've been smuggled into their ranks."

"They don't trust me yet."

"No. I didn't expect they would—very much. . . . But let's carry on our visual performance. I wouldn't flipflop over to the enemy side just because you're here, Kit; but when I am badly shaken, I lose discretion and ordinary carefulness. Svantozik will accept that."

He gathered her back to him. She responded hungrily. He felt so much of himself return to his abused being, that his brain began to spark, throwing up schemes and inspecting them, discarding them and generating new ones, like a pyrotechnic display, like merry hell.

He said at last, while she quivered on his lap: "I think I have a notion. We'll have to play things as they lie, and prearrange a few signals, but here's what we'll try for." He felt her stiffen in his embrace. "Why, what's the matter?"

She asked, low and bitter: "Were you thinkin' o' your work all the time—just now?"

"Not that alone." He permitted himself the

briefest grin. "Or, rather, I enjoyed my work immensely."

"But still—Oh, never mind. Go on." She slumped.

Flandry scowled. But he dared not stop for side issues. He said: "Tell Svantozik, or whoever deals with you, that you played remorseful in my presence, but actually you hate my inwards, and my outwards too, because—uh—"

"Judith!" she snarled.

He had the grace to blush. "I suppose that's as plausible a reason as any, at least in Ardazirho eyes."

"Or human. If you knew how close I was to—No. Go on."

"Well, tell the enemy that you told me you'd betrayed me in a fit of pique, and now you regretted it. And I, being wildly in love with you—which again is highly believable—" She gave his predictable gallantry no response whatsoever. "I told you there was a possible escape for you. I said this: The Ardazirho are under the impression that Ymir is behind them. Actually, Ymir leans toward Terra, since we are more peace-minded and therefore less troublesome. The Ymirites are willing to help us in small ways; we keep this fact secret because now and then it saves us in emergencies. If I could only set a spaceship's signal to a certain recognition pattern, you could try to steal that ship. The Ardazirho would assume you headed for Walton's fleet, and line out after you in that direction. So you could give them the slip, reach Ogre, transmit the signal pattern, and request transportation to safety in a force-bubble ship."

Her eyes stretched wide with terror. "But if Svantozik hears that—an' 'tisn't true—"

"He won't know it's false till he's tried, will he?"

answered Flandry cheerfully. "If I lied, it isn't your fault. In fact, since you hastened to tattle, even about what looked like an escape for you, it'll convince him you're a firm collaborationist."

"But—no, Dominic. 'Tis . . . I don't dare—"

"Don't hand me that, Kit. You're one girl in ten to the tenth, and there's nothing you won't dare."

Then she did begin to sob.

After she had gone, Flandry spent a much less happy time waiting. He could still only guess how his enemy would react: an experienced human would probably not be deceived, and Svantozik's ignorance of human psychology might not be as deep as hoped. Flandry swore and tried to rest. The weariness of the past days was gray upon him.

When his cell door opened, he sprang up with a jerkiness that told him how thin his nerves were worn.

Svantozik stood there, four guards poised behind. The Ardazirho officer flashed teeth in a grin. "Good hunting, Captain," he greeted. "Is your den comfortable?"

"It will do," said Flandry, "until I can get one provided with a box of cigars, a bottle of whisky, and a female."

"The female, at least, I tried to furnish," riposted Svantozik.

Flandry added in his suavest tone: "Oh, yes, I should also like a rug of Ardazirho skin."

One of the guards snarled. Svantozik chuckled. "I too have a favor to ask, Captain," he said. "My brothers in the engineering division are interested in modifying a few spaceships to make them more readily usable by humans. You understand how such differences as the location of the thumb, or that lumbar

conformation which makes it more comfortable for
us to lie prone on the elbows than sit, have in-
fluenced the design of our control panels. A man
would have trouble steering an Ardazirho craft. Yet
necessarily, in the course of time, if the Great Hunt
succeeds and we acquire human subjects—we will
find occasion for some of them to pilot some of our
vehicles. The Kittredge female, for example, could
profitably have a ship of her own, since we antici-
pate usefulness in her as a go-between among us and
the human colonists here. If you would help her—
simply in checking over one of our craft, and drawing up suggestions—"

Flandry grew rigid. "Why should I help you at
all?" he said through clenched jaws.

Svantozik shrugged. "It is very minor assistance.
We could do it ourselves. But it may pass the time for
you." Wickedly: "I am not at all sure that good treatment, rather than abuse, may not be the way to
break down a man. Also, Captain, if you must have
a rationalization, think: here is a chance to examine
one of our vessels close up. If later, somehow, you
escape, your own service would be interested in
what you saw."

Flandry stood a moment, altogether quiet.
Thought lanced through him. *Kit told. Svantozik
naturally prefers me not to know what she did tell.
So he makes up this story—offers me what he hopes
I'll think is a God-sent opportunity to arrange for
Kit's escape—*

He said aloud, urbanely: "You are most kind, my
friend of the Janneer Ya. But Miss Kittredge and I
could not feel at ease with ugly guards like yours
drooling over our shoulders."

He got growls from two warriors that time. Svantozik hushed them. "That is easily arranged," he said. "The guards can stay out of the control turret."

"Excellent. Then, if you have some human-made tools—"

They went down hollow corridors, past emplacements where artillery slept like nested dinosaurs, across the furious arctic day, and so to a spaceship near the outworks. Through goggles, the man studied her fiercely gleaming shape. About equivalent to a Terran Comet class. Fast, lightly armed, a normal complement of fifteen or so, but one could handle her if need be.

The naked hills beyond wavered in heat. When he had stepped through the airlock, he felt dizzy from that brief exposure.

Svantozik stopped at the turret companionway. "Proceed," he invited cordially. "My warriors will wait here until you wish to return—at which time you and the female will come dine with me and I shall provide Terran delicacies." Mirth crossed his eyes. "Of course, the engines have been temporarily disconnected."

"Of course," bowed Flandry.

Kit met him as he shut the turret door. Her fingers closed cold on his arm. "Now what'll we do?" she gasped.

"Easy, lass." He disengaged her. "I don't see a bugscrambler here." *Remember, Svantozik thinks I think you are still loyal to me. Play it, Kit, don't forget, or we're both done!* "There are four surly-looking guards slouched below," he said. "I don't imagine Svantozik will waste his own valuable time in their company. A direct bug to the office of someone who knows Anglic is more efficient. Consider me making obscene gestures at you, O great unseen audience. But is anyone else aboard, d'you know?"

"N-no—" Her eyes asked him, through fear: *Have you forgotten? Are you alerting them to your plan?*

Flandry wandered past the navigation table to the main radio transceiver. "I don't want to risk someone getting officious," he murmured. "You see, I'd first like to peek at their communication system. It's the easiest thing to modify, if any alterations are needed. And it could look bad, unseen audience, if we were surprised at what is really a harmless inspection." *I trust,* he thought with a devil's inward laughter, *that they don't know I know they know I'm actually supposed to install a password circuit for Kit.*

It was the sort of web he loved. But he remembered, as a cold tautening, that a bullet was still the ultimate simplicity which clove all webs.

He took the cover off and began probing. He could not simply have given Kit the frequencies and wave shapes in a recognition signal: because Ardazirho equipment would not be built just like Terran, nor calibrated in metric units. He must examine an actual set, dismantle parts, test them with oscilloscope and static meters—and, surreptitiously, modify it so that the required pattern would be emitted when a single hidden circuit was closed.

She watched him, as she should if she expected him to believe this was her means of escape. And doubtless the Ardazirho spy watched too, over a bugscreen. When Flandry's job was done, it would be Svantozik who took this ship to Ogre, generated the signal, and saw what happened.

Because on the question of whose side the Ymirite Dispersal truly was on, overrode everything else. If Flandry had spoken truth to Kit, the lords of Urdahu must be told without an instant's pause.

The man proceeded, making up a pattern as he went and thinking wistfully how nice it would be if Ymir really did favor Terra. Half an hour later he re-sealed the unit. Then he spent another hour osten-tatiously strolling around the turret examining all controls.

"Well," he said at last, "we might as well go home, Kit."

He saw the color leave her face. She knew what the sentence meant. But she nodded. "Let's," she whispered.

Flandry bowed her through the door. As she came down the companionway, the guards at its base got up. Their weapons aimed past her, covering Flandry, who strolled with a tigerish leisure.

Kit pushed through the line of guards. Flandry, still on the companionway, snatched at his pocket. The four guns leaped to focus on him. He laughed and raised empty hands. "I only wanted to scratch an itch," he called.

Kit slipped a knife from the harness of one guard and stabbed him in the ribs.

Flandry dived into the air. A bolt crashed past him, scorching his tunic. He struck the deck with flexed knees and bounced. Kit had already snatched the rifle from the yelling warrior she had wounded. It thundered in her hand, point-blank. Another Ardazirho dropped. Flandry knocked aside the gun of a third. The fourth enemy had whipped around towards Kit. His back was to Flandry. The man raised the blade of his hand and brought it down again, chop to the skull-base. He heard neckbones splinter. The third guard sprang back, seeking room to shoot. Kit blasted him open. The first one, stabbed, on his knees, reached for a dropped rifle.

Flandry kicked him in the larynx.

"Starboard lifeboat!" he rasped.

He clattered back into the turret. If the Ardazirho watcher had left the bugscreen by now, he had a few minutes' grace. Otherwise, a nuclear shell would probably write his private doomsday. He snatched up the navigator's manual and sprang out again.

Kit was already in the lifeboat. Its small engine purred, warming up. Flandry plunged through the lock, dogged it behind him. "I'll fly," he panted. "I'm more used to non-Terran panels. You see if you can find some bailing out equipment. We'll need it."

Where the devil was the release switch? The bugwatcher had evidently quit in time, but any moment now he would start to wonder why Flandry and Party weren't yet out of the spaceship—

There! He slapped down a lever. A hull panel opened. Harsh sunlight poured through the boat's viewscreen. Flandry glanced over its controls. Basically like those he had just studied. He touched the *Escape* button. The engine yelled. The boat sprang from its mother ship, into the sky.

Flandry aimed southward. He saw the fortress whirl dizzily away, fall below the horizon. And still no pursuit, not even a homing missile. They must be too dumbfounded. It wouldn't last, of course. . . . He threw back his head and howled out all his bottled-up laughter, great gusts of it to fill the cabin and echo over the scream of split atmosphere.

"What are you doin'?" Kit's voice came faint and frantic. "We can't escape this way. Head spaceward before they overhaul us!"

Flandry wiped his eyes. "Excuse me," he said. "I was laughing while I could." Soberly: "With the blockade, and a slow vessel never designed for hu-

man steering, we'd not climb 10,000 kilometers
before they nailed us. What we're going to do is bail
out and let the boat continue on automatic. With
luck, they'll pursue it so far before catching up that
they'll have no prayer of backtracking us. With still
more luck, they'll blow the boat up and assume we
were destroyed too."

"Bail out?" Kit looked down at a land of stones
and blowing ash. The sky was like molten steel.
"Into that?" she whispered.

"If they do realize we jumped," said Flandry, "I
trust they'll figure we perished in the desert. A natural conclusion, I'm sure, since our legs aren't so
articulated that we can wear Ardazirho spacesuits."
He grew grimmer than she had known him before.
"I've had to improvise all along the way. Quite probably I've made mistakes, Kit, which will cost us a
painful death. But if so, I'm hoping we won't die for
naught."

XIV

Even riding a grav repulsor down, Flandry felt how
the air smote him with heat. When he struck the
ground and rolled over, it burned his skin.

He climbed up, already ill. Through his goggles,
he saw Kit rise. Dust veiled her, blown on a furnace
wind. The desert reached in withered soil and bony
crags for a few kilometers beyond her, then the heat-
haze swallowed vision. The northern horizon
seemed incandescent, impossible to look at.

Thunder banged in the wake of the abandoned
lifeboat. Flandry stumbled toward the girl. She
leaned on him. "I'm sorry," she said. "I think I
twisted an ankle."

"And scorched it, too, I see. Come on lass, not far now."

They groped over tumbled gray boulders. The weather monitor tower rippled before their eyes, like a skeleton seen through water. The wind blasted and whined. Flandry felt his skin prickle with ultraviolet and bake dry as he walked. The heat began to penetrate his bootsoles.

They were almost at the station when a whistle cut through the air. Flandry lifted aching eyes. Four torpedo shapes went overhead, slashing from horizon to horizon in seconds. The Ardazirho, in pursuit of an empty lifeboat. If they had seen the humans below—No. They were gone. Flandry tried to grin, but it split his lips too hurtfully.

The station's equipment huddled in a concrete shack beneath the radio transmitter tower. The shade, when they had staggered through the door, was like all hopes of heaven. Flandry uncorked a water bottle. That was all he had dared take out of the spaceboat supplies; alien food was liable to have incompatible proteins. His throat was too much like a mummy's to talk, but he offered Kit the flask and she gulped thirstily. When he had also swigged, he felt a little better.

"Get to work, wench," he said. "Isn't it lucky you're in Vixen's weather engineering department, so you knew where to find a station and what to do when we got there?"

"Go on," she tried to laugh. It was a rattling in her mouth. "You built your idea aroun' the fact. Let's see, now, they keep tools in a locker at every unit—" She stopped. The shadow in this hut was so deep, against the fury seen through one little window, that she was almost invisible to him. "I can tinker with the sender, easily enough," she said. Slow terror rose in her voice. "Sure, I can make it 'cast your message, 'stead o' telemeterin' weather data. But . . . I just now get to thinkin' . . . s'pose an Ardazirho reads it? Or s'pose nobody does? I don't know if my service is even bein' manned now. We could wait here, an' wait, an'—"

"Easy." Flandry came behind her, laid his hands on her shoulders and squeezed. "Anything's possible. But I think the chances favor us. The Ardazirho can hardly spare personnel for something so routine and, to them, unimportant, as weather adjustment. At the same time, the human engineers are very probably still on the job. Humanity always continues as much in the old patterns as possible, people report to their usual work, hell may open but the city will keep every lawn mowed . . . Our real gamble is that whoever spots our call will have the brains, and the courage and loyalty, to act on it."

She leaned against him a moment. "An' d'you think there's a way for us to be gotten out o' here, under the enemy's nose?"

An obscure pain twinged in his soul. "I know it's unfair, Kit," he said. "I myself am a hardened sinner and this is my job and so on, but it isn't right to hazard all the fun and love and accomplishment waiting for you. It must be done, though. My biggest hope was always to steal a navigation manual. Don't you understand, it will tell us where Ardazir lies!"

"I know." Her sigh was a small sound almost lost in the boom of dry hot wind beyond the door. "We'd better start work."

While she opened the transmitter and cut out the meter circuits, Flandry recorded a message: a simple plea to contact Emil Bryce and arrange the rescue

from Station 938 of two humans with vital material
for Admiral Walton. How that was to be done, he
had no clear idea himself. A Vixenite aircraft would
have little chance of getting this far north undetected
and undestroyed. A radio message—no, too easily in-
tercepted, unless you had very special apparatus—a
courier to the fleet—and if that was lost, another and
another—

When she had finished, Kit reached for the second
water bottle. "Better not," said Flandry. "We've a
long wait."

"I'm dehydrated," she husked.

"Me too. But we've no salt; heat stroke is a real
threat. Drinking as little as possible will stretch our
survival time. Why the devil aren't these places air
conditioned and stocked with rations?"

"No need for it. They just get routine inspection
. . . at midwinter in these parts." Kit sat down on the
one little bench. Flandry joined her. She leaned into
the curve of his arm. A savage gust trembled in the
hut walls, the window was briefly blackened with
flying grit.

"Is Ardazir like this?" she wondered. "Then 'tis a
real hell for those devils to come from."

"Oh, no," answered Flandry. "Temulak said their
planet has a sane orbit. Doubtless it's warmer than
Terra, on the average, but we could stand the temperature in most of its climatic zones, I'm sure. A hot
star, emitting strongly in the UV, would split water
molecules and kick the free hydrogen into space
before it could recombine. The ozone layer would
give some protection to the hydrosphere, but not
quite enough. So Ardazir must be a good deal drier
than Terra, with seas rather than oceans. At the same
time, judging from the muscular strength of the

natives, as well as the fact they don't mind Vixen's air pressure, Ardazir must be somewhat bigger. Surface gravity of one-point-five, maybe. That would retain an atmosphere similar to ours, in spite of the sun."

He paused. Then: "They aren't fiends, Kit. They're fighters and hunters. Possibly they've a little less built-in kindliness than our species. But I'm not even sure about that. We were a rambunctious lot too, a few centuries ago. We may well be again, when the Long Night has come and it's root, hog, or die. As a matter of fact, the Ardazirho aren't even one people. They're a whole planetful of races and cultures. The Urdahu conquered the rest only a few years ago. That's why you see all those different clothes on them—concession to parochialism, like an ancient Highland regiment. And I'll give odds that in spite of all their successes, the Urdahu are not too well liked at home. Theirs is a very new empire, imposed by overwhelming force; it could be split again, if we used the right tools. I feel almost sorry for them, Kit. They're the dupes of someone else—and Lord, what a someone that is! What a genius!"

He stopped, because the relentless waterless heat had shrivelled his gullet. The girl said, low and bitter: "Go on. Sympathize with Ardazir an' admire the artistry o' this X who's behind it all. You're a professional too. But my kind o' people has to do the dyin'."

"I'm sorry." He ruffled her hair.

"You still haven't tol' me whether you think we'll be rescued alive."

"I don't know." He tensed himself until he could add: "I doubt it. I expect it'll take days, and we can only hold out for hours. But if the ship comes—no, damn it, *when* the ship comes!—that pilot book will be here."

"Thanks for bein' honest, Dominic," she said. "Thanks for everything."

He kissed her, with enormous gentleness.

After that they waited.

The sun sank. A short night fell. It brought little relief, the wind still scourging, the northern sky still aflame. Kit tossed in a feverish daze beside Flandry. He himself could no longer think very clearly. He had hazed recollections of another white night in high-altitude summer—but that had been on Terra, on a cool upland meadow of Norway, and there had been another blonde girl beside him—her lips were like roses. . . .

The whistling down the sky, earthshaking thump of a recklessly fast landing, feet that hurried over blistering rock and hands that hammered on the door, scarcely reached through the charred darkness of Flandry's mind. But when the door crashed open and the wind blasted in, he swam up through waves of pain. And the thin face of Chives waited to meet him.

"Here, sir. Sit up. If I may take the liberty—"

"You green bastard," croaked Flandry out of nightmare, "I ordered you to—"

"Yes, sir. I delivered your tape. But after that, it seemed advisable to slip back and stay in touch with Mr. Bryce. Easy there, sir, if you please. We can run the blockade with little trouble. Really, sir, did you think *natives* could bar your own personal space-craft? I shall prepare medication for the young lady, and tea is waiting in your stateroom."

XV

Fleet Admiral Sir Thomas Walton was a big man, with gray hair and bleak faded eyes. He seldom wore any of his decorations, and visited Terra only on business. No sculp, but genes and war and unshed tears, when he watched his men die and then watched the Imperium dribble away what they had gained, had carved his face. Kit thought him the handsomest man she had ever met. But in her presence, his tongue locked with the shyness of an old bachelor. He called her Miss Kittredge, assigned her a private cabin in his flagship, and found excuses to avoid the officer's mess where she ate.

She was given no work, save keeping out of the way. Lonely young lieutenants buzzed about her, doing their best to charm and amuse. But Flandry was seldom aboard the dreadnought.

The fleet orbited in darkness, among keen sardonic stars. Little could actively be done. Ogre must be watched, where the giant planet crouched an enigma. The Ardazirho force did not seek battle, but stayed close to Vixen where ground support was available and where captured robofactories daily swelled its strength. Now and then the Terrans made forays. But Walton hung back from a decisive test. He could still win—*if* he used his whole strength and if Ogre stayed neutral. But Vixen, the prize, would be a tomb.

Restless and unhappy, Walton's men muttered in their ships.

After three weeks, Captain Flandry was summoned to the admiral. He whistled relief. "Our scout must have reported back," he said to his assistant. "Now maybe they'll take me off this damned garbage detail."

The trouble was, he alone had been able to speak Urdahu. There were a hundred Ardazirho prisoners, taken off disabled craft by boarding parties. But the officers had destroyed all navigational clues and died, with the ghastly gallantry of preconditioning. None of the enlisted survivors knew Anglic, or co-operated with the Terran linguists. Flandry had passed on his command of their prime tongue, electronically; but not wishing to risk his sanity again, he had done it at the standard easy pace. The rest of each day had been spent interrogating—a certain percentage of prisoners were vulnerable to it in their own language. Now, two other humans possessed Urdahu: enough of a seedbed. But until the first spies sent to Ardazir itself got back, Flandry had been left on the grilling job. Sensible, but exhausting and deadly dull.

He hopped eagerly into a grav scooter and rode from the Intelligence ship to the dreadnought. It was Nova class; its hull curved over him, monstrous as a mountain, guns raking the Milky Way. Otherwise he saw only stars, the distant sun Cerulia, the black nebula. Hard to believe that hundreds of ships, with the unchained atom in their magazines, prowled for a million kilometers around.

He entered the No. 7 lock and strode quickly towards the flag office. A scarlet cloak billowed behind him; his tunic was peacock blue, his trousers like snow, tucked into half-boots of authentic Cordovan leather. The angle of his cap was an outrage to all official dignity. He felt like a boy released from school.

"Dominic!"

Flandry stopped. "Kit!" he whooped.

She ran down the corridor to meet him, a small lonely figure in brief Terran dress. Her hair was still a gold helmet, but he noted she was thinner. He put hands on her shoulders and held her at arm's length.

"The better to see you with," he laughed. And then, soberly: "Tough?"

"Lonesome," she said. "Empty. Nothin' to do but worry." She pulled away from him. "No, darn it, I hate people who feel sorry for themselves. I'm all right, Dominic." She looked down at the deck and knuckled one eye.

"Come on!" he said.

"Hm? Dominic, where are you goin'? I can't— I mean—"

Flandry slapped her in the most suitable place and hustled her along the hall. "You're going to sit in on this! It'll give you something to hope for. March!"

The guard outside Walton's door was shocked. "Sir, my orders were to admit only you."

"One side, junior." Flandry picked up the marine by the gun belt and set him down a meter away. "The young lady is my portable expert on hyper-squidgeronics. Also, she's pretty." He closed the door in the man's face.

Admiral Walton started behind his desk. "What's this, Captain?"

"I thought she could pour beer for us," burbled Flandry.

"I don't—" began Kit helplessly. "I didn't mean to—"

"Sit down." Flandry pushed her into a corner chair. "After all, sir, we might need first-hand information about Vixen." His eyes clashed with Walton's. "I think she's earned a ringside seat," he added.

The admiral sat unmoving a moment. Then his mouth crinkled. "You're incorrigible," he said. "And spare me that stock answer, 'No, I'm Flandry.' Very well, Miss Kittredge. You understand this is under top security. Captain Flandry, you know Commander Sugimoto."

Flandry shook hands with the other Terran, who had been in charge of the first sneak expedition to Ardazir. They sat down. Flandry started a cigarette. "D'you find the place all right?" he asked.

"No trouble," said Sugimoto. "Once you'd given me the correlation between their astronomical tables and ours, and explained the number system, it was elementary. Their star's not in our own catalogues, because it's on the other side of that dark nebula and there's never been any exploration that way. So you've saved us maybe a year of search. Incidentally; when the war's over the scientists will be interested in the nebula. Seen from the other side, it's faintly luminous: a proto-sun. No one ever suspected that Population One got *that* young right in Sol's own galactic neighborhood! Must be a freak, though."

Flandry stiffened. "What's the matter?" snapped Walton.

"Nothing, sir. Or maybe something. I don't know. Go on, Commander."

"No need to repeat in detail," said Walton. "You'll see the full report. Your overall picture of Ardazirho conditions, gained from your interrogations, is accurate. The sun is an A4 dwarf—actually no more than a dozen parsecs from here. The planet is terrestroid, biggish, rather dry, quite mountainous, three satellites. From all indications—you know the techniques, sneak landings, long-range telescopic spying, hidden cameras, random samples—the Urdahu hegemony is recent and none too stable."

"One of our xenologists spotted what he swore was a typical rebellion," said Sugimoto. "To me, his films are merely a lot of red hairy creatures in one kind of clothes, firing with gunpowder weapons at a modern-looking fortress where they wear different clothes. The sound track won't mean a thing till your boys translate for us. But the xenologist says there are enough other signs to prove it's the uprising of a backward tribe against more civilized conquerors."

"A chance, then, to play them off against each other," nodded Flandry. "Of course, before we can hope to do that, Intelligence must first gather a lot more information. Advertisement."

"Have you anything to add, Captain?" asked Walton. "Anything you learned since your last progress report?"

"No, sir," said Flandry. "It all hangs together pretty well. Except, naturally, the main question. The Urdahu couldn't have invented all the modern paraphernalia that gave them control of Ardazir. Not that fast. They were still in the early nuclear age, two decades ago. Somebody supplied them, taught them, and sent them out a-conquering. Who?"

"Ymir," said Walton flatly. "Our problem is, are the Ymirites working independently, or as allies of Merseia?"

"Or at all?" murmured Flandry.

"Hell and thunder! The Ardazirho ships and heavy equipment have Ymirite lines. The governor of Ogre ties up half our strength simply by refusing to speak. A Jovian colonist tried to murder you when you were on an official mission, didn't he?"

"The ships could be made that way on purpose, to mislead us," said Flandry. "You know the Ymirites are not a courteous race: even if they were, what difference would it make, since we can't investigate them in detail? As for my little brush with Horx—"

He stopped. "Commander," he said slowly, "I've

learned there are jovoid planets in the system of Ardazir. Is any of them colonized?"

"Not as far as I could tell," said Sugimoto. "Of course, with that hot sun . . . I mean, we wouldn't colonize Ardazir, so Ymir—"

"The sun doesn't make a lot of difference when atmosphere gets that thick," said Flandry. "My own quizzing led me to believe there are no Ymirite colonies anywhere in the region overrun by Ardazir. Don't you think, if they had interests there at all, they'd *live* there?"

"Not necessarily." Walton's fist struck the desk. "Everything's 'not necessarily,'" he growled like a baited lion. "We're fighting in a fog. If we made an all-out attack anywhere, we'd expose ourselves to possible Ymirite action. This fleet is stronger than the Ardazirho force around Vixen—but weaker than the entire fleet of the whole Ardazirho realm—yet if we pulled in reinforcements from Syrax, Merseia would gobble up the Cluster! But we can't hang around here forever, either, waiting for somebody's next move!"

He stared at his big knobby hands. "We'll send more spies to Ardazir," he rumbled. "Of course some'll get caught, and then Ardazir will know we know, and they'll really exert themselves against us. . . . By God, maybe the one thing to do is smash them here at Vixen, immediately, and then go straight to Ardazir and hope enough of our ships survive long enough to sterilize the whole hell-planet!"

Kit leaped to her feet. "No!" she screamed.

Flandry forced her down again. Walton looked at her with eyes full of anguish. "I'm sorry," he mumbled. "I know it would be the end of Vixen. I don't want to be a butcher at Ardazir either . . . all their little cubs, who never heard about war—But what can I do?"

"Wait," said Flandry. "I have a hunch."

Silence fell, layer by layer, until the cabin grew thick with it. Finally Walton asked, most softly: "What is it, Captain?"

Flandry stared past them all. "Maybe nothing," he said. "Maybe much. An expression some of the Ardazirho use: the Sky Cave. It's some kind of dark hole. Certain of their religions make it the entrance to hell. Could it be—I remember my friend Svantozik too. I surprised him, and he let out an oath which was not stock. *Great unborn planets*. Svantozik ranks high. He knows more than any other Ardazirho we've met. It's little enough to go on, but . . . can you spare me a flotilla, Admiral?"

"Probably not," said Walton. "And it couldn't sneak off. One ship at a time, yes, we can get that out secretly. But several. . . . The enemy would detect their wake, notice which way they were headed, and wonder. Or wouldn't that matter in this case?"

"I'm afraid it would." Flandry paused. "Well, sir, can you lend me a few men? I'll take my own flitter. If I'm not back soon, do whatever seems best."

He didn't want to go. It seemed all too likely that the myth was right and the Sky Cave led to hell. But Walton sat watching him, Walton who was one of the last brave and wholly honorable men in all Terra's Empire. And Kit watched him too.

XVI

He would have departed at once, but a stroke of luck —*about time*, he thought ungratefully—made him decide to wait another couple of days. He spent them on the *Hooligan*, not telling Kit he was still with the fleet. If she knew he had leisure, he would never catch up on some badly needed sleep.

The fact was that the Ardazirho remained unaware that any human knew their language, except a few prisoners and the late Dominic Flandry. So they were sending all messages in clear. By now Walton had agents on Vixen, working with the underground, equipped to communicate undetected with his fleet. Enemy transmissions were being monitored with growing thoroughness. Flandry remembered that Svantozik had been about to leave, and requested a special lookout for any information on this subject. A scanner was adjusted to spot that name on a recording tape. It did so; the contents of the tape were immediately relayed into space; and Flandry listened with sharp interest to a playback.

It was a normal enough order, relating to certain preparations. Mindhunter Svantozik of the Janneer Ya was departing for home as per command. He would not risk being spotted and traced back to Ardazir by some Terran, so would employ only a small ultra-fast flitter. (Flandry admired his nerve. Most humans would have taken at least a Meteor class boat.) The hour and date of his departure were given, in Urdahu terms.

"Rally 'round," said Flandry. The *Hooligan* glided into action.

He did not come near Vixen. That was the risky business of the liaison craft. He could predict the exact manner of Svantozik's takeoff: there was only one logical way. The flitter would be in the middle of a squadron, which would roar spaceward on a foray. At the right time, Svantozik would give his own little boat a powerful jolt of primary drive; then, orbiting with cold engines away from the others, let distance accumulate. When he felt sure no Terran had spied him, he would go cautiously on gravs until well clear—then switch over into secondary and exceed the velocity of light. So small a craft, so far away from Walton's bases, would not be detected: especially with enemy attention diverted by the raiding squadron.

Unless, to be sure, the enemy had planted himself out in that region, with foreknowledge of Svantozik's goal and sensitive pulse-detectors running wide open.

When the alarm buzzed and the needles began to waver, Flandry allowed himself a yell. "That's our boy!" His finger stabbed a button. The *Hooligan* went into secondary with a wail of abused converters. When the viewscreens had steadied, Cerulia was visibly dimming to stern. Ahead, outlined in diamond constellations, the nebula roiled ragged black. Flandry stared at his instruments. "He's not as big as we are," he said, "but travelling like goosed lightning. Think we can overhaul short of Ardazir?"

"Yes, sir," said Chives. "In this immediate volume of space, which is dustier than average, and at these pseudo-speeds, friction becomes significant. We are more aerodynamic than he. I estimate twenty hours. Now, if I may be excused, I shall prepare supper."

"Uh-uh," said Flandry emphatically. "Even if he isn't aware of us yet, he may try evasive tactics on general principles. An autopilot has a randomizing predictor for such cases, but no poetry."

"Sir?" Chives raised the eyebrows he didn't have.

"No feel . . . intuition . . . whatever you want to call it. Svantozik is an artist of Intelligence. He may also be an artist at the pilot panel. So are you, little chum. You and I will stand watch and watch here. I've assigned a hairy great CPO to cook."

"Sir!" bleated Chives.

Flandry winced. "I know. Navy cuisine. The sacrifices we unsung heroes made for Terra's cause—"

He wandered aft to get acquainted with his crew. Walton had personally chosen a dozen for this mission: eight humans; a Scothanian, nearly human-looking but for the horns in his yellow hair; a pair of big four-armed gray-furred shaggy-muzzled Gorzuni; a purple-and-blue giant from Donarr, vaguely like a gorilla torso centauroid on a rhinoceros body. All had Terran citizenship, all were career personnel, all had fought with every weapon from axe to operations analyzer. They were as good a crew as could be found anywhere in the known galaxy. And far down underneath, it saddened Flandry that not one of the humans, except himself, came from Terra.

The hours passed. He ate, napped, stood piloting tricks. Eventually he was close upon the Ardazirho boat, and ordered combat armor all around. He himself went into the turret with Chives.

His quarry was a squat, ugly shape, dark against the distant star-clouds. The viewscreen showed a slim blast cannon and a torpedo launcher heavier than most boats that size would carry. The missiles it sent must have power enough to penetrate the *Hooligan*'s potential screens, make contact, and vaporize the target in a single nuclear burst.

Flandry touched a firing stud. A tracer shell flashed out, drawing a line of fire through Svantozik's boat. Or, rather, through the space where shell and boat coexisted with differing frequencies. The conventional signal to halt was not obeyed.

"Close in," said Flandry. "Can you phase us?"

"Yes, sir." Chives danced lean triple-jointed fingers over the board. The *Hooligan* plunged like a stooping osprey. She interpenetrated the enemy craft, so that Flandry looked for a moment straight through its turret. He recognized Svantozik at the controls, in person, and laughed his delight. The Ardazirho slammed on pseudo-deceleration. A less skillful pilot would have shot past him and been a million kilometers away before realizing what had happened. Flandry and Chives, acting as one, matched the maneuver. For a few minutes they followed every twist and dodge. Then, grimly, Svantozik continued in a straight line. The *Hooligan* edged sideways until she steered a parallel course, twenty meters off.

Chives started the phase adjuster. There was an instant's sickness while the secondary drive skipped through a thousand separate frequency patterns. Then its in-and-out-of-space-time matched the enemy's. A mass detector informed the robot, within microseconds, and the adjuster stopped. A tractor beam clamped fast to the other hull's sudden solidity. Svantozik tried a different phasing, but the *Hooligan* equalled him without skipping a beat.

"Shall we lay alongside, sir?" asked Chives.

"Better not," said Flandry. "They might choose to blow themselves up, and us with them. Boarding tube."

It coiled from the combat airlock to the other hull, fastened leech-like with magnetronic suckers, and clung. The Ardazirho energy cannon could not be brought to bear at this angle. A missile flashed from their launcher. It was disintegrated by a blast from the *Hooligan's* gun. The Donarrian, vast in his armor, guided a "worm" through the boarding tube to the opposite hull. The machine's energy snout began to gnaw through metal.

Flandry sensed, rather than saw, the faint ripple which marked a changeover into primary drive. He slammed down his own switch. Both craft reverted simultaneously to intrinsic sublight velocity. The difference of fifty kilometers per second nearly ripped them across. But the tractor beam held, and so did the compensator fields. They tumbled onward, side by side.

"He's hooked!" shouted Flandry.

Still the prey might try a stunt. He must remain with Chives, parrying everything, while his crew had the pleasure of boarding. Flandry's muscles ached with the wish for personal combat. Over the intercom now, radio voices snapped: "The worm's pierced through, sir. Our party entering the breach. Four hostiles in battle armor opposing with mobile weapons—"

Hell broke loose. Energy beams flamed against indurated steel. Explosive bullets burst, sent men staggering, went in screaming fragments through bulkheads. The Terran crew plowed unmercifully into the barrage, before it could break down their armor. They closed hand to hand with the Ardazirho. It was not too uneven a match in numbers: six to four, for half Flandry's crew must man guns against possible missiles. The Ardazirho were physically a bit stronger than humans. That counted little, when fists beat on plate. But the huge Gorzuni, the barbarically shrill Scothanian with his wrecking bar of collapsed alloy, the Donarrian happily ramping and roaring and dealing buffets which stunned through all insulation—they ended the fight. The enemy navigator, preconditioned, died. The rest were extracted from their armor and tossed in the *Hooligan's* hold.

Flandry had not been sure Svantozik too was not channeled so capture would be lethal. But he had doubted it. The Urdahu were unlikely to be that prodigal of their very best officers, who if taken prisoner might still be exchanged or contrive to escape. Probably Svantozik had simply been given a bloc against remembering his home sun's coordinates, when a pilot book wasn't open before his face.

The Terran sighed. "Clear the saloon, Chives," he said wearily. "Have Svantozik brought to me, post a guard outside, and bring us some refreshments." As he passed one of the boarding gang, the man threw him a grin and an exuberant salute. "Damn heroes," he muttered.

He felt a little happier when Svantozik entered. The Ardazirho walked proudly, red head erect, kilt somehow made neat again. But there was an inward chill in the wolf eyes. When he saw who sat at the table, he grew rigid. The fur stood up over his whole lean body and a growl trembled in his throat.

"Just me," said the human. "Not back from the Sky Cave, either. Flop down." He waved at the bench opposite his own chair.

Slowly, muscle by muscle, Svantozik lowered himself. He said at last, "A proverb goes: 'The hornbuck may run swifter than you think.' I touch the nose to you, Captain Flandry."

"I'm pleased to see my men didn't hurt you. They had particular orders to get you alive. That was the whole idea."

"Did I do you so much harm in the Den?" asked Svantozik bitterly.

"On the contrary. You were a more considerate host than I would have been. Maybe I can repay that." Flandry took out a cigarette. "Forgive me. I have turned the ventilation up. But my brain runs on nicotine."

"I suppose—" Svantozik's gaze went to the view-screen and galactic night, "you know which of those stars is ours."

"Yes."

"It will be defended to the last ship. It will take more strength than you can spare from your borders to break us."

"So you are aware of the Syrax situation." Flandry trickled smoke through his nose. "Tell me, is my impression correct that you rank high in Ardazir's space service and in the Urdahu *orbekh* itself?"

"Higher in the former than the latter," said Svantozik dully. "The Packmasters and the old females will listen to me, but I have no authority with them."

"Still—look out there again. To the Sky Cave. What do you see?"

They had come so far now that they glimpsed the thinner part of the nebula, which the interior luminosity could penetrate, from the side. The black cumulus shape towered ominously among the constellations; a dim red glow along one edge touched masses and filaments, as if a dying fire smouldered in some grotto full of spiderwebs. Not many degrees away from it, Ardazir's sun flashed sword blue.

"The Sky Cave itself, of course," said Svantozik wonderingly. "The Great Dark. The Gate of the Dead, as those who believe in religion call it. . . ." His tone, meant to be sardonic, wavered.

"No light, then? Is it black to you?" Flandry nodded slowly. "I expected that. Your race is red-blind. You see further into the violet than I do; but in your eyes, I am gray and you yourself are black. Those atrociously combined red squares in your kilt all look equally dark to you." The Urdahu word he used for "red" actually designated the yellow-orange band; but Svantozik understood.

"Our astronomers have long known there is invisible radiation from the Sky Cave, radio and shorter wavelengths," he said. "What of it?"

"Only this," said Flandry, "that you are getting your orders from that nebula."

Svantozik did not move a muscle. But Flandry saw how the fur bristled again, involuntarily, and the ears lay flat.

The man rolled his cigarette between his fingers, staring at it. "You think the Dispersal of Ymir lies behind your own sudden expansion," he said. "They supposedly provided you with weapons, robot machinery, knowledge, whatever you needed, and launched you on your career of conquest. Their aim was to rid the galaxy of Terra's Empire, making you dominant instead among the oxygen breathers. You were given to understand that humans and Ymirites simply did not get along. The technical experts on Ardazir itself, who helped you get started, were they Ymirite?"

"A few," said Svantozik. "Chiefly, of course, they were oxygen breathers. That was far more convenient."

"You thought those were mere Ymirite clients, did you not?" pursued Flandry. "Think, though. How do you know any Ymirites actually were on Ardazir? They would have to stay inside a force-bubble ship all the time. Was *anything* inside that ship, ever, except a remote-control panel? With maybe a dummy

Ymirite? It would not be hard to fool you that way. There is nothing mysterious about vessels of that type, they are not hard to build, it is only that races like ours normally have no use for such elaborate additional apparatus—negagrav fields offer as much protection against material particles, and nothing protects against a nuclear shell which has made contact.

"Or, even if a few Ymirites did visit Ardazir . . . how do you know they were in charge? How can you be sure that their oxygen-breathing 'vassals' were not the real masters?"

Svantozik laid back his lip and rasped through fangs: "You flop bravely in the net, Captain. But a mere hypothesis—"

"Of course I am hypothesizing." Flandry stubbed out his cigarette. His eyes clashed so hard with Svantozik's, flint gray striking steel gray, that it was as if sparks flew. "You have a scientific culture, so you know the simpler hypothesis is to be preferred. Well, I can explain the facts much more simply than by some cumbersome business of Ymir deciding to meddle in the affairs of dwarf planets useless to itself. Because Ymir and Terra have never had any serious trouble. We have no interest in each other! They know no terrestroid race could ever become a serious menace to them. They can hardly detect a difference between Terran and Merseian, either in outward appearance or in mentality. Why should they care who wins?"

"I do not try to imagine why," said Svantozik stubbornly. "My brain is not based on ammonium compounds. The fact is, however—"

"That a few individual Ymirites, here and there have performed hostile acts," said Flandry. "I was the butt of one myself. Since it is not obvious why they would, except as agents of their government, we have assumed that that was the reason. Yet all the time another motive was staring us in the face. I knew it. It is the sort of thing I have caused myself, in this dirty profession of ours, time and again. I have simply lacked proof. I hope to get that proof soon.

"When you cannot bribe an individual—blackmail him!"

Svantozik jerked. He raised himself from elbows to hands, his nostrils quivered, and he said roughly: "How? Can you learn any sordid secrets in the private life of a hydrogen breather? I shall not believe you even know what that race would consider a crime."

"I do not," said Flandry. "Nor does it matter. There is one being who could find out. He can read any mind at close range, without preliminary study, whether the subject is naturally telepathic or not. I think he must be sensitive to some underlying basic life energy our science does not yet suspect. We invented a mind-screen on Terra, purely for his benefit. He was in the Solar System, on both Terra and Jupiter, for weeks. He could have probed the inmost thoughts of the Ymirite guide. If Horx himself was not vulnerable, someone close to Horx may have been. Aycharaych, the telepath, is an oxygen breather. It gives me the cold shudders to imagine what it must feel like, receiving Ymirite thoughts in a protoplasmic brain. But he did it. How many other places has he been, for how many years? How strong a grip does he have on the masters of Urdahu?"

Svantozik lay wholly still. The stars flamed at his back, in all their icy millions.

"I say," finished Flandry, "that your people have been mere tools of Merseia. This was engineered over a fifteen-year period. Or even longer, perhaps. I do not know how old Aycharaych is. You were unleashed against Terra at a precisely chosen moment —when you confronted us with the choice of losing the vital Syrax Cluster or being robbed and ruined in our own sphere. You, personally, as a sensible hunter, would cooperate with Ymir, which you understood would never directly threaten Ardazir, and which would presumably remain allied with your people after the war, thus protecting you forever. But dare you cooperate with Merseia? It must be plain to you that the Merseians are as much your rivals as Terra could ever be. Once Terra is broken, Merseia will make short work of your jerry-built empire. I say to you, Svantozik, that you have been the dupe of your overlords, and that they have been the helpless, traitorous tools of Aycharaych. I think they steal off into space to get their orders from a Merseian gang—which I think I shall go and hunt!"

XVII

As the two flitters approached the nebula, Flandry heard the imprisoned Ardazirho howl. Even Svantozik, who had been here before and claimed hard agnosticism, raised his ruff and licked dry lips. To red-blind eyes, it must indeed be horrible, watching that enormous darkness grow until it had gulped all the stars and only instruments revealed anything of the absolute night outside. And ancient myths will not die: within every Urdahu subconscious, this was still the Gate of the Dead. Surely that was one reason the Merseians had chosen it for the lair from which they controlled the destiny of Ardazir. Demoralizing awe would make the Packmasters still more their abject puppets.

And then, on a practical level, those who were summoned—to report progress and receive their next instructions—were blind. What they did not see, they could not let slip, to someone who might start wondering about discrepancies.

Flandry himself saw sinister grandeur: great banks and clouds of blackness, looming in utter silence on every side of him, gulfs and canyons and steeps, picked out by the central red glow. He knew, objectively, that the nebula was near-vacuum even in its densest portions: only size and distance created that picture of caverns beyond caverns. But his eyes told him that he sailed into Shadow Land, under walls and roofs larger than planetary systems, and his own tininess shook him.

The haze thickened as the boats plunged inward. So too did the light, until at last Flandry stared into the clotted face of the infra-sun. It was a broad blurred disc, deep crimson, streaked with spots and bands of sable, hazing at the edges into impossibly delicate coronal arabesques. Here, in the heart of the nebula, dust and gas were condensing, a new star was taking shape.

As yet it shone simply by gravitational energy, heating as it contracted. Most of its titanic mass was still ghostly tenuous. But already its core density must be approaching quantum collapse, a central temperature of megadegrees. In a short time (a few million years more, when man was bones and not even the wind remembered him) atomic fires would kindle and a new radiance light this sky.

Svantozik looked at the instruments of his own flitter. "We orient ourselves by these three cosmic radio sources," he said, pointing. His voice fell flat in a stretched quietness. "When we are near the . . . headquarters . . . we emit our call signal and a regular ground-control beam brings us in."

"Good." Flandry met the alien eyes, half frightened and half wrathful, with a steady compassionate look. "You know what you must do when you have landed."

"Yes." The lean grim head lifted. "I shall not betray anyone again. You have my oath, Captain. I would not have broken troth with the Packmasters either, save that I think you are right and they have sold Urdahu."

Flandry nodded and clapped the Ardazirho's shoulder. It trembled faintly beneath his hand. He felt Svantozik was sincere, though he left two armed humans aboard the prize, just to make certain the sincerity was permanent. Of course, Svantozik might sacrifice his own life to bay a warning—or he might have lied about there being only one installation in the whole nebula—but you had to take some risks.

Flandry crossed back to his own vessel. The boarding tube was retracted. The two boats ran parallel for a time.

Great unborn planets. It had been a slim clue, and Flandry would not have been surprised had it proved a false lead. But . . . it has been known for many centuries that when a rotating mass has condensed sufficiently, planets will begin to take shape around it.

By the dull radiance of the swollen sun, Flandry saw his goal. It was, as yet, little more than a dusty, gassy belt of stones, strung out along an eccentric orbit in knots of local concentration, like beads.

Gradually, the forces of gravitation, magnetism, and spin were bringing it together; ice and primeval hydrocarbons, condensed in the bitter cold on solid particles, made them unite on colliding, rather than shatter or bounce. Very little of the embryo world was visible: only the largest nucleus, a rough asteroidal mass, dark, scarred, streaked here and there by ice, crazily spinning; the firefly dance of lesser meteors, from mountains to dust motes, which slowly rained upon it.

Flandry placed himself in the turret by Chives. "As near as I can tell," he said, "this is going to be a terrestroid planet."

"Shall we leave a note for its future inhabitants, sir?" asked the Shalmuan, dead-pan.

Flandry's bark of laughter came from sheer tension. He added slowly, "It does make you wonder, though, what might have happened before Terra was born—"

Chives held up a hand. The red light pouring in turned his green skin a hideous color. "I think that is the Merseian beam, sir."

Flandry glanced at the instruments. "Check. Let's scoot."

He didn't want the enemy radar to show two craft. He let Svantozik's dwindle from sight while he sent the *Hooligan* leaping around the cluster. "We'd better come in about ten kilometers from the base, to be safely below their horizon," he said. "Do you have them located, Chives?"

"I think so, sir. The irregularity of the central asteroid confuses identification, but. . . . Let me read the course, sir, while you bring us in."

Flandry took the controls. This would come as close to seat-of-the-pants piloting as was ever possible in space. Instruments and robots, faster and more precise than live flesh could ever hope to be, would still do most of the work; but in an unknown, shifting region like this, there must also be a brain, continuously making the basic decisions. *Shall we evade this rock swarm at the price of running that ice cloud?*

He activated the negagrav screens and swooped straight for his target. No local object would have enough speed to overcome that potential and strike the hull. But sheer impact on the yielding force field could knock a small vessel galley west, dangerously straining its metal.

Against looming nebular curtains, Flandry saw two pitted meteors come at him. They rolled and tumbled, like iron dice. He threw in a double vector, killing some forward velocity while he applied a "downward" acceleration. The *Hooligan* slid past. A jagged, turning cone, five kilometers long, lay ahead. Flandry whipped within meters of its surface. Something went by, so quickly his eyes registered nothing but an enigmatic firestreak. Something else struck amidships. The impact rattled his teeth together. A brief storm of frozen gases, a comet, painted the viewscreens with red-tinged blizzard.

Then the main asteroid swelled before him. Chives called out figures. The *Hooligan* slipped over the whirling rough surface. "Here!" cried Chives. Flandry slammed to a halt. "Sir," added the Shalmuan. Flandry eased down with great care. Silence fell. Blackness lowered beyond the hull. They had landed.

"Stand by," said Flandry. Chives' green face grew mutinous. "That's an order," he added, knowing how he hurt the other being, but without choice in the matter. "We may possibly need a fast get-away. Or a fast pursuit. Or, if everything goes wrong, someone to report back to Walton."

"Yes, sir." Chives could scarcely be heard. Flandry left him bowed over the control panel.

His crew, minus the two humans with Svantozik, were already in combat armor. A nuclear howitzer was mounted on the Donarrian's centauroid back, a man astride to fire it. The pieces of a rocket launcher slanted across the two Gorzunis' double shoulders. The Scothanian cried a war chant and swung his pet wrecking bar so the air whistled. The remaining five men formed a squad in one quick metallic clash.

Flandry put on his own suit and led the way out.

He stood in starless night. Only the wan glow from detector dials, and the puddle of light thrown in vacuum by a flashbeam, showed him that his eyes still saw. But as they adjusted, he could make out the very dimmest of cloudy red above him, and blood-drop sparks where satellite meteors caught sunlight. The gravity underfoot was so low that even in armor he was near weightlessness. Yet his inertia was the same. It felt like walking beneath some infinite ocean.

He checked the portable neutrino tracer. In this roil of nebular matter, all instruments were troubled, the dust spoke in every spectrum, a million-year birth cry. But there was clearly a small nuclear-energy plant ahead. And that could only belong to one place.

"Join hands," said Flandry. "We don't want to wander from each other. Radio silence, of course. Let's go."

They bounded over the invisible surface. It was irregular, often made slick by frozen gas. Once there

was a shudder in the ground, and a roar travelling
through their bootsoles. Some giant boulder had
crashed.

Then the sun rose, vast and vague on the topplingly
near horizon, and poured ember light across ice
and iron. It climbed with visible speed. Flandry's
gang released hands and fell into approach tactics:
dodge from pit to crag, wait, watch, make another
long flat leap. In their black armor, they were merely
a set of moving shadows among many.

The Merseian dome came into view. It was a blue
hemisphere, purple in this light, nestled into a broad
shallow crater. On the heights around there squatted
negafield generators, to maintain a veil of force
against the stony rain. It had been briefly turned off
to permit Svantozik's landing: the squat black flitter
sat under a scarp, two kilometers from the dome. A
small fast warcraft—pure Merseian, the final proof
—berthed next to the shelter, for the use of the twenty or so beings whom it would accommodate. The
ship's bow gun was aimed at the Ardazirho boat.
Routine precaution, and there were no other defenses. What had the Merseians to fear?

Flandry crouched on the rim and tuned his radio.
Svantozik's beam dispersed enough for him to listen
to the conversation: "—no, my lords, this visit is on
my own initiative. I encountered a situation on Vixen
so urgent that I felt it should be made known to you
at once, rather than delaying to stop at Ardazir—"
Just gabble, bluffing into blindness, to gain time for
Flandry's attack.

The man checked his crew. One by one, they
made the swab-O sign. He led them forward. The
force field did not touch ground; they slithered beneath it, down the crater wall, and wormed towards

the dome. The rough, shadow-blotted rock gave ample cover.

Flandry's plan was simple. He would sneak up close to the place and put a low-powered shell through. Air would gush out, the Merseians would die, and he could investigate their papers at leisure. With an outnumbered band, and so much urgency, he could not afford to be chivalrous.

"—thus you see, my lords, it appeared to me the Terrans—"

"*All hands to space armor! We are being attacked!*"

The shout ripped at Flandry's earphones. It had been in the Merseian Prime language, but not a Merseian voice. Somehow, incredibly, his approach had been detected.

"*The Ardazirho is on their side! Destroy him!*"

Flandry hit the ground. An instant later, it rocked. Through all the armor, he felt a sickening belly blow. It seemed as if he saw the brief thermonuclear blaze through closed lids and a sheltering arm.

Without air for concussion, the shot only wiped out Svantozik's boat. Volatilized iron whirled up, condensed, and sleeted down again. The asteroid shuddered to quiescence. Flandry leaped up. There was a strange dry weeping in his throat. He knew, with a small guiltiness, that he mourned more for Svantozik of the Janneer Ya than he did for the two humans who had died.

"*—attacking party is about sixteen degrees north of the sunrise point, 300 meters from the dome—*"

The gun turret of the Merseian warship swivelled about.

The Donarrian was already a-gallop. The armored man on his back clung tight, readying his weapon. As the enemy gun found its aim, the nuclear howitzer spoke.

That was a lesser blast. But the sun was drowned in its noiseless blue-white hell-dazzle. Half the spaceship went up in a fiery cloud, a ball which changed from white to violet to rosy red, swelled away and was lost in the nebular sky. The stern tottered, a shaken stump down which molten steel crawled. Then, slowly, it fell. It struck the crater floor and rolled earthquaking to the cliffs, where it vibrated and was still.

Flandry opened his eyes again to cold wan light. "Get at them!" he bawled.

The Donarrian loped back. The Gorzuni were crouched, their rocket launcher assembled in seconds, its chemical missile aimed at the dome. "Shoot!" cried Flandry. It echoed in his helmet. The cosmic radio noise buzzed and mumbled beneath his command.

Flame and smoke exploded at the point of impact. A hole gaped in the dome, and air rushed out. Its moisture froze; a thin fog overlay the crater. Then it began to settle, but with slowness in this gravitational field, so that mists whirled around Flandry's crew as they plunged to battle.

The Merseians came swarming forth. There were almost a score, Flandry saw, who had had time to throw on armor after being warned. They crouched big and black in metal, articulated tail-plates lashing their boots with rage. Behind faceless helmets, the heavy mouths must be drawn into snarls. Their hoarse calls boomed over the man's earphones.

He raced forward. The blast from their sidearms sheeted over him. He felt heat glow through insulation, his nerves shrank from it. Then he was past the concerted barrage.

A dinosaurian shape met him. The Merseian held a blaster, focused to needle beam. Its flame gnawed at Flandry's cuirass. The man's own energy gun spat —straight at the other weapon. The Merseian roared and tried to shelter his gun with an armored hand. Flandry held his beam steady. The battle gauntlet began to glow. The Merseian dropped his blaster with a shriek of anguish. He made a low-gravity leap towards his opponent, whipped around, and slapped with his tail.

The blow smashed at Flandry. He went tumbling across the ground, fetched against the dome with a force that stunned him, and sagged there. The Merseian closed in. His mighty hands snatched after the Terran's weapon. Flandry made a judo break; yanking his wrist out between the Merseian's fingers and thumb. He kept his gun arm in motion, till he poked the barrel into the enemy's eye slit. He pulled the trigger. The Merseian staggered back. Flandry followed, close in, evading all frantic attempts to break free of him. A second, two seconds, three, four, then his beam had pierced the thick super-glass. The Merseian fell, gruesomely slow.

Flandry's breath was harsh in his throat. He glared through the drifting red streamers of fog, seeking to understand what went on. His men were outnumbered still, but that was being whittled down. The Donarrian hurled Merseians to earth, tossed them against rocks, kicked and stamped with enough force to kill them through their armor by sheer concussion. The Gorzuni stood side by side, a blaster aflame in each of their hands; no metal could long withstand that concentration of fire. The Scothanian bounced, inhumanly swift, his wrecking bar leaping in and out like a battle axe—strike, pry, hammer at vulnerable joints and connections, till something gave way and air bled out. And the humans were live machines, bleakly wielding blaster and slug gun, throwing grenades and knocking Merseian weapons aside with karate blows. Two of them were down, dead; one slumped against the dome, and Flandry heard his pain over the radio. But there were more enemy casualties strewn over the crater. The Terrans were winning. In spite of all, they were winning.

But—

Flandry's eyes swept the scene. Someone, somehow, had suddenly realized that a band of skilled space fighters was stealing under excellent cover towards the dome. There was no way Flandry knew of to be certain of that, without instruments he had not seen planted around. Except—

Yes. He saw the tall gaunt figure mounting a cliff. Briefly it was etched against the bloody sun, then it slipped from view.

Aycharaych had been here after all.

No men could be spared from combat, even if they could break away. Flandry bounded off himself.

He topped the ringwall in three leaps. A black jumble of rocks fell away before him. He could not see any flitting shape, but in this weird shadowy land eyes were almost useless at a distance. He knew, though, which way Aycharaych was headed. There was only one escape from the nebula now, and the Chereionite had gotten what information he required from human minds.

Flandry began to travel. Leap—not high, or you will take forever to come down again—long, low bounds, with the dark metallic world streaming away beneath you and the firecoal sun slipping towards night again: silence, death, and aloneness. If you die here, your body will be crushed beneath falling continents, your atoms will be locked for eternity in the core of a planet.

A ray flared against his helmet. He dropped to the ground, before he had even thought. He lay in a small crater, blanketed with shadow, and stared into the featureless black wall of a giant meteor facing away from the sun. Somewhere on its slope—

Aycharaych's Anglic words came gentle, "You can move faster than I. You could reach your vessel before me and warn your subordinate. I can only get in by a ruse, of course. He will hear me speak on the radio in a disguised voice of things known only to him and yourself, and will not see me until I have been admitted. And that will be too late for him. But first I must complete your life, Captain Flandry."

The man crouched deeper into murk. He felt the near-absolute cold of the rock creep through armor and touch his skin. "You've tried often enough before," he said.

Aycharaych's chuckle was purest music. "Yes, I really thought I had said farewell to you, that night at the Crystal Moon. It seemed probable you would be sent to Jupiter—I have studied Admiral Fenross with care—and Horx had been instructed to kill the next Terran agent. My appearance at the feast was largely sentimental. You have been an ornament of my reality, and I could not deny myself a final conversation."

"My friend," grated Flandry, "you're about as sentimental as a block of solid helium. You wanted us to know about your presence. You foresaw it would alarm us enough to focus our attention on Syrax, where you hinted you would go next—what part of our attention that superb red-herring operation had not fastened on Ymir. You had our Intelligence men swarming around Jupiter and out in the Cluster, going frantic in search of your handiwork: leaving you free to manipulate Ardazir."

"My egotism will miss you," said Aycharaych coolly. "You alone, in this degraded age, can fully appreciate my efforts, or censure them intelligently when I fail. This time, the unanticipated thing was that you would survive on Jupiter. Your subsequent assignment to Vixen has, naturally, proven catastrophic for us. I hope now to remedy that disaster, but—" The philosopher awoke. Flandry could all but see Aycharaych's ruddy eyes filmed over with a vision of some infinitude humans had never grasped. "It is not certain. The totality of existence will always elude us: and in that mystery lies the very meaning. How I pity immortal God!"

Flandry jumped out of the crater.

Aycharaych's weapon spat. Flame splashed off the man's armor. Reflex—a mistake, for now Flandry knew where Aycharaych was, the Chereionite could not get away—comforting to realize, in this querning of worlds, that an enemy who saw twenty years ahead, and had controlled whole races like a hidden fate, could also make mistakes.

Flandry sprang up on to the meteor. He crashed against Aycharaych.

The blaster fired point-blank. Flandry's hand chopped down. Aycharaych's wrist did not snap across, the armor protected it. But the gun went spinning down into darkness. Flandry snatched for his own weapon. Aycharaych read the intention and closed in, wrestling. They staggered about on the meteor in each other's arms. The sinking sun poured its baleful light across them: and Aycharaych could see better by it than Flandry. In minutes, when night fell, the man would be altogether blind and the

Chereionite could take victory.

Aycharaych thrust a leg behind the man's and pushed. Flandry toppled. His opponent retreated. But Flandry fell slowly enough that he managed to seize the other's waist. They rolled down the slope together. Aycharaych's breath whistled in the radio, a hawk sound. Even in the clumsy spacesuit, he seemed like water, nearly impossible to keep a grip on.

They struck bottom. Flandry got his legs around the Chereionite's. He wriggled himself on to the back and groped after flailing limbs. A forearm around the alien helmet—he couldn't strangle, but he could immobilize and—his hands clamped on a wrist. He jerked hard.

A trill went through his radio. The struggle ceased. He lay atop his prisoner, gasping for air. The sun sank, and blackness closed about them.

"I fear you broke my elbow joint there," said Aycharaych. "I must concede."

"I'm sorry," said Flandry, and he was nothing but honest. "I didn't mean to."

"In the end," sighed Aycharaych, and Flandry had never heard so deep a soul-weariness, "I am beaten not by a superior brain or a higher justice, but by the brute fact that you are from a larger planet than I and thus have stronger muscles. It will not be easy to fit this into a harmonious reality."

Flandry unholstered his blaster and began to weld their sleeves together. Broken arm or not, he was taking no chances. Bad enough to have that great watching mind next to his for the time needed to reach the flitter.

Aycharaych's tone grew light again, almost amused: "I would like to refresh myself with your pleasure. So, since you will read the fact anyway in our papers, I shall tell you now that the overlords of Urdahu will arrive here for conference in five Terran days."

Flandry grew rigid. Glory blazed within him. A single shellburst, and Ardazir was headless!

Gradually the stiffness and the splendor departed. He finished securing his captive. They helped each other up. "Come along," said the human. "I've work to do."

XVIII

Cerulia did not lie anywhere near the route between Syrax and Sol. But Flandry went home that way. He didn't quite know why. Certainly it was not with any large willingness.

He landed at Vixen's main spaceport. "I imagine I'll be back in a few hours, Chives," he said. "Keep the pizza flying." He went lithely down the gangway, passed quarantine in a whirl of gold and scarlet, and caught an airtaxi to Garth.

The town lay peaceful in its midsummer. Now, at apastron, with Vixen's atmosphere to filter its radiation, the sun might almost have been Sol: smaller, brighter, but gentle in a blue sky where tall white clouds walked. Fields reached green to the Shaw; a river gleamed; the snowpeaks of the Ridge hovered dreamlike at world's edge.

Flandry looked up the address he wanted in a public telebooth. He didn't call ahead, but walked through bustling streets to the little house. Its peaked roof was gold above vine-covered walls.

Kit met him at the door. She stood unmoving a long time. Finally she breathed: "I'd begun to fear you were dead."

"Came close, a time or two," said Flandry awkwardly.

She took his arm. Her hand shook. "No," she said, "Y-y-you can't be killed. You're too much alive. Oh, come in, darlin'!" She closed the door behind him.

He followed her to the living room and sat down. Sunlight streamed past roses in a trellis window, casting blue shadows over the warm small neatness of furnishings. The girl moved about, dialling the public pneumo for drinks, chattering with frantic gaiety. His eyes found it pleasant to follow her.

"You could have written," she said, smiling too much to show it wasn't a reproach. "When the Ardazirho pulled out o' Vixen, we went back to normal fast. The mailtubes were operatin' again in a few hours."

"I was busy," he said.

"An' you're through now?" She gave him a whisky and sat down opposite him, resting her own glass on a bare sunbrowned knee.

"I suppose so." Flandry took out a cigarette. "Until the next trouble comes."

"I don't really understan' what happened," she said. " 'Tis all been one big confusion."

"Such developments usually are," he said, glad of a chance to speak impersonally. "Since the Imperium played down all danger in the public mind, it could hardly announce a glorious victory in full detail. But things were simple enough. Once we'd clobbered the Ardazirho chiefs at the nebula, everything fell apart for their planet. The Vixen force withdrew to help defend the mother world, because revolt was breaking out all over their little empire. Walton followed. He didn't seek a decisive battle, his fleet being less than the total of theirs, but he held them at bay while our psychological warfare teams took

Ardazir apart. Another reason for avoiding open combat as much as possible was that we wanted that excellent navy of theirs. When they reconstituted themselves as a loose federation of coequal *orbekhs*, clans, tribes, and what have you, they were ready enough to accept Terran supremacy—the Pax would protect them against one another!"

"As easy as that." A scowl passed beneath Kit's fair hair. "After all they did to us, they haven't paid a millo. Not that reparations would bring back our dead, but—should they go scot free?"

"Oh, they ransomed themselves, all right." Flandry's tone grew sombre. He looked through a shielding haze of smoke at roses which nodded in a mild summer wind. "They paid ten times over for all they did at Vixen: in blood and steel and agony, fighting as bravely as any people I've ever seen for a cause that was not theirs. We spent them like wastrels. Not one Ardazirho ship in a dozen came home. And yet the poor proud devils think it was a victory!"

"What? You mean—"

"Yes. We joined their navy to ours at Syrax. They were the spearhead of the offensive. It fell within the rules of the game, you see. Technically, Terra hadn't launched an all-out attack on the Merseian bases. Ardazir, a confederacy subordinate to us, had done so! But our fleet came right behind. The Merseians backed up. They negotiated. Syrax is ours now." Flandry shrugged. "Merseia can afford it. Terra won't use the Cluster as an invasion base. It'll only be a bastion. We aren't brave enough to do the sensible thing; we'll keep the peace, and to hell with our grandchildren." He smoked in short ferocious drags. "Prisoner exchange was a condition. All prisoners, and the Merseians meant *all*. In plain language, if they couldn't have Aycharaych back, they wouldn't withdraw. They got him."

She looked a wide-eyed question.

"Never mind," said Flandry scornfully. "That's a mere detail. I don't suppose my work went quite for nothing. I helped end the Ardazir war and the Syrax deadlock. I personally, all by myself, furnished Aycharaych as a bargaining counter. I shouldn't demand more, should I?" He dropped his face into one hand. "Oh, God, Kit, how tired I am!"

She rose, went over to sit on the arm of his chair, and laid a palm on his head. "Can you stay here an' rest?" she asked softly.

He looked up. A bare instant he paused, uncertain himself. Then rue twisted his lips upwards. "Sorry. I only stopped in to say goodbye."

"What?" she whispered, as if he had stabbed her. "But, Dominic—"

He shook his head. "No," he cut her off. "It won't do, lass. Anything less than everything would be too unfair to you. And I'm just not the forever-and-ever sort. That's the way of it."

He tossed off his drink and rose. He would go now, even sooner than he had planned, cursing himself that he had been so heedless of them both as to return here. He tilted up her chin and smiled down into the hazel eyes. "What you've done, Kit," he said, "your children and their children will be proud to remember. But mostly . . . we had fun, didn't we?"

His lips brushed hers and tasted tears. He went out the door and walked down the street again, never looking back.

A vague, mocking part of him remembered that he had not yet settled his bet with Ivar del Bruno. And why should he? When he reached Terra, he would have another try. It would be something to do.

Lurex and Gold:
Poul Anderson's Dominic Flandry Series
by
Sandra Miesel

Science fiction critic Algis Budrys once speculated that "Dominic Flandry could have sprung from no union less than that of Diana the Huntress and David Niven, with all the early personality advantages one would derive from such a fortune."[1] From his sleek seal-brown hair to his soft beefleather boots, Flandry is the epitome of rakish elegance, a devil in velvyl whose smile "had bowled over female hearts from Scotha to Antares." ("A Plague of Masters," 1961, chapter 6) Poul Anderson's debonair Naval Intelligence agent exerts his agile body and nimble wits preserving the moribund Terran Empire a thousand years hence. As Flandry says, "What was the use of this struggle to keep a decaying civilization from being eaten alive, if you never got a chance at any of the decadence yourself?" ("The Game of Glory," 1958) His life is a glittering web woven of lurex and genuine gold.

Yet Flandry is a voluptuary with a conscience, a hedonist subject to bouts of *Angst*. " 'We're hollow and corrupt,' " he says of his class, " 'and death has marked us for its own. Ultimately, though we disguise it, however strenuous and hazardous our amusements are, the only reason we can find for living is to have fun. And I'm afraid that isn't reason enough.' " ("Hunters of the Sky Cave," 1959, chapter 8) Flandry often broods over the price of his pleasures. He desperately needs to believe in the merit of the bargains he strikes to prolong the Empire's lifespan. He takes some grim satisfaction in tabulating the billions of man-years of peace his exploits have bought for others and in predicting that colonies he has saved will outlive the Empire. The last knight of Terra is a failed gentleman, but a species of gentleman nonetheless.

It is this combination of opposing traits that makes Flandry so memorable. His charm has a certain bittersweet "Gallic" flavor, a blend of cynicism and idealism. Initially, Anderson intended him to be a science fictional cousin of the Saint, not another James Bond. (Remember, Fleming's hero postdates Anderson's.) Moreover, the Terran officer's relationship with his intrepid alien servant Chives has faint traces of Bertie Wooster's with Jeeves or Lord Peter Wimsey's with Bunter.

But Anderson's restless imagination was not content to remain with his original premises. Fifteen years after the first Flandry story appeared, he shifted the series from template to developmental mode and transformed his hero into a futuristic Horatio Hornblower. The Terran is a born aristocrat and the Briton an incorrigible bourgeois but Ensign Flandry's rise is meant to match Midshipman Hornblower's.

Like C.S. Forester, Anderson was faced with the challenge of extrapolating his hero's youth from his maturity: seven stories about Captain Flandry (1951 –61) precede *Ensign Flandry* (1966). Unlike Forester, he also had to expand and justify the imaginary universe which his hero inhabits and invent settings for his heroics. Most of the time Anderson manages to achieve psychological and historical consistency and accommodate scientific advances. This makes his Flandry cycle a more technically interesting example of series-writing than his David Falkayn cycle which appeared in correct chronological order.

Furthermore, since Flandry has survived through 28 of Anderson's first 32 years as a professional writer, these works record fluctuations in the author's sentiments and skills like annual growth rings on a tree. The Flandry saga exemplifies Anderson's adventure fiction and summarizes many of his own personal interests, opinions and tastes. The perceptive reader will recognize that Anderson is a scientifically educated man who reads history, favors limited government, delights in nature, adores women, and enjoys Mozart, Hiroshige, Scotch, and *Alice in Wonderland*.

Flandry's first home was in the pulp magazines alongside such bold adventurers as C.L. Moore's Northwest Smith and Leigh Brackett's Eric John Stark. The influence of these early peers lingers in his flamboyant garb and flair for melodrama. Nowadays, sf protagonists seldom worry about the tilt of their bonnets nor ride rockets to probable doom sipping Lapsang Soochong tea.

Flandry's earliest escapades, "Tiger by the Tail" (1951), "Honorable Enemies" (1951), and "Warriors from Nowhere" (1954), are simply entertainments. Their pseudo-medieval and quasi-Oriental settings are conventional, their casts of curvaceous ladies, brash barbarians, rotten noblemen, and alien menaces are drawn from the basic Planet Stories Repertory Company. (Special revisions for this edition justify such matters as inhabited worlds around Betelgeuse.)

Against this background, Flandry's impudent roguery blazes up like a nova. Although his novelty failed to excite pulp readers (a group as tradition-bound as Kabuki fanciers), it laid the groundwork for his subsequent popularity. Thus "Tiger by the Tail" remains enjoyable while "Witch of the Demon Seas," its running mate from the very same issue of *Planet Stories*, is mercifully forgotten. "Tiger by the Tail" has survived changes in taste partly because its sardonic plot reads like a sword 'n blaster version of Mark Twain's "Man That Corrupted Hadleyburg."

A whole new audience was waiting for Flandry after the demise of the pulps, an audience with higher expectations of its amusements. By then Anderson's talent had matured. He was able to spin cleverer puzzles at longer lengths using stronger characters. For instance, compare Aycharaych's first appearance in "Honorable Enemies" with his next encore in "Hunters of the Sky Cave." Eight years' more writing experience had equipped the author to present his ambiguous villain more skillfully.

Anderson had also shaken off pulp conventions sufficiently to realize that aliens are not merely humans disguised with horns, tails, and tinted skins. He no longer copies past cultures as closely as he did in "Tiger by the Tail" where the Celtic and Nordic prototypes of the Scothani are perhaps too obvious despite rationalizations. The Ice People of "A Message in Secret" (1959), the hydrogen-breathing Ymirites and lupine Ardazirho of "Hunters of the Sky Cave" are more pleasingly original. The "otherness" of the latter two races is heightened by playing them off against the essentially American colonists of Vixen.

However, colonial societies can still be plausibly modeled on past historic ones, especially when a pattern of ethnic immigration is assumed. Anderson maintains that preserving a cultural, religious, or political heritage will motivate extrasolar colonization. Therefore he presents Boer-Bantus on Nyanza in "The Game of Glory," Russo-Mongols on Altai in "A Message in Secret," and Malays on Unan Besar in "A Plague of Masters." At this point, Anderson had not quite perfected his procedures: his repetitions are too neat, he arbitrarily borrows personal and geographical names, and he overlooks data—the natives of Unan Besar are more likely to be Moslems than polytheists. But each planetary society is richly colorful and shows the regional differences appropriate to a world. None is in danger of being mistaken for the state of Delaware.

Furthermore, from the warm shallow seas of Nyanza to the wind-scourged deserts of Vixen, each people occupies a thoroughly realized environment complete with marvelous scenery. This is an arctic forest on Altai:

> White slender trees with intricate, oddly geometric branches flashed like icicles, like jewels. Their thin, bluish leaves vibrated continuously. It seemed that they should tinkle, that the whole forest was glass. ("A Message in Secret," chapter 8)

Compare it with a stand of gigantic Trees on tropical Unan Besar:

> The great Trees were. . . incredibly massive, organic mountains with roots like foothills. They shot straight up for fifty meters or so, then

began to branch, broadest at the bottom, tapering to a spire. The slim higher boughs would each have made a Terran oak; the lowest were forests in themselves, forking again and yet again, the five-pointed leaves (small, delicately serrated, green on top but with a golden underside of nearly mirror brightness) outnumbering the visible stars. ("A Plague of Masters," chapter 13)

These stories demonstrate Anderson's growing fascination with extraterrestrial astrophysics and ecology as well as his ability to express it in hard data. (They coincide with his first major attempt at world-building, "The Man Who Counts"/*War of the Wing-Men*, 1958.) Thereafter, each place Flandry visits is more exotically alien than the last.

The other development to be noted over the course of a decade is the deepening sense of melancholy that tinges the stories. (Anderson's series typically grow darker the longer he writes them.) To quote Budrys again, "The devil-may-care hero of the earliest stories became the socially conscious inner-directed man. . . , the seeker-out-of-extracurricular adventure. . . . What he gave away prodigally in his first flush of manhood he regrets in his prime, and now he takes it."[2] Flandry's old sense of fun has not vanished—he could still trade quips with his own executioner—but he knows his former hopes for a Terran Renaissance are vain. He and the Empire he serves have reached their autumn season. " 'We who see winter coming can also see it won't be here till after our lifetimes. . . so we shiver a bit, and swear a bit, and go back to playing with a few bright dead leaves.' " ("Hunters of the Sky Cave," chapter 8)

Finally, Anderson took an impulsive step that significantly altered the direction of the series. He

tied Flandry's universe to that of his other popular
character Nicholas van Rijn by mentioning the latter
is a legendary folk hero on Unan Besar. (This is an
appropriate place for van Rijn's reputation to survive
since he is half-Indonesian.) Uniting these two
blocks of stories gave Anderson the nucleus of a
future history 5000 years long which now numbers
more than 40 separate items including 11 full-length
novels. It is the most remarkable achievement of its
kind in sf.

Since this splice was made in 1961, a pre-
occupation with the historical process itself has
come to dominate the whole series. In the rise and
fall of Technic civilization Anderson has found a
theme engrossing enough to engage all his talents. It
allows him to combine political, social, and
philosophical commentary with scientific specu-
lations. It also encourages him to go on design-
ing worlds and cultures but adds the challenging constraint that these creations be mutually
consistent. A few flaws have unavoidably crept
into Anderson's scenario despite a voluminous set
of background notes that "bulges out a looseleaf
binder." As he explains, "Perfect consistency is
possible only to God Himself, and a close study of
Scripture will show that He doesn't always make
it."[3]

Not only does cross-referencing amuse reader and
writer alike, it also transmits information. Instead of
mentioning Unan Besar's successful re-entry into
Technic civilization, Anderson shows Flandry eating
imported Unan Besarian fish in *A Stone in Heaven*
23 years after the events in "A Plague of Masters."
Genealogical references indicate whether characters
met or shirked their duty to build a better universe
for their offspring. Each time Anderson traces a

family connection he proclaims his faith in the continuity of life: "children *are* the future." Note that he bridges the 700-year gap between his principal heroes with a bond of flesh. Van Rijn's descendant Tabitha Falkayn has a brief affair with Flandry's ancestor Philippe Rochfort in *The People of the Wind* (1973).

Such attention to detail reflects the same spirit of craftsmanship that prompted medieval stonemasons to carve the hidden parts of their work as carefully as the visible ones. Consider an obscure bit of irony in *Ensign Flandry:* peacemongering Lord Hauksberg's name means "Hawk's Mountain." His policies are clearly doomed from the start because his title, Viscount of Ny Kalmar, and space yacht, the *Droning Margrete,* point to the ill-fated Union of Kalmar established by medieval Danish queen Margaret I.

Anderson will always make allusions whether anyone notices or not. However, those who do notice leave the author pleasantly bemused and receptive to their suggestions. Several Flandry fans independently concluded that the lost colonists of Kirkasant in "Starfog" (1967) were descended from some of the McCormac exiles in *The Rebel Worlds* (1969). Their arguments persuaded Anderson to accept this unplanned connection as true.

History, politics, philosophy, the sciences—these are the factors shaping the final batch of Flandry tales and related works. The series has grown in scope and intricacy far beyond its frivolous origins, much to the surprise of the author himself. "That aimless, hedonistic boy who did them, in a hurry because he needed more beer, does seem rather a stranger now," says Anderson, echoing Flandry's own sentiments as he looks back across the same span of years at his younger self in *A Knight of Ghosts and Shadows* (1974).

World-building skills honed to unrivaled keenness over the decades have been lavished on these stories. The aliens are a roll call of wonders: the feline Tigeries and cetacean Seatrolls of Starkad *(Ensign Flandry)*, the composite Didonians *(The Rebel Worlds)*, and the lyncean Ramnuans *(A Stone in Heaven)*. The three colonial planets are among Anderson's loveliest: snowy Slavic Dennitza *(A Knight of Ghosts and Shadows)*, ecologically sane Freehold ("Outpost of Empire," 1967), and austere Aeneas *(The Rebel Worlds* and *The Day of Their Return*, 1973). The last of these is especially noteworthy. It is a cool, dry globe ruled by mind and might, fittingly paired with a steamy hot, barbaric world called Dido. Aeneas has a tripartite social system on the traditional Indo-European model while the bizarre natives of Dido possess tripartite bodies. Compare this description of an Aenean landscape to the glimpses of Altai and Unan Besar quoted earlier:

> The sun was almost down. Rays ran gold across the Antonine Seabed, making its groves and plantations a patchwork of bluish-green and shadows, burning on its canals, molten in the mists that curled off a salt marsh. Eastward, the light smote crags and cliffs where the ancient continental shelf of Ilion lifted a many-tiered, wind-worn intricacy of purple, rose, ocher, tawny, black up to a royal blue sky. *(The Rebel Worlds*, chapter 6)

But these novels subordinate aesthetic delights and even adventurousness to political observations. *Ensign Flandry* reflects the early stages of the Viet Nam War, *The Rebel Worlds* denounces radicalism,

A *Circus of Hells* (1970) depicts the social impact of corruption, *The Day of Their Return* warns against charismatic movements, *A Knight of Ghosts and Shadows* examines nationalism, and *A Stone in Heaven* exposes a would-be Hitler. Anderson regards politics as the cutting edge of history. Every situation, even something so petty as urban graft, is shown to have historical repercussions—there are no trivial deeds or minor events. Men forge their own tomorrows, blow by puny blow.

The tomorrows thus wrought take shapes both fair and foul. Technic civilization is a western-flavored, technophilic global order that arises during the twenty-first century after an era of chaos. Discovery of faster-than-light travel soon permits interstellar exploration and colonization. Human expansion beyond Earth is known as the Breakup. Trade among colonial and alien societies is controlled by the merchant-adventurers of the Polesotechnic League under conditions reminiscent of the European Age of Exploration. Nicholas van Rijn and his protégé David Falkayn flourish late in this period just as civilization is beginning to break down under the pressure of institutionalized greed. The bloody Time of Troubles follows. Manuel Argos founds the Terran Empire—the Principate phase of Technic civilization—and restores galactic order. His empire expands (peacefully and otherwise) to embrace a sphere 400 light-years in diameter until it collides with a younger and fiercer Imperium, the Roidhunate of Merseia. Dominic Flandry is born late in the Principate and lives into the Interregnum that follows, ending his days as a trusted Imperial advisor. The Empire degenerates into a cruel Dominate and the Long Night Flandry has labored so hard to postpone falls at last. But civilization will eventually revive and a new cycle will commence.[4]

This is a plausible enough scenario despite its patchwork origins because Anderson sewed his imaginary future out of recurring motifs from the real past. His sound instincts for historical pattern-making were augmented after 1973 by the theories of historian and sf fan John K. Hord. Hord's system (as yet unpublished) is an attempt to go beyond Spengler and Toynbee by actually quantifying the historical process. He showed Anderson how well the Terran Empire fitted his model. Anderson enthusiastically resolved to make the fit even closer by altering dates and adopting Hord's terminology. The long conversation between Flandry and Chunderban Desai in Chapter Three of *A Knight of Ghosts and Shadows* summarizes Hord's scheme and *A Stone in Heaven* is dedicated to him.

Aside from this influence, Anderson has become much more specific in his use of historical analogies in the past decade. Originally, Terra and Merseia were generalized Old and New Empires. Gradually, they began to resemble Rome and Persia. Although the Merseians have Welsh-sounding names and the self-discipline of samurai, they are Sassanid Persians in their social and political arrangements, their hunters' ethos, their romantic masculinity, and their militant xenophobia. Transforming the hostile "gatortails" into complex beings who promise their cubs stars for playthings is a fine example of Anderson's ability to refine his starting materials. (cf. chapter 3 of *Ensign Flandry*. *A Circus of Hells* shows the danger of admiring Merseians too much.)

The Terran Empire's Roman aspects are more obvious. Terra's dynasties—the Argolids, Wangs, and

Molitors—are roughly comparable to Rome's Julio-Claudians, Antonines, and Severi. The emperors Flandry serves correspond to specific Roman ones: Georgios is Marcus Aurelius, Josip is Commodus, Hans Molitor is Septimus Severus, Dietrich is Geta, and Gerhart is Caracalla. (Flandry himself has the cynical gallantry of a Byzantine aristocrat.) Terra and Merseia are doomed to exhaust each other as the Eastern Roman Empire and Sassanid Persia did. Does some future cognate of Islam await its turn on the galactic stage?

Yet however grand the scale of events he dramatizes, Anderson steadfastly treats history as the sum total of individual moral choices. He extols freedom, not mystical Necessity although he knows full well the grief free actions may breed. Every decision plants a seed that can bring forth fruits never foreseen. If Falkayn had not saved and humiliated the Merseians in "Day of Burning" (1967), they would not have survived to menace Flandry's society. But likewise, if Falkayn had not founded the colony of Avalon and his descendants successfully defended it against Terra in *The People of the Wind*, an Avalonian native would not have been on hand to save the Empire in *The Day of Their Return*.

Flandry, who is Falkayn's counterpart even to his initials, demonstrates this truth with even grimmer clarity. His biography is a record of choice and consequence, sin and retribution. The nexus points in his life inevitably involve women, "The aliens among us!" (*A Circus of Hells*, chapter 20). This dramatic pattern expresses the author's own admitted gynolatry. Mistreating women is one of the worst things he can imagine Flandry—or anyone else—doing. Note that the killing of little girls is the ultimate outrage throughout Anderson's work.

"Seeing the anguish upon her, Flandry knew in full what it meant to make an implement of a sentient being." *(Ensign Flandry,* chapter 13) These lines might apply to any number of Flandry's affairs. Maternal neglect explains but scarcely excuses his behavior. He is also a seducer, an exploiter, and a betrayer of women. Even his dangerous feud with his superior Fenross starts over a woman. Sadly, his best and bravest ladies lose the most because they care the most. Flandry's callousness towards Persis *(Ensign Flandry)* and Djana *(A Circus of Hells)* costs him both of his great loves, Kathryn *(The Rebel Worlds)* and Kossura *(A Knight of Ghosts and Shadows).* Eventually, after years of pointless dalliance with bored noblewomen and expensive whores, he finds a measure of peace with Miriam, the daughter of his old mentor Captain Abrams. She is one woman he never deceives *(A Stone in Heaven).*

Furthermore, there is also a malign influence over-shadowing Flandry, insuring he reaps even more sorrow than he sows. This is his great nemesis Aycharaych,[5] the agent and witness of his woes. This alien genius darkens Flandry's life for more than a decade before they meet in person. Merseian master-spy Aycharaych surely has a hand in the Starkad plot that brings Flandry and Persis together. Aycharaych's special mind-training techniques arm Djana with the power she uses to curse Flandry so effectively. The two agents clash repeatedly and inconclusively until Aycharaych's machinations destroy both Flandry's favorite child and intended bride. He then destroys what Aycharaych loves best and scars his own spirit with the fury of his vengeance.

Aycharaych claims kinship with his foe.

" 'Dominic, we share a soul, you and I. We have always been alone.' " *(A Knight of Ghosts and Shadows*, chapter 20. In a sense, the "Tom O'Bedlam" quote of the title applies to both beings.) But is the charge true? Granted that both enjoy their work and justify it by appealing to the value of the ends they seek. Nevertheless, Flandry still retains a sense of righteousness even when cataloging his own vices. Aycharaych's principles transcend the normal categories of good and evil. He is in fact the galaxy's sublimest sadist, virtuoso in an art " 'whose materials are living beings.' " *(A Knight of Ghosts and Shadows*, chapter 3) His enthralling charm is satanic at the core.

Aycharaych, the last member of a supremely gifted Elder Race, guards his charnel homeworld Chereion. (Note the probably accidental associations in that name—Chiron, Charon, and carrion.) He kills without compunction to protect what is already dead. Aycharaych's depravity is best measured against the standards of a race as wise and ancient as his own—the Ice People of Altai. These beings are stewards of an evolving biosphere, not lifeless relics. They possess in truth the enlightenment he feigns.

Flandry's service to dying Terra is not really comparable. His true allegiance is to the Empire's Pax rather than to the Empire as such—he calls himself a " 'civilization loyalist,' " not an imperialist in *A Knight of Ghosts and Shadows* (chapter 11). "Dead's dead," he says elsewhere, "My job is to salvage the living." *(The Rebel Worlds*, chapter 8) Human and other civilizations can survive Terra's fall. New births will surely follow her death as long as thinking beings endure.

Ironically, Aycharaych is defeated by qualities he

disdains—physical force, emotional violence, moral principle. Try as he may, he cannot really appreciate the intensity of love, courage, loyalty, or self-sacrifice in lesser beings and so miscalculates at critical moments. This recalls Anderson's *Operation Chaos* (1971) in which an ordinary American couple defeats the hosts of Hell. Moreover, there is something of Faerie in Aycharaych's subtle beauty and artfulness. Like the elves of fable, he finds the weight of his centuries oppressive and wonders about the effect of mortality on men: " 'What depth does the foreknowledge of doom give to your loves?' " (*A Knight of Ghosts and Shadows*, chapter 9) Anderson's judgment on the elves in *The Broken Sword* (1971) can be applied to Aycharaych: " 'Happier are all men than the dwellers in Faerie—or the gods, for that matter, ... Better a life like a falling star, bright across the dark, than a deathlessness which can see naught above or beyond itself.' "

Failure and death are the only certainties in this universe. There is no lasting shield against the pitiless arrow of Time. Yet intelligent beings prove their worth by the manner in which they meet their fates. " 'If we're doomed to tread out the measure, we can try to do so gracefully,' " says Flandry. (*A Knight of Ghosts and Shadows*, chapter 3) The loom of history captures such experiences for us to share. No matter that here Anderson's threads happen to be imaginary rather than real. Whatever the scale—personal, dynastic, or cosmic—all the patterns he designs for his Technic Civilization tapestry convey the same message: " 'We're mortal—which is to say, we're ignorant, stupid, and sinful—but those are only handicaps. Our pride is that nevertheless, now and then, we do our best. A few times we succeed. What more dare we ask for?' " (*Ensign Flandry*, chapter 18)

So despite all his flaws and denials of virtue, this ill-starred knight, Dominic Flandry, is truly a hero. He accepts the terrible consequences of doing the wrong thing for the right reason. He trades his own peace of soul for other beings' happiness. Even Aycharaych admires his bold, unyielding spirit. " 'Your instincts are such that you can never accept dying.' " ("Hunters of the Sky Cave," chapter 2) Flandry has won the right to boast with Kipling's battered chevalier:

"Ay, they were strong, and the fight was long;
But I paid as good as I got!"[6]

* * *

FOOTNOTES

[1]"Galaxy Bookshelf," *Galaxy* (June 1967), pp. 188–89. Flandry is actually the illegitimate son of an opera diva and a nobly-born space captain with antiquarian interests.

[2]"Galaxy Bookshelf," *Galaxy* (February 1966), p. 139.

[3]These and other unattributed remarks are from personal communications between Anderson and Miesel.

[4]For a detailed account of Technic history, see my essay "The Price of Buying Time" published by Ace Books, 1979, an Afterword to *A Stone in Heaven*, the final(?) novel of the Flandry series.

[5]These remarks incorporate some suggestions from critic Patrick McGuire.

[6]"The Quest"